NEVER AGAIN

E A Preece

Never Again

Copyright © 2023 by E A Preece

Paperback ISBN: 978-1-63812-573-0
Ebook ISBN: 978-1-63812-572-3

All rights reserved. No part in this book may be produced and transmitted in any form or by any means, electronic, or mechanical, including photocopying, recording, or by any information storage and retrieval system, without permission in writing from the copyright owner.

The views expressed in this work are solely those of the author and do not necessarily reflect the views of the publisher hereby disclaims any responsibility for them.

Published by Pen Culture Solutions   01/30/2023

Pen Culture Solutions
1-888-727-7204 (USA)
1-800-950-458 (Australia)
support@penculturesolutions.com

Dedicated to Adrienne,
Sandy and Jean, who
always believed in me.

Chapter 1

The sun came up over the mountains, slowly awakening the valley below with the vibrant colors of bright pink and orange. Morning chased away the dark, inch by inch until the valley floor below was bathed in beautiful yellow sunshine. Mornings in the mountains were beautiful.

Mandy woke with a start. She could have sworn she heard something in the house. She threw back the covers and stood beside the bed, listening. The house was quiet. Her heart was racing. A shiver ran down her back and arms. She slowly moved down the hallway. In the kitchen, coffee was already made and the warm aroma assaulted her senses, immediately calming her. No one was in her house.

As she stepped out onto her back deck, coffee in hand, Mandy looked all around her. Her awareness of her surroundings hadn't eased in the five years she had lived in Jackson. The wraparound deck that outlined her log home showed nothing other than what had been there last night. No footprints. All the chairs were where they should be. She knew her constant vigil would never go away, not completely. It had kept her alive the last six years. It was nice it wasn't so intense anymore. So why was she so edgy today? She tried to put it out of her mind as she walked to the barn but she knew better. It would sit in the back, waiting for a noise that would make her jump or a feeling that would wash over her.

The horses were in the pen and nickering as she walked towards the barn. She stopped and watched Phoenix, her eight - year old gelding. He was the leader, after her, of her little herd of four horses. He was pacing, stopping every few yards and look around. He came up to the fence, waiting for his morning rub on his velvet nose. As Mandy stroked his neck, she checked out the other three. They all looked good. Her mare was on alert, though not as much as Phoenix. The two younger horses weren't really concerned. They would follow their leaders. Mandy walked into the barn to get the hay and get horses fed. They could get very demanding when hungry. She filled the water trough and headed back to the house.

As she started up the steps, she heard a diesel coming down her driveway. The house was set back from the road about half a mile. Evergreens were in the front of the property so the house couldn't be seen from the road. She wasn't expecting anyone. She went into the house and stood next to the cupboard where one of her guns was kept. It was the easiest to get to. She waited. The driveway came around to the back of the house and was a turnaround that went over by the barn and horse pens. A big blue GMC pulled up and stopped by the back door. She relaxed.

Michael Johnson was just stepping out of the truck when Mandy came out of the door.

"Hey, Michael! You're up early. Want some coffee?'

At 57, Michael was a handsome man. His black hair had turned to steel gray in the past few years but it looked good on him. Gave him that distinguished appearance. He was a rancher and been for most of his life. With that came a business sense in order to run a large ranch that had been in his family for generations. But other than the obvious, there was an air about Michael.

He looked up at Mandy and grinned as he said, "Do you really think I came over this early to say hi?"

Mandy smiled back. "No, I don't suppose you did. Come on in."

With Mandy pouring coffee, Michael asked, "What's up with Phoenix? He's not eating."

Mandy looked out the window. Phoenix was still pacing the front of the pen, grabbing a mouth full of hay and looking up the driveway.

"He's been like that all morning."

"He's always so aware. I wonder what's up. He's not upset about me so it makes me wonder."

"Me, too,"

They chatted as old friends do about the weather with winter coming, horses, cattle, cost of feed. Michael wanted to be sure Mandy had enough hay to get through til next summer. He knew she did but it was a good excuse to see her. Mandy had bought the property from Michael. She had come to town from nowhere, gave no information as to what brought her to Jackson, only that she was looking for some property to buy. The waitress at one of the coffee shops in town gave her Michael's name and address as she had heard he had a small place for sale. It was 20 acres with a log home, six stall barn, pens and equipment shed. The whole property was fenced and crossed fenced and about 10 miles out of town, which suited Mandy. She had given him cash for the place and they had remained friends.

As Michael got ready to leave, he stopped, hand on the door handle.

"Would you like to have dinner with me tonight?"

Mandy looked at him and smiled.

"I would love to have dinner with you tonight. Any place particular?"

"I thought we could try that new steakhouse on the other side of town."

"I heard that's good. Want me to meet you there?"

"No, silly," Michael grinned. "My mom would shoot me if I did that. I'll pick you up about 6:00. That work?"

"Absolutely. See you then." Mandy started to walk to the house and turned back. "Tell your mom thank you."

"She'll appreciate the acknowledgment." Michael continued to grin as he drove out of the driveway. It had taken him four and a half years to ask her out and she said yes. It was going to be a great day!

Mandy walked back to the house grinning. She caught herself as she walked in the back door. She had always thought Michael was a nice man and he was good looking. Being 6'2" was another strong point. She liked tall men. Not just because of her own height of 5'8" but tall men usually carried themselves well. Michael did. He knew himself – knew his strengths and weaknesses. He knew exactly who he was. With age, came maturity – if you were lucky. There was something to be said for being around the block a few times.

As she started picking up the house, Mandy started thinking. This would be the first date in many years. She wasn't seen in public much and wasn't real comfortable with it. She grabbed another cup of coffee and sat in her chair. Okay. She need to think this through and stop being terrified of "ifs" and "maybes" but she couldn't help it. Six years in hiding kept you on guard. It kept you alive. She had no close friends. Only her children knew where she was. Would she be endangering them with this date?

"Girl, knock it off," she scolded herself. "It's only a dinner date. Nothing more. No one's found you yet. The trial's over. It's not a major production. Don't make it one." So, she got up out of her chair, poured another cup of coffee and put it out of her head. When she finished folding laundry and putting it away, she put on her boots and headed out to the horses. She had training to do.

Mandy spent the remainder of the day outside. Phoenix and Kona, her seven- year old mare, were pretty well trained. They didn't take as much time as the two younger horses, Chico and Cheyenne. Mandy hadn't had them as long. They were doing well, both were very smart and wanted to please. Phoenix had calmed down a bit but not completely. Kona stayed on alert. The younger horses followed the leaders. They could feel the tension but weren't really concerned at this point.

By the time she got back in the house, it was 5:00. Michael would be there in an hour. Mandy showered and put on makeup. That was a first in a long time. Deciding to wear black jeans, a lavender camisole, black boots and her short black leather jacket. She blew dried her dark auburn hair, checking to be sure the gray wasn't showing. It was long, past her shoulders. As she looked in the mirror, she was still surprised at who was staring back at her. She didn't look in the mirror much. She couldn't get use to who looked back. She didn't look anything like herself or what she used to look like. She had a smaller nose, fuller lips and not such a square jaw line. The only thing the same was her dark brown eyes. She liked what she saw. It was just so different.

As she adjusted her jacket, she heard Michael's truck pull up. She hurried down the hall, grabbing her lipstick, cell phone (she hated taking it with her but it was a necessity, just in case) and her coin purse of which all would go into the inside pocket just as Michael knocked on the door.

"Wow!" he said when she opened the door. "You clean up pretty good."

"So do you," Mandy grinned back. Looking up at him, he was the same guy who was there this morning only more polished. He wore his hair a bit longer than what was stylish but it looked good on him. He wore black jeans, a pale blue shirt and brown suede bomber jacket. His blue eyes were that dark, midnight blue that seemed to see through to her soul.

"Ready?"

"Yea. Go ahead and I'll set the alarm."

"You have an alarm? Here? When did you do that?"

"Yes, I have an alarm HERE! I put it in about a week after I moved in. I know it's a bit strange but I live alone." She offered no other explanation.

Truth was, Michael knew about the alarm. He has seen the installation being done when he had ridden over one day after she moved in. He had kept a close eye on her because she was here by herself. And he was interested. She never volunteered any information and he hadn't asked. It didn't take a brain surgeon to see she wasn't ready to talk about it, whatever it was.

"I do like what you've done with this place," Michael commented as he opened the door for her. Getting into the driver's seat, he continued, "This place needed some care for a long time and I just didn't have the time to do it. You've made it a really nice home."

"Thanks. I really didn't do that much. At least it doesn't seem so because I've done it over time. Just needed to make it mine."

"I've only been in two rooms and I've seen paint, light fixtures, ceiling fans, faucets, sinks, flooring. Not to mention the kitchen looks brand new."

Mandy laughed.

"It's not. I painted the cupboards, put in the soap stone counters. The island was made from two old doors that had windows in them and the ends were old window frames. Just put in new glass. I redid the laundry room as the pipes needed replacing so I opened it up and made it the mudroom, too. I put in a jetted tub in the master bath, new tile flooring in there and the guest bath. Both are the lighter gray of the kitchen. The mud room is part of the smallest bedroom. The other part of that bedroom I added into the workout room. I painted the other rooms, put carpet in the master and guest rooms. There's a doorway from the living room into my office. That's about it."

"You only redid the whole house!" Michael was amazed. She had done all the work herself. Talking about materials used and how the wiring was done, she knew her stuff. Most people would have been scared to death to attempt any of it. Not Mandy.

They talked all the way to Matt's Steakhouse. The parking lot was full. It appeared to be a popular place.

Matt's was a huge log building. It had always been a restaurant of some sort but the new owner had completely remodeled it. It was done with comfort and class. The antiques and pictures were from the area, local artists and scenes of the mountains, streams and wild life. The restaurant and bar were separated by the entryway. The bar with a small lounge was to the left while the dining room was straight ahead. It was all very open. The back of the dining room was all windows that looked out over a meadow with the tree line starting on the other side. As they were led to their table, the forest was outlined in the orange of the setting sun.

They settled into their perspective sides of the table and ordered drinks - white wine for Mandy. Dark beer for Michael.

He studied Mandy as they waited for their drinks. She really was a beautiful woman. Her dark brown eyes against her olive complexion looked as though they held the secrets of a thousand years. His curiosity about her past was up and what was so bad that she never spoke of anything regarding it. Never any old friends or childhood memories. The only thing she had said about her marriage was that it had been a mistake. That was true for about half the vows ever said. No help there.

"What?" she asked.

"Excuse me?"

"You were staring at me. Do I have lipstick on my teeth or toothpaste on my lip?"

Michael laughed.

"No. I'd have told you long before now."

"Thank God!"

Michael loved her sense of humor. She didn't take herself seriously and wasn't vain about how beautiful she was. She didn't really pay much attention to her looks-definitely not "high maintenance". She didn't need to be the center of attention. In fact, she preferred to stay in the back ground. There was some self – protection going on. You could feel it. It was subtle but there. She looked before she made a leap – checking all aspects before jumping in.

Just then, their drinks arrived.

"Tell me how you learned about renovation."

Mandy looked at him. The answer could have come from a hundred million people so she felt safe in answering him. She leaned back against the booth, twirling her wine glass, not completely relaxing.

"My dad was a contractor. He renovated a lot of the old historical homes and did finish work on new construction. I use to go with him as a kid. I got bored doing kid stuff so I asked if I could help. He gave me little things to do, like get tools, As I got older and understood more, he gave me bigger jobs. He was a wonderful teacher. Very meticulous. He wanted everything perfect. He told me that's what people paid him for and they only deserved the best he could give them. He never cut corners or used cheap product. He said his name was on his work and it would only take one crappy job to ruin him."

"He taught you well. What about your mom?"

"She died when I was three. Hit by a car."

"Oh, man. I'm sorry. That must've been rough." Michael couldn't imagine kids growing up without parents, though his own had. It was something that had always tugged at his heart.

"It had it's moments but I didn't understand until I was older. To me it was normal – just me and dad." She paused. "What about you? What have you done to get where you are?" The change in subject wasn't lost on Michael.

"You know my family's ranched here since the early 1800s. Hopefully, it will continue and be passed down to generations after me. I graduated, did several years in the service, got married, had three kids, lost my wife along the way. Came back to the ranch and went to night school for a degree in Business and Ranch Management and have just kept working the ranch. I got lucky with my kids. All three are involved with the ranch to some degree. My daughter Alex is the one who moved away. She's an attorney in Green River so she isn't that far away – a couple of hours. Both my sons you already know about. Kenny and his wife do a lot. They have ever since they came back from Iraq – they met there. Dustin works the ranch full time. His wife is an ER nurse at the hospital here. But on her days off, she's on a horse right beside Dustin. Says it's her therapy." Michael paused.

"I can relate to that," Mandy grinned. "They have a way of doing that."

"They sure do. Can make any day brighter. We have 10,000 acres so there's a lot of land for therapy sessions. And, then, my parents are still very much involved with the ranch. They travel a lot but never for extended periods of time. I have two other brothers that are also involved. My brother David and his wife Carmen live behind me and are as involved as I am. I do most of the cattle part, Larry does the farming and David does the breeding aspect. He's the science nerd of our family but the man is incredible. Larry's wife died several years ago and he's just started seeing a lady who owns the Jackson Cafe a few months back. You know her. She's the one who told you about your property." Michael paused again. Relating the facts about his life made him wish he'd chosen a better life partner. But if he had, he wouldn't be here right now looking at this gorgeous woman. Fair trade.

"How do you make it work? So many different people and different personalities. That could be really tough."

Michael laughed. He leaned back and took a drink of his beer.

"The hardest thing in the world." he said, smiling. "Communication. Sounds so easy but it's not. It takes everyone working together, listening to each other and respecting each other. Don't get me wrong. We have our moments but all in all, we do pretty well. At least we have. Our formula works for us."

"That's all you can ask for."

Their waitress came and took their orders. Michael had ordered appetizers with the drinks and that was served as their waitress left. The sauteed shrimp was delicious. Michael laughed as he wiped butter from Mandy's chin.

"Butter is better in your mouth."

"No joke." Mandy smiled as she wiped her mouth.

"Tell me about your kids. You don't say much about them but your whole face lights up when you talk about them."

"They are my life. Always have been. Just wish I could see them more."

"Why don't you? I know they've been out here several times and you've been to see them."

"They are grown and have their own lives," Mandy hedged. "Marie's an attorney with her practice in Stockton and Brad's in Flagstaff. He owns an electronics company there. They're busy." Even as she spoke, Mandy wanted to see them. It hurt that she couldn't just pick up the phone and call anytime she wanted or drop by their house. But it wasn't safe. They knew that and understood it, though they didn't like it either. That's why the infrequent visits meant so much to all of them. It was just too dangerous.

"We should get our daughters together. I imagine they would have a lot to talk about." Michael ate another shrimp. "What else?"

Mandy looked at him.

"You face says there's more."

"And where did you learn to read people so well? I know being around cows didn't give you such insight. Horses, yea. Umm, cows? Not so much."

Michael grinned. She was avoiding the subject again. That's okay. Obviously, it was a bit touchy. He went along with her. Mandy wasn't someone you demanded answers from. Trust was earned.

"My stint in the service. Learned a few things that have been useful throughout the years."

"What branch were you in?"

"Army."

"Where were you stationed."

"All over the world. I was a Ranger and then asked to join Delta Force."

Mandy looked at him. She'd had an uncle who was a Navy SEAL so she had an understanding of the military structure. It said a lot about this man. She had known him for five years but didn't know much about him. She knew he was divorced but didn't know why. With him being in Delta Force, she understood why he seem so relaxed but she'd noticed nothing got past him. He saw everything around him. He was like the horses today – on alert. But for Michael, it was natural.

Their dinner was served then. Mandy asked for coffee and some water. Michael noticed she didn't order anymore wine.

The steak was delicious and Mandy savored every bite. Other people's cooking was always better than her own. Not that she was a bad cook. It was just boring when you cooked for one. She loved it when Marie and Brad came to visit. She cooked the whole time they were there and sent home packages of dinners and desserts. And don't forget the cookies! She was an avid baker. But it just being her, she made something fast. Too much to do with the property and horses. There wasn't a lot of time to cook. Her favorite dinner was steak and salad. This was done to perfection.

"How's your steak?" Michael asked.

"Perfect. Yours?"

"Great. I heard they brought in a chef from Chicago."

"That's interesting. It must be a bit of culture shock for him."

"I imagine so. But, then, a lot of people get tired of the city and just want a simpler way of life."

They chit chatted through the rest of the meal and sat drinking coffee while the table was cleared. Mandy excused herself, grabbed her jacket and headed for the restroom. She was aware of people looking at her as she past tables and only hoped it wasn't something embarrassing like her jeans unzipped. That would just top off a perfect evening!

Mandy had washed her hands and was applying her lipstick when her cell phone rang. She froze, staring at her jacket. Her cell never rang. Only Brad, Marie and one other person had the number. It was only for emergencies. She picked it up and saw the return number – 818 area code with 911 behind it. She hit ignore and grabbed the counter, trying to breathe. She took several deep breaths…in, out, in, out, trying to think. Damn! Why was he looking for her now? What had caused the call? How close was he to finding her? Too many questions and no answers. She knew she needed a phone booth. All calls could be traced but she wasn't going to make it easy.

What about Michael? How was she going to do this? She knew she'd have to lie to him and that he would most likely pick up on it.

There was no doubt. He had been in such an elite area of the military, it would be ingrained in him by now. She didn't know if she could pull it off. She definitely didn't want to involve anyone in this mess. It was too dangerous. Just thinking about it made her stomach hurt. Thoughts flew through her head. The horses, her house. Would she ever see any of it again? Who would take care of them if she had to leave? Would she ever be able to come home?

"Okay, calm down." she told herself. "No answers yet. Don't blow it out of proportion, until you know. Just breathe."

Mandy put her phone back in her pocket and put on her jacket. As she walked back to the table, shivers ran down her spine as she neared a specific table. A man was on a cell phone, his back to her. His friend sat across from him, watching the conversation that was taking place.

"No. We haven't seen her. I'm not sure she is here. I've checked with local people and no seems to know her. Are you sure of the information given?" That was all she heard as she walked by. She casually turned and saw his face. As she turned around, a memory hit her. That was what woke her up this morning! That face! Where did she know that face from? Crap! Who was he? More questions. No answers. She took several deep breaths and hoped she looked herself as she sat down.

"You okay?" Michael asked, concern in his voice. He had watched her as she past the table of the two men and saw the look on her face when she turned back around. She was stressed before she walked past the table and seeing the one guy seemed to blow her out of the water. What kind of trouble could anyone get into in a restroom?

"Yea. I'm fine." Mandy smiled. She prayed she could pull this off. Michael was such a nice person.

"What are you doing tomorrow?"

Mandy looked at Michael. So many smart remarks ran through her head and she almost laughed. She always did that when stressed…… made up things in her head to laugh at. God! She was so demented.

"I've got several things to do. I may have to leave town for a while and need to get things taken care of first. Someone to come in and take care of the horses, stop the mail. That kind of stuff." It wasn't a complete lie. For all she knew, she'd be gone by noon tomorrow and no telling when she'd be back.

"Have time for a ride?"

"If I'm not leaving, that would be great. Could we stop at a phone booth on the way back so I can see if I'll be leaving? As soon as I know the particulars, I can make a decision."

"Sure, but you can use my cell or they have a phone booth here. It's down the hall from the restrooms."

"No. Anywhere we can stop will be good."

That didn't make sense. He knew she had to know calls could be traced. Her son was an electronics geek.

As they walked out, they past the table of the two men again. Neither looked up. A shiver ran down her spine again. Michael paid the bill at the register and they walked out, Michael reaching for her hand as they walked to the truck. She looked up at him and smiled. Funny how such a small gesture could put things in perspective. This felt so good, so right. And such perfect timing. Yea. Right.

They stopped at a truck stop outside of town. Mandy went to the phone inside and dialed the number. It was answered on the first ring.

"Mandy?"

"Yea, Sally. What's up?"

The voice on the other end of the line was a detective from the LA County Sheriff's Department.

"I heard something that wasn't good. I waited 'til I could validate it before I called. He's looking for you and heard you were somewhere near Jackson. He's sent two men to see if they can locate you. By all the reports I've heard, they haven't been successful but I didn't know how close that was to you. I called so you'd be on guard….well, more so than normal."

"Why's he looking for me now? He hasn't bothered in six years, at least that I know of. What has caused this?"

"I don't know. I do know he's tried in the past but hasn't put too much effort into it. About three months ago, I started hearing rumors on the street but I didn't pay much attention as there wasn't anything solid. Then, this afternoon, I had a snitch tell me Jim sent two guys to Jackson. There's been rumors about financial issues."

"I would imagine the alimony must be adding up," Mandy commented. "But I had nothing to do with that. That was the judge."

She thought for a minute. She knew she should be relatively safe for the moment. The plastic surgeon had done a wonderful job putting her back together. She didn't recognize herself so she knew other people wouldn't. It also stood to reason that with all the damage done to her, she wouldn't be able to live any type of normal life, let alone one that was physically demanding. Good thing the doctors listened when she said to exaggerate her injuries. They did, but not by much. The detective, Sally Shore, didn't know anything about Mandy's lifestyle and Mandy wanted to keep it that way.

"They're here. I just passed them."

"Damn. Can you give me anything?"

"No. I just overheard a conversation on a cell phone." She gave a vague description of the two men. Sally had been with Mandy all through the trial. She stood by her, literally, when she went to the divorce hearing as Mandy was in casts and bandages around her face. Only her eyes, nose and mouth showed at all. They had become very close in those months. But when the bandages came off, Mandy told Sally she couldn't see her. If Sally didn't know what Mandy looked like, she wouldn't know the changes and that could keep them both safe. "Let me know if you hear anything else."

"I will. And, Mandy, stay safe. You're always in my thoughts and prayers."

"Thanks, Sally. You're in mine." Mandy hung up and stood for a moment, thinking. Then she went back to the truck and Michael.

Chapter 2

"What's the verdict?" Michael could see more strain around Mandy's eyes as she got in the truck.

"I'll be leaving tomorrow."

Michael turned the truck away from Jackson and headed out to Mandy's. He was trying to figure out the situation and what the hell was going on. He made small conversation on the way back. How he loved the Tetons and always thought about coming back to them when he'd been out on a mission. They kept him grounded and focused. Mandy barely said a word, lost in her own thoughts.

As Michael put the truck in park at Mandy's, she turned to face him, one hand on the door handle.

"Thank you for a wonderful dinner."

"My pleasure. I hope we can do it again."

That brought a smile to her face.

"I'd invite you in for coffee but I have to pack."

"Anything I can do to help?"

Mandy turned back to look at him. "Could you take care of my horses until I get back?" She didn't add "if I get back" but you could tell it was in the back of her mind. "I know it's an imposition but I have to know they're taken care of."

"That's no problem. Want me to take them to my house? I have a big pasture they could have. They'd think they were on vacation."

"That would be great. Thank you." She got out of the truck and walked around to the driver's side. So many things were going through her head. She saw the horses walking along a beach with flowers around their necks. Lord! She needed to be in survival mode, not Fantasy Island.

"Really," she said, leaning against his door. "Thank you for tonight. I really did enjoy myself."

"You're more than welcome. Anything else I can do?"

"Oh, no. You're doing more than enough now. I really do appreciate it." She started walking towards the house.

"Mandy. Wait." Michael was out of the truck and following her. As he caught up with her, she saw the intensity on his face.

"I know something's wrong. I don't know what but I know you're scared to death and I want to help."

She stood looking at him, a million thoughts going through her head in a split second. She knew she had to trust someone and with Michael's background, it could be him. Right now, that scared the hell out of her. She stared at him for several more seconds.

"Want some coffee?"

"Sure."

Michael walked into the kitchen as Mandy turned off the alarm. He was leaning against the counter as she came.

"What? No coffee made?" She turned and grinned at him, trying to keep it light. Light was something far from reality at this point.

"Mom told me it was rude to go through people's cupboards."

"Your mom is such a smart lady."

Mandy relaxed the minute she got in the house. This was her turf. She was safe here. Well, safer than anywhere else at the moment. It showed in her body language as she made coffee. She put out her hand for Michael's jacket and put hung it on a hook next to hers in the mudroom.

"Have a seat," she said as she reached for the mugs. Michael sat at the island. Just then, her cell phone rang. She got it out of her jacket pocket and looked at the screen. Brad. 911. She raised her index finger to Michael.

"Hi, honey." She was trying to keep the edge out of her voice. "When? I heard earlier that there were two and they couldn't find anything." There was a long pause. Michael came around and poured the two mugs of coffee and sat back at the island, watching Mandy.

"Okay. I will. Give me some time to figure this out. I'll let you know as soon as I do. I know, baby. I love you, too." She hung up.

"That was my son."

"Kinda figured it was one of them. Bad news?"

"Nothing I wasn't expecting. Just not so soon."

"Let me help." It was said quietly, softly.

Mandy looked at him. She knew he was serious in the offer. Her gut said to trust him. She was terrified. There was so much to lose now. A lot more than before. She wasn't even the same person she had been. She took a deep breath. If she couldn't trust herself and the instincts God gave her, she couldn't trust anyone.

"It scares me. It could get ugly and it would tear me apart if something happened to you."

Michael put down his coffee and came over to stand in front of her. He didn't touch her. He stood there, looking down at her and seeing someone who had been through hell and was willing to go again to survive, as long as no one else got hurt.

"Tell ya what. Tell me what it is and let me judge. And just for the record, I know it's asking a lot for you to trust me with this. If I decide not to, your secret is safe with me. I won't violate the trust."

Mandy looked up at him. She knew this was a crossroads. Lord. She was so tired of carrying this burden alone. Okay. If it was a mistake, just meant she'd die sooner rather than later.

"Get your coffee. We can talk while I pack."

They walked down the hall to Mandy's bedroom. She flipped on the light and pulled a large duffel bag from the closet. Michael sat in a chair in a corner of the room. As Mandy grabbed clothes and toiletries, she told Michael of her past.

Mandy met Jim when she was a senior in high school. He was the "older man," being four years older than her. They dated for a couple of years and got married. The kids soon followed. Jim did well at the construction company he'd gone to work for out of high school. He'd started as a laborer and worked his way up to foreman. When the owner decided to retire, he asked Jim if he wanted to buy the business. He did and that was when everything started to fall apart.

Jim bid on a strip mall out in the San Fernando Valley. His bid was too low and the job cost a lot more than the bid. Mandy had tried to tell him when she saw the bid sheets. She knew about bidding jobs from her dad but Jim wouldn't listen to her. The business pulled out of it, barely breaking even. But Jim learned from that mess and soon the business was thriving. It expanded and they had jobs all over California and Nevada. Jim was the man to know in construction. If he couldn't do the job, he knew who could. At home, his family didn't want anything to do with him. He'd become abusive and neglectful.

By the time the kids were through high school, they'd had enough of Jim. They begged Mandy to leave him. It took her another two years after they both were in college.

Her saving grace was horses. She had started riding when the kids were little and it became her salvation. She had found a trainer who had been down many of life's bumpy roads. Horses had literally saved Kelly. She taught Mandy how to let them save her.

Then, eight years ago, Mandy left. By this time, Jim's business was a multi-million dollar corporation. He thought he owned the world. He kept cheating, kept abusing. One day, Mandy just walked out the front door and never looked back.

She got a small apartment closer to her trainer. Jim had no idea about her and horses so as he continued to search, he never looked in that area. He looked for her all over the state.

Over the years, Mandy had stashed cash. She knew the day would come when she would leave and she needed to be as prepared as possible. Because she had, she had one less thing to worry about.

She lost contact with her best friend, Katie. They had grown up together and shared the adventures of teenagers. But after she left, Mandy was scared to contact her. She didn't know what Jim would do. She stayed to herself. She needed time to heal and sort things out.

One day in August, Marie called in a panic. She said Brad had called her and that Jim had found her. She was incoherent. Mandy could only make out something about a contract being put out on her. Before Marie could finish the sentence, Mandy's door had flown open. She ran to the door, dropping the phone. She got to the door and was trying to shut it when she got hit in the face. Everything became a blur. She remembered incredible pain in her face and her stomach, arms and legs being broke. She vaguely remembered hearing sirens. Marie had heard the whole thing. She had called 911.

Mandy woke up in the hospital three weeks later. Both Brad and Marie were there. She saw the look on their faces and prayed to God she never had to see that again. It broke her heart. She saw uniforms when the door opened but nothing registered as to why they were there.

Nothing could be proven that Jim ordered the attack. Mandy met Detective Sally Shore with LA County Sheriff's Office. She worked all the leads, stayed by Mandy. She was with her when Mandy went to the divorce hearing, in a wheelchair, one arm and one leg still in casts. Her face was completely bandaged. Only her eyes, nose and mouth showed. Both her checks had been broken along with her jaw and her left eye socket. She had two surgeries to repair internal damage.

The judge was mad and told Jim so. He ordered all medical bills to be paid by Jim regarding the attack, along with $10,000 a month alimony and to sign a lifetime restraining order. He told him if he ever heard of Jim going near Mandy again, he would personally see that he spent a minimum of ten years in prison.

Life was surreal. Brad had set up a bank account in the Bahamas for her money to be transferred from the courts every month so Jim couldn't trace it. She was put into rehab at a center in the Sierra Nevada Mountains that was known for their security. There, she healed from the last of the surgeries and started the up-hill battle to walk again. Only Brad and Marie saw her. She kept in contact with Sally by phone but was too scared to contact Katie. She didn't know what would happen to her.

A year later she was released from the rehab center. She got ID in her mom's name and got a small apartment in San Diego. She was now Diane Amanda Leeds. She took martial arts training, learned to shoot with a 9mil that she bought. She got back on a horse at another stable and finally felt free again. She saw the kids as much as possible, whenever they could lose whoever Jim had following them. They got pretty inventive in their deceptions.

She bought Phoenix and Kona from an auction, he was two and Kona was a yearling. She started training them with everything she learned from Kelly. She had them about six months when she decided she wanted a home. She was tired of the city and had gotten a taste of the peace and different energy level nature gave. She traded her SUV for her Chevy pickup and bought a horse trailer. She made a road trip to Jackson, driving up through Nevada, Idaho and a small part of Montana. She checked out the area. It felt right so she went into town to see about property for sale. She had called Michael when Amy at the cafe had given her his number. She got the address and drove out to it. She wandered the property, checking out what she could. Then she called Michael to see the inside. She'd already made up her mind that she wanted the place. The inside of the home didn't matter. Whatever needed to be fixed, she could do. The barn was good and so were the other two out buildings. Fence was good. She gave Michael cash and it was done. The rest, he already knew.

Michael never said a word as Mandy talked. She amazed him. He knew she was giving him a short version of what happened. Her instincts were incredible. She had come along way by herself.

Just when Mandy closed her duffel bag, her phone rang. All color drained from her face. It rang two more time before she answered.

"Mom, dad found you. Brad just called me." Marie's voice had the same edge as all those years ago. "He doesn't want to stop monitoring whatever he has set up so he told me to call. You have to get out of there. Now."

"I know, honey. I've talked to Brad and Sally. I'm leaving tonight, as soon as I can get the horses settled."

"Where are you going?"

"I don't know right now. I'll figure it out as I go." Mandy motioned to Michael to come with her and grabbed her bag.

"Mom, be safe. Don't let that son of a bitch hurt you again."

"Not if I can help it. This time, he won't catch me by surprise. Tell Brad. I'll call as soon as I can. I love you."

"We love you, too. Be careful."

Mandy hung up and looked at Michael. He was standing in the mudroom, holding Mandy's heavier jacket out to her.

"I'm sorry. Jim's found me. Brad's been monitoring him and just found out. I don't know how much time I have. I gotta go."

"Would you accept a suggestion?"

"As long as you can suggest and walk at the same time." She put her coat on and headed out the door to the barn.

"What about going up to my cabin? No one will find you there. It's fifteen miles up in the back country. Only way there is by horseback or hiking."

Mandy stopped. It was a tempting offer.

"Why are you so willing to help me?"

"Well, for starters, I've had a crush on you since you moved here." They continued walking. "Then, this was our first real date of which I'm looking forward to more of and then, this guy's a bastard and needs to be stopped. Not just from hurting you again but stopped. Period."

Mandy smiled. She was a bit surprised at Michael's feeling but the truth was she also wanted Jim stopped. She was scared the only way that would happen was if one of them was dead. She didn't want it to come to that but knew that it could.

"What do we do?"

"Let me call Kenny. Have him bring the horse trailer tonight. We load up your horses and go to the ranch. We leave from there in the morning. That will give us time to get some things in place."

"What things?"

"I've lived here most of my life. I know people here and I've a few buddies from the service that I can call that aren't far."

"You've stayed in contact with the guys from Delta Force?"

"Some of them and a few others."

Mandy thought for a minute. It was either go with Michael or go it alone. She was tired of running, of always being on guard. This was where she had made her home and where she wanted to stay. She just needed some time to think.

"Call Kenny."

Michael called.

"He'll be here in 20 minutes."

"Okay. Let's go to the barn."

The horses were a bit surprised for the lights to come on. Mandy haltered each one and was putting some grooming supplies in a saddlebag when Kenny drove in. She had only met Michael's sons a few times but not his daughter Alex. She hoped she would get the chance for him to meet Brad and Marie. What a thing to think about now.

Kenny had driven the truck around so it was facing out and was opening the trailer door when Mandy and Michael came out leading Phoenix and Kona.

Kenny was a younger version of his father. Same build, same walk. The only difference was Kenny had dark brown hair but he had the same blue eyes.

"How ya doin', Mandy? Dad gave me the short version of what's happenin'. I'm really sorry you have to go through this again." His concern was written on his face. Mandy was a bit taken back. She hadn't expected such compassion.

"Thanks, Kenny, but I'll be okay. It's just a mess right now."

"Yea. No stinkin' joke. And pretty scary, I'd bet."

"You'd win there."

They got all four horses loaded and Kenny left, saying he would have them in the barn when they got there. Mandy headed to the house as Michael closed up the barn. He had just come in the door when Mandy thought she heard a car. Michael hit the light switch. She grabbed his hand and headed back to her room, picking up her duffel as she pulled him into her closet. As soon as they were in there, she shut the door and turn on the light. She walked to the back of the closet and moved her small rattan dresser. Michael immediately saw the handle. The door slid silently to the right. Mandy stepped through into a hallway with Michael right behind her. She pulled the dresser back in place, closed the door and flipped two light switches. The hallway lit up with a low beam light.

"One shuts off the light in the closet," she whispered. He nodded and followed her lead. She had turned to the right and stopped in front of a door, listening. They could hear footsteps and low voices but not what was being said. The footsteps receded. A few minutes later, they heard a car start up and pull away. They waited until it was silent, then Mandy stepped forward and reached into the wall. There was a click and an opening appeared where Mandy had pushed. She pushed again and the wall gave way. You couldn't tell from the rest of the outside logs because of the overhang.

"Pretty neat trick."

"Didn't I tell you my dad did renovations?"

"Yea. Just didn't expect that."

"Nice to know I can surprise you."

"Smart ass under stress?"

"Have to," she replied. "Otherwise, I'd cry."

As Michael started the truck, he said, "Scoot down on the floorboard. You can get up as soon as I'm sure no one's following us."

Mandy got on the floor. It was a bit cramped but she leaned her head on the seat and tried to get as comfortable as possible. Michael's ranch was about five miles past Mandy's. She watched him as he shifted gears, eyes constantly watching the road and checking the mirrors.

"Okay. Come on up. I think we're good. I can't imagine anyone letting us get this far ahead when they don't know the area."

Mandy crawled up on the seat,

"Damn. Getting older sure isn't for sissies." She put on her seat belt and stretched her legs.

"Where's your gun?"

"Which one?"

"The one you're most comfortable with."

"One on me. Two in my bag. Four back at the house."

"Any good?"

Mandy looked at him. Michael could feel her stare.

"I'm not a perfect marksman but I can hit what I'm aiming at with any of 'em. I have a 410 shotgun, just in case. I'm a third- degree black belt and can shoot a bow."

It was Michael's turn to stare.

"Damn, woman. I just wanted to know if you'd have my back if I needed you."

"I got yours. You got mine?" The teasing had come back into her voice.

"Try me."

"Are we still talking about back up?"

"Maybe. Maybe not."

"Tell your mom she raised a smart ass."

"She knows."

They'd driven in silence for a minute when Michael noticed lights behind them, coming up fast. He took the next right and pulled into a grove of trees, shut the engine and lights. They waited. About 30 seconds passed and a car went speeding by. They could see the brake lights as the car slowed, obviously looking for them. Michael figured his plate had been run when they saw his truck at Mandy's. But here, he had his truck registered at his post office box. It was allowed as he was ex Special Forces. He couldn't be traced to the ranch from the truck registration or driver's license. They were far enough off the road and hidden by the trees. They waited. The car drove back and forth. The road Michael turned onto was nothing more than a path, really. You wouldn't know it was there unless you really did know it was there. The car drove up towards Michael's. A few minutes later, it came back and headed towards town. They'd given up. Would most likely try again tomorrow.

Michael's house was set back about a mile from the main road. It was mostly pasture in front, then a small rise. Coming down the backside was a grove of evergreens and the main house was set at the west edge of the grove. Dustin and Kenny's houses were set further back. None of the houses were in close proximity to each other for privacy but none were far from the barn. As they pulled in, Kenny's truck was gone and the security light was on over the barn door.

They walked into the barn and checked on the horses. Everyone was fine, munching on the bit of hay that Kenny had given them. They nickered when they saw Mandy and she checked all them, just making sure they were okay. She knew what sudden change could do to horses but hers were fine. Michael shut off the light and they walked to the house.

Chapter 3

Michael's house was definitely male. The house was big but felt empty. Michael wasn't there much since the guys had their own places and Alex was in Green River.

Michael showed Mandy the guest room that had it's own bath. She was grateful as she needed a few minutes of down time.

"How about some coffee? I usually drink decaf at night."

Mandy smiled. "That would be great."

"Consider it done."

Fifteen minutes later, Mandy walked into the kitchen. She looked pale and tired. Michael was taking this all in stride. It made her wonder but she put it in the back of her mind. She'd figure it out later.

Mandy sat at the table where a coffee mug had been placed. Michael was pouring another and came to sit across from her. She sipped, a distant look in her eye. So many thoughts going through her head. She was trying to slow them down and it was proving to be a challenging process. Slowly, things were coming into order from the chaos.

"Guess I was a bit zoned there for a minute."

"Don't sweat it. You've had a lot to absorb tonight,"

"I want to go home in the morning." Before Michael could respond, Mandy continued. "I've been running for eight years. That was when I first left Jim. It was a year later that he found me and tried to kill me. I spent 18 months being somewhat physically, emotionally and spiritually repaired. The last five and a half years have been here, always living in fear that he would find me. Now he has. This has to stop. I can't run anymore. There's no freedom in that and no freedom is no life. I love my home. I want to see my kids anytime I want and I don't want to look over my shoulder anymore. I'm tired of this. The only way to end it, is to confront him. I'd rather it be on my turf.".

Michael looked at her. She was terrified. You could see it in her face, how tightly she held herself. But there was also a determination in her eye, in her voice when she spoke. She had heart.

"Tell ya what. See if you like this idea. I'll come back to the house with you. Wait a minute. Don't say no just yet. Hear me out. They'll think twice about confronting any man that's with you. Men who abuse women, do it for control over someone they consider weaker than themselves. They don't want to come up against someone they could possibly lose to. That'd mean a loss of power and they won't risk that. And I won't have to lose any sleep wondering if you're okay."

Mandy looked into her coffee cup, contemplating what he had said. It would be so nice to say yes to this. But if anything happened to Michael, she wouldn't be able to live with herself. If something happened to anyone, for that matter. She really didn't see a way out of this. She looked up.

"I can't let you do that. You have no idea of what he's like and I can't risk something happening to you. He'd kill the horses if he thought he could get to me that way, if he knew about them. The only reason he hasn't gone after Marie and Brad is because they were there. They were also in the courtroom and heard all the testimony at the divorce hearing. They know he wasn't convicted of anything because the guy he hired couldn't be found. I'd bet some major money that's who he sent out here and who we saw at Matt's tonight." She paused, recognition on her face. "It just dawned on me. That's who I saw. The guy on the phone. He seemed familiar but I couldn't place him. He's the one who tried to kill me." Her hands were shaking as she took a sip of coffee.

"All the more reason for me to be there," Michael said as he covered her hand with his own. "I can handle my own. I may not know Jim but I've known men like him and they aren't worth a shit. If I take a punch, I guarantee I can give back worse than I get. So let's just get some sleep tonight and go back in the morning. We can figure out a game plan better with some rest."

Mandy looked at him. She was a pretty logical person. She knew he made sense and she really didn't have an excuse to say no, other than her own fear. Fear was an emotion she could face and, also, down play. It would be nice to have some back up.

"Okay. Let's talk in the morning."

They walked down the hall. As they came to the guest room, Mandy turned to Michael.

"Thank you."

"No problem. Feels good to help someone other than a cow that got herself in a jam. You're a lot prettier and smell better."

Mandy smirked. "I'm glad I smell better than a cow. 'Night."

Michael bent and kissed her cheek. "Get some sleep." He walked down the hall to his room and Mandy shut her door. Lord. She hoped she could.

Mandy had been awake for several hours when the sun came up. She'd thought of several scenarios and tried to figure every possible move Jim's men could make. She knew her own capabilities. She also knew how to compensate for her weaknesses. She didn't know what to expect from Michael. He'd do whatever he'd do. She knew he'd been up most of the night. She'd heard him moving in his room. He had finally quieted down about three hours ago.

She got up. She'd showered the night before which is why she got any sleep at all. She got dressed and grabbed her boots, deciding she couldn't think anymore without coffee. Michael walked in as she was pouring water in the coffee maker.

"Hey, sunshine," he smiled as he opened the refrigerator and grabbed the orange juice.

"Hi. Did you get any sleep?"

"A bit. You?"

"Some. I was trying to figure out situations and reactions. Finally decided I needed coffee to think straight."

"How about coffee and breakfast? Then we can head to your place."

"Personally, I'm not hungry. Coffee's good for me."

Michael started making breakfast and soon the smells of bacon and scrambled eggs filled the kitchen. Mandy put two more pieces of bread in the toaster.

"Okay, I lied," she grinned. "Breakfast would be good."

"It's the bacon. Always makes me hungry. Good thing I made extra."

They ate in silence for a few moments, each in their own thoughts. Michael looked at Mandy, at the concentration on her face.

"What are you thinking?"

"That I'm 55 years old and this is bullshit."

"That is very true." She had always seemed at peace to Michael even when you could feel the underlying current of tension. All these years of coming by to check on her, working on fencing or chatting on the deck or in the kitchen. She had learned to hide not only physically but also her feelings. He was guessing that was about to end.

"I've never tried to make any trouble for Jim. I just wanted to be left alone. I've no interest in him. I don't want his damn money. I had no choice in that. The judge was pissed. He knew Jim had hired those men. He thought it was the only way to get Jim's attention so he made the alimony payments huge and lifelong. It's been so many years and damn it, I'm pissed! I don't like being pushed and he's pushing. But," she said, calming down a bit, "I don't think he's going to be prepared for me. He won't expect the person I've become. He'll expect the woman I was and I'm nothing like her anymore. I don't even look like her, let alone feel like her. It's so strange. It's like the person I was is a distant memory….out there somewhere and I can barely connect with her. The only connection I have to the past is my kids."

Michael had sat, drinking his coffee and listening. As Mandy talked, he watched the emotion on her face. He knew what she meant. Being in combat or on missions, he's had to leave the person he was behind and become someone else. He could relate to what she was saying.

"What have you got planned for him?"

"I don't know. Just have to wait and see how this plays out. I do know I want to confront him face to face. Sending these guys is total crap and it pisses me off he doesn't have the guts to face me. But just have to wait and see. You ready?"

"Yep." Michael stood. Mandy put dishes in the sink. She grabbed her jacket and bag and headed out the door. The sun was just coming up over the mountains. It was so beautiful with all the colors. She wanted to see more beautiful sunrises.

"You really don't have to do this," Mandy said as they got in the truck. "This is my issue and I'll take care of it."

"Damn," Michael said, grinning. "We forgot to talk about that this morning. Guess we'll just have to play it by ear."

Mandy smiled back.

"Okay. But if anything happens to you, I can't tell you how much trouble you'll be in."

"Don't know anyone else I'd rather be in trouble with."

They parked the truck by the barn and turned the horses out in the pasture. Mandy checked the water tank and watched them for a moment. She wanted to keep this picture of them in her mind in case she never saw them again. Seeing them happy, running and bucking and playing helped, a bit.

They drove in silence. The tension built as they got closer. All was quiet as they drove down the drive. Pulling around to the back of the house, they saw the back door open. Why wasn't the alarm going off?

"Where's the wiring to the house?"

"Along the side we just past."

"Stay here. I'll check it."

"Yea, right," Mandy muttered as she got out of the truck. Michael threw her a look that she threw right back.

"My house. My rules."

The line had been cut. Whoever had installed the system had put the line in plain sight. A lot of good that did. Michael looked at Mandy and raised a finger to his lips. She nodded and stood back. Someone could still be in the house. The house was completely still. As he slowly pushed the door open, he heard a low, deep growl. He looked at Mandy.

"When did you get a dog?"

Mandy ran up to the door.

"He's a stray that's been coming around for the last few weeks. Better let me go first."

She walked through the doorway and called softly, "Max? Com' ere, boy. It's okay."

Michael heard the clicking of nails and whimpering. Mandy had dropped to her knees and was hugging one of the biggest dogs Michael had ever seen. He was definitely a mixture of breeds but looked mostly like German Shepard and Malamute. He was licking Mandy's face, tail wagging that was blowing dog hair all over. Mandy was laughing and talking to him all at the same time. He stopped when Michael came in. He didn't growl or bristle, just looked at him.

"He's okay, Max. He's a friend,"

Max came up to Michael and sniffed his hand. Then he pushed his head under his hand so Michael would scratch his ears.

"Guess you're accepted," Mandy grinned. She stood and looked around. Nothing was completely torn up but you could tell someone had been through the mudroom and the kitchen. The disarray stopped at the dining room, where dog hair began.

"Guess they met Max here." Mandy stepped around the table and walked through the rest of the house. Michael and Max followed. Nothing was disturbed.

"Maybe they were looking for confirmation this was my house."

"They didn't find anything in the kitchen?"

"No. I keep all my personal stuff packed away. I've been too scared someone would find me and go after Brad or Marie."

"We never stop being parents, do we?" Michael commented.

"I think he must have come in behind whoever it was and then met them in the dining room," Mandy mused. "I wonder why they didn't shoot him. Maybe they didn't have any guns. Thank God." Her hand dropped to Max's head to gently rub his ears as she was thinking. She turned and walked through the mudroom to the garage, pulling her gun out of her pocket as she walked. Maybe they went out there. As she opened the door and turned on the lights, she sensed rather than saw that someone had been out there. As she scanned the garage, she saw the corner of the cover over her car didn't look right. As she walked around her vehicles, she saw a hand print on the rear quarter panel of her truck. They had been in the garage. She turned and walked out the side door to the barn. Same thing there. Nothing big out of order but you could feel someone had been there. Grain bins weren't down completely, a stall door wasn't latched. Things Mandy did automatically. So now they knew her property but they didn't know all of it. Only what Mandy allowed them to see. Jim must not be thinking right to not give any knowledge of her. But, then, he only knew so much and he didn't know who she was now.

As Mandy was walking back into the house, Michael was checking the pens. There were footprints all along the fence. If Max had stopped them in the house, they must have investigated the outside before going in, obviously realizing she wasn't home.

Mandy was checking several drawers when Michael came in.

"All your weapons where they should be?"

"How'd you know that's what I was looking for?"

"You said you had four back at the house last night and that's what I'd do if I was you. I'd need to know if they were there. Are they?"

"Yea."

"Good."

Max decided his job of guarding was done for now. He stood in the mudroom and whined. Mandy filled his bowls with fresh food and water. He ate and then promptly went to his bed in the living room under the window and went to sleep, head on his paws. Michael smiled. It all made perfect sense. He didn't say anything as Mandy went about putting her house back in order. As she was finishing up, her cell rang.

"Hi, honey. No, I'm home. Yea, I know. Someone was here after I left last night. No, I'm not leaving. This is it, Brad. I'm done running. He will deal with me on my turf and my terms, if he even realizes this is my house. I think Max must have scared them off and Michael is here with me." Pause. "Max is a stray dog that's decided to stay and Michael is who I bought the property from." Another pause. "Okay. I'll see ya soon." She turned and looked at Michael.

"My son is coming. Seems he's a bit concerned."

"I gathered that. I think he needs to be concerned. This could get ugly."

"He knows that. He's also concerned about you. He wants to know what our relationship is and if he needs to be worried about you."

"Oh, yea?" Michael looked at Mandy. "I'm glad he's concerned but I'm not a threat to anyone but Jim."

"I hope so. You need to know I've never asked anyone for help. What I've done, I've done by myself because I was so scared of what would happen. I haven't even spoke to my best friend. Brad has no idea of why I've allowed you in. Why I trust you. He doesn't know anything about except your name so he's going to be a bit......curious. He will tell Marie and they both will do as much research on you that they can find before they get here. I know that. He didn't have to say anything. They won't get stupid. They are both logical people. I raised them to think. The only issue they won't listen to all sides on is Jim. They know what he tried to do. They don't care how he tries to justify it. There is no justification."

"Can I put my card on the table?"

"Please do. An up-front man would be so refreshing."

"I've always known you've been through some sort of trauma. You tried to hide it and did a pretty good job. I've watched you heal in the last few years and the last few months, you've started to relax. My intentions last night were to take you to dinner, dazzle you with my wit, humor, charm and good looks," he said with a smirk, "and hope to get to know a small amount more about you. I want to know you, what you think, what you feel. I got a small dose of that in the last 12 hours and I stand by what I said. I'm not asking you to be my girlfriend, to move in with me or get married or any of that. I' saying I want us to get to know each more and see where it leads. Maybe it's for the long haul. Maybe not. But I think we've both been through enough shit that we deserve to find out." He had moved to stand in front of her and now put his hands on her shoulders.

"What d'ya think?"

Mandy hugged him. She looked up.

"I think we do, too." She leaned against his chest and they just stood there, holding each other. They could have stayed that way, arms wrapped around each other, safe, warm and secure. Allowing to feel things that had been lacking in both their lives. Suddenly, both of them stiffened. A car was coming. Max was immediately at Mandy's side. His hair stood up on his back and he rumbled his deep growl.

Mandy moved to the kitchen, pulling her gun out of her pocket and dropping her arm to the side of her leg. She looked out the window. A black Dodge Charger with tinted windows had pulled in behind Michael's truck. Two men got out. The same two men that were at Matt's last night. Her gut instinct had been right. She had been the topic of conversation.

They weren't particularly large men but by the way they carried themselves, Mandy knew they were in shape. They dressed in slacks and leather jackets – obviously from LA. She guessed them to be in their late 30s or early 40s. Mandy stepped out on the porch with Max beside her and Michael a step behind.

"Can I help you?"

They weren't expecting anyone to come out of the house. For it to possibly be the woman they were looking for, a big man and a huge dog took them by surprise.

"We're looking for Amanda Thompson. We understand she lives around here."

"No on here by that name." Mandy's voice was mater of fact.

"Do you know where she lives?'

"No."

"You fit the general description of here."

"About a third of the women in Wyoming fit my general description."

"I think we found her." The guy who had been on the phone at Matt's made the statement.

Mandy had been leaning on the screen door. As she stepped forward, she also moved her right arm forward. They still couldn't see her gun because of the shadowed porch.

"Sorry to disappoint you."

Both men started to reach inside their jackets. Michael stepped up. In his hand was his .9 mil, pointed directly at them.

"I think you need to listen. She said she's not who you're looking for. Now get off the property."

Mandy raised her gun.

"You need to leave. Now. Don't come back."

Max growled. He bared his teeth and stepped in front of Mandy. The two men looked at each other and started to back away.

"He won't be happy with your answer."

"Since I don't know who 'HE' is, I don't care."

They walked backwards to the car, got in and left, raising dust as they drove out the driveway.

"They'll be back."

"I know," Mandy replied. Her arm was shaking. She looked down at her gun and started to laugh.

"What's so funny?"

"I left the safety on." She walked back into the house and put her gun in the drawer.

Michael sat at the table with Max at his side. He reached down to pet him and seemed to be lost in his own thoughts.

"When they tell Jim I had a gun, a man with a gun and huge dog, he'll think for a bit and then send them back to get tougher. How the hell did he find me?"

"I don't know but we better figure it out." Michael paused. "You've never aimed a gun at anything, have you?"

"Does a target count?"

"No."

"Well, then, no. I can hit the bull's eye dead on even when it's moving. But I know a living thing is different."

"Yes, it is. There may come a time when you won't be able to think about it. Your survival or someone with you may depend on it."

"I know. By the time I've come to terms with it, it may be too late. That scares the hell outa me."

"Just think about it. Face it in your mind as much as you can. Imagine all the feelings of the situation. The fear. The anger. Imagine pulling that trigger. Imagine it until it's not so scary. It still will be but hopefully, it won't paralyze you."

"You know a lot about this. Part of your military training?" Mandy was pouring coffee as she she spoke. She handed Michael his and sat down. She wasn't shaking as much.

"Yea. Sometimes you're faced with things you'd rather not have to. And I trained a lot of people. We had the benefit of physical scenarios that we could practice with until the fear wasn't as strong. They could still be scared but could think it through and handle the situation. They learned to use the fear to stay alert. You don't have that option."

"How long were you in?" Mandy was trying to talk about anything other than what they had just faced. She needed some time to process it, a little at a time.

"Twenty years."

Mandy looked at him. It didn't take a genius to figure out he had been gone most of the time the kids had been growing up.

"And yes, that is part of what destroyed my marriage. In all fairness, I could've had any job and it wouldn't have lasted."

Mandy waited. She knew what was going through his head. There was no rushing it.

"Allison is a complicated woman. She comes from the Baker Ranch up in the northeast part of the state. She grew up around a lot of money, politics and power. Her dad had a lot to do with the Cattleman's Association and was Lt. Governor for several years. Her mom was an attorney with the State Attorney General's office. We met when I was home on leave between the transition of leaving the Rangers and joining Delta Force. There was a formal dinner at the Governor's mansion for all the returning soldiers. Full dress uniform, ball gowns. I don't think there's been anything like that done in over 30 years. She came up and asked me to dance. When I looked at her, I thought I'd found heaven. She was breathtakingly beautiful. I never did find out why she picked me. I thought it was because I'd been promoted to Delta Force and she was attracted to the excitement and danger. Anyway, I was home for six weeks and we were inseparable. When I got my orders for training in South Carolina, she wanted to go with me. I said only if she married me. We got married and went south." Michael paused to sip some coffee.

"I had 18 months of training and got orders to go to the Middle East with my team. By this time, Allison was pretty well established in the community and was finishing law school. She wanted to finish her last year and then start practicing law. She found out she was pregnant with Kenny about two months before I left. So we were planning for the baby, She'd be graduating by the time I got back. I wasn't to be gone more than four months. We were pretty excited at that point. Of course, her parents wanted her to come home but Allison wanted to stick it out on post. She had her doctors there and had made some really good friends. I'll give her that. I went over -seas and she stayed on base. The mission lasted five months instead of four and when I got back, something was different. I couldn't put my finger on it but as soon as I got off the plane, I could feel it. But with the baby coming and all the excitement surrounding that, I just kinda ignored it."

"Kenny was born and three months later, I went out on another mission. I was gone for another few months and then home for a few.

That's how it was. I never knew when I'd be going or where or for how long. It was hard on her, taking care of a new baby and starting a new job. She did try and gave it everything she had. I was proud of her for that. I went on missions and she went to work for Legal Aid in town. About six months after Kenny was born, I came home to find out she was pregnant again. But, like I said, something wasn't right. It was starting to feel sort of normal by now. We had Dustin. I started to hate leaving them. All I wanted to do was take them home so my kids could grow up in the country and learn about life by living it instead of seeing it on TV. We talked about it a lot. About coming back home to the ranch.

"My parents weren't old by any means but they had worked their whole lives on our ranch and it was time for them to reap some of the rewards. My brothers were helping so it wasn't like the ranch wasn't being taken care of. Dad and I talked a lot about me leaving the service. He was always worried I wouldn't make it back to see my mountains. And Allison was pregnant again. Only I knew the baby wasn't mine. We hadn't had sex in over two months before I left. I guess she figured I was just some dumb soldier who wouldn't figure it out."

Michael was quiet for a few minutes. He looked at Mandy. She held his gaze.

"To make a long story short, I went out on one last mission. I had already decided to get out of the field. I knew we were headed for divorce. I just didn't know when. I had a suspicion that Dustin wasn't mine either but I didn't care. I loved him. I was the only dad he'd ever known. I had two sons. Period. When I came back from the last mission, Allison was in the hospital. She had delivered at seven and half months. I went directly to the hospital from the plane. Allison was still in recovery and Alex in in the NICU. After I checked on Allison and spoke to the nurses, I went to see my daughter. I didn't care that she wasn't mine. She would have my last name and we were still married at the time. She was mine. She broke my heart. She was lying there with all these tubes stuck in her in the incubator. The nurses told me she was in good shape for being premature. Her lungs weren't fully developed but she was a fighter. I had to put on a gown and gloves. There were these holes in the incubator where you put your arms through in order to hold her hand or touch her. We couldn't hold her yet. I had her little hand in mine and was rubbing the top of it. She opened her eyes and looked at me for about four seconds. She did this little sigh and went back to sleep. She had coal black eyes and olive complexion. I'm part Blackfoot but not enough for it to show up that much. She was a beautiful baby. For two days, I was back and forth to the hospital, sitting with Allison and Alex. They finally released Allison and we split our time between the hospital and home. One of us was always with the boys and a neighbor came over to help Allison when I was gone. We got to bring Alex home about a month later.

"All during this time, we never talked about anything. We did surface stuff, the kids, chores. I didn't love her anymore. I hadn't for several years and I knew she didn't love me. Here we were. Stair step kids and no future together. I had put in for a position as training officer in Ft. Hood, TX. It was closer to home and I could get up to the ranch several times a year, schedule permitting. I hadn't said anything to Allison about it.

"One day, about two months after Alex was born, I got a call from one of her girlfriends. Pretty ironic as that was the same day I had decided to tell Allison we needed to have a talk. Celeste had been Allison's friend since we had moved to the base. She asked me to meet her for lunch off base so I knew something was up.

"I met her at this little hole in the wall cafe. I had discovered it several years previously and like to go there when I just needed some down time. Celeste was waiting for me. She was married to the base commander and knew just about everything that went on base. We talked for a long time. She confirmed my suspicions about the kids and that Allison was planning on leaving me in the next few weeks. I asked her why she was telling me this when she was supposed to be Allison's friend. She said because a person was a friend, that didn't give the other person the right to involve them in something that person didn't believe in. She said my job was tough enough without having to come home to this kind of bullshit. She was pretty pissed.

"I went home and asked Allison to get a sitter so we could go out to dinner. I let her know we needed to talk without the kids. At dinner I let her know I didn't love her anymore and I knew she didn't love me. I wanted to end this amicably for the sake of the kids. She agreed. I let her know I wanted joint custody of the kids. She asked me if I would consider full legal custody. That blew me away. We talked about why and what that would mean. She had been offered a job at the federal attorney general's office that did the investigation and prosecution of drug smugglers. She felt that if I had the kids, they would be safer because she didn't know what she'd be going up against. I still believe that it gave her more freedom and she wouldn't have to feel guilty about not being there for them. I got the kids. We worked out a schedule so she could see them. I never mentioned that I knew about Dustin and Alex. She never offered the information but I had them tested. Biologically, they aren't mine. I just needed to know for my own sake. I didn't want to get caught by surprise at some point in the future. I've never told them. They have no idea as far as I know. Anyway, we moved to Ft Hood and came up here whenever we could. I worked the ranch when we were here and the kids loved it. I went to night school in TX and got my degree in Ranch Management and Business. I retired from the service at 39. We moved here permanently. Allison kept in touch with the kids but didn't see them much after about the first two years. She'd send them birthday and Christmas cards but didn't come to see them. She was always working some case. They had a hard time with that, especially Kenny. I put us all into counseling. Alex didn't really think much about it. Her family didn't have Allison in it. I just wanted a solid base for when the questions started. Dustin had his moments but Kenny was almost five when we split up so it was rougher on him. But we got through it and here we are. I really think it made us stronger."

Mandy didn't say anything. She was having a hard time understanding how anyone, especially a woman, could walk away from their children for a career. It was beyond her comprehension and she really didn't care to try and understand it. She took Michael's mug and refilled it.

"You're awfully quiet."

"I don't understand how anyone could leave their babies for a career. But thank God she had enough sense to let you have them and there wasn't a custody battle. I am so thankful those sweet little kids had you."

"There wouldn't have been a custody fight. The service doesn't have a very high opinion of someone who cheats on their spouse while they're deployed. And Allison is very intelligent. She knew not to even go there. All the stops would have been pulled if I felt those kids were in any danger. Even though she gave them up, I have to believe that she did, and still does, care about them. Some people just weren't made to be parents."

Mandy could only nod her agreement. She remembered once when Jim had hit her so hard, she had literally flown across the room, hitting her head on the wall and falling to the floor. The kids had been screaming as Brad was only four and Marie two. Both of them had been hitting Jim in the legs and screaming not to hit mommy again. Yea, some people need to be shot for their non-parenting skills.

"Waiting around is going to drive me crazy with the horses gone. I'm trying to figure out how Jim found me. No one knows I'm here and he doesn't know the name my ID is under." She paused. "Do you work out?"

"Yea. About three to four times a week."

"Want to spar with me?"

"Sure. You any good?"

"Are we still talking about sparring?"

"Maybe. Maybe not."

Mandy just grinned as she walked down the hall.

"Meet ya in the workout room."

Michael took his bag to the guest room and changed. This could be fun, depending on how good she really was. He was betting she was top of the third degree. Mandy didn't come across as someone who didn't give her all.

They warmed up and worked out on the equipment in the room. Then all the equipment was pushed to the side and the mats brought out. They sparred for the better part of two hours. Both took their falls. By the time they were done, they were both lying on the mats, literally in pools of sweat and breathing hard. They were a good match.

"You really need to go for your fourth- degree belt," Michael said, once he could talk.

"Ya think?"

"Yea. I've got my fourth degree and you stayed with me all the way."

"Nice to know since I haven't had a master in several years."

Mandy stood up.

"I'm in the shower."

"Need any help? I'm great at washing backs."

"I bet you are but I'm good."

"Yea. I bet you are."

Mandy threw him a grin as she walked out of the room. A shower would be good right now. The sexual tension was a bit hard to deal with. God. You'd think they were a couple of hormonal teenagers.

The warm water felt wonderful as it ran down her body. Mandy lathered up and was trying to keep things in perspective. She was attracted to Michael. Anyone in their right mind would be but now? Really? It just seemed so bizarre when Jim was after her again. What was that saying? God's timing is perfect. Okay. She'll go with that and see where this leads.

Max was in her room when she came out of the shower. She was expecting the door to be open but it wasn't. Interesting. Now she had a stray dog that shut doors. Maybe she was just losing her mind. Oh, well. Now was as good a time as any. She put on lotion and clean clothes. As she dressed, she thought of who had any information on her. Only the kids. Sally only had the cell number. None of this made any sense. She wondered if the call to Brad and Marie could have been monitored. She'd have to ask Brad. He'd know. Maybe Michael would, too.

Michael found Mandy out on the back porch when he came out. She'd poured two iced teas that were sitting on the table between the two chairs. It was going to be cool tonight but now it was nice out. She smiled at him as he sat down.

"Feel better?"

"Yea. I feel great. That was a good workout."

"Glad to oblige, sir. That tea's for you." Michael drank down half the glass. His hair was drying in the slight breeze. He was fresh, clean and relaxed. Since he didn't know what else was coming, that was a good thing.

"Do you think anyone could have monitored Brad or Marie's phones?"

"That's a possibility. Still thinking how you were found?"

"Yea. They're the only ones who know where I am. Sally can only reach me by cell and it's a burner. I don't talk to anyone else."

"I'm no computer geek but I know that would most likely take a satellite. That would mean connections. I know the government uses them to track and the big software companies like Microsoft can, also. I don't know all the details on how it's done, though."

"But you know more than I do and Brad probably knows more than both of us since he's had Jim's phone monitored."

"I have to agree with you there."

Mandy's cell phone rang. It was Sally.

"Hey, Sal. I have a bit of back up here. No. I'm not doing this alone." Mandy explained what had transpired. "And they've been here. No shots fired. I'm figuring they'll be back. Okay. I will. Have you any idea how I was found? Have you heard anything?"

Mandy chuckled. "Consider it done. Talk to you soon." She turned to Michael. "Word in LA's that Jim's sending more people. Sally will see what she can find out."

Chapter 4

"It's time I made a few calls." Michael walked down to his truck and pulled his cell phone from the console. He dialed a number and leaned against the rear fender. Mandy watched him from the porch. His eyes never left her face as he spoke. She got out of the chair and walked towards him.

"More like our mission in northeast India. We don't know how many or when they're coming. We just got word he's sending more men. Mandy's son's coming in tonight and I've got Kenny and Dustin close by if I need them. Okay. Thanks, Marty. See ya then." He hung up and dialed another number.

"Hey, how's it going? Good. Are you going to be in cell range today? I might need you guys over here at Mandy's. No, that's why the horses are in the little pasture. No, no need to now. Just wanted to know you could get here. Okay. Stay sharp. We don't know what's out there yet. Yea, you too, son."

Mandy was leaning against the truck door, watching him.

"Jim's not a nice guy. He's got connections to some ugly people."

"I know. What I don't know is why he still wants me dead. I'm not a threat. The last contact we had was in the courtroom when we got divorced. The look on his face was pure hate. I just wish I knew why."

"Sometimes people change. Something in their brain disconnects and it's all short-circuited. The only thing you did was something in their mind. He sounds like a control freak and has been going on a down- hill spiral for years."

"That's all true. But something had to trigger this and I don't know what."

"And you may never know."

"That scares the hell outa me. If this doesn't come to some sort of resolution, what will it be the next time?"

"There's not gonna be a next time. Jim knows that. He also knows you're not alone. He'll pull out all the stops. No matter what the reason was in the beginning, it doesn't matter anymore."

Mandy was quiet. She knew he was right. She was terrified someone would get hurt or killed. There were people coming to help her that she didn't even know.

"The police have already been notified. They're more than willing to do what they can."

"Yea. I have to be dead before they'll do anything. Not much said for past history, huh?" She held a lot of anger towards law enforcement in general. Criminals had more rights than honest people. Wouldn't want to offend the poor, misguided creatures. She had tried for several years to get LA County to listen to her. It wasn't until she was almost dead that someone listened. Thank God that someone was Sally.

"I talked to the sheriff. I had him call your friend in LA. Personally, I think Jim's so powerful, they don't want to screw up anything in nailing him. I think he's involved in a lot more than you know about."

"That's comforting," Mandy said sarcastically. "But it makes sense. What I know is bad enough. What makes you think so?"

"Just a gut feeling. Something's not right about all this. It just seems to be so far off. What else has this guy been into that he hasn't been caught with? I have a call in to a friend of mine at the FBI. Maybe he can find out."

Mandy stood staring out to the pastures and the mountains. Her hand dropped to Max's head. Michael was voicing things she had thought for years. There had been the late nights, quiet phone calls, the sudden trips out of town with no explanation. She'd always thought it was another woman. Lord knows there had been enough of them. But what if it had been something else. She remembered trips to Mexico that were supposed to be business. She had no reason to think it was anything else at the time. Now, as she thought about it, she wondered who would hire an American when there were so many people out of work there. He was always nervous when he came home but gave the reasoning of permits and licensing – all issues he knew Mandy would never question. She questioned everything now. The bastard wanted her dead.

"Penny for your thoughts?"

"I'm sorry," Mandy smiled. "Just trying to piece some things together."

"Hind sight's always twenty/twenty."

"I have something to show you." She moved off the truck towards the pasture, Max at her side.

They walked across the pasture to the tree line of evergreens that was at the edge of Mandy's property. They had just entered the first trees when Max turned around, facing the house. He growled deep in his chest and the hair stood up on his back. Mandy looked towards the house. The Charger had returned and four men stepped from it. They went to the house and walked in. She looked at Michael. He saw the fear and anger on her face.

"Do you have your gun?"

"No. It's in the truck."

"Is it locked?"

He gave her that "you've got to be kidding" look.

"Are we too far away to lock it?"

"I don't know. I've never had to try," he said as he pulled the key out of his pocket. He hit the "Lock" on the fob. The light flashed, indicating it was locked.

They stepped back into the shadows of the trees with Mandy tugging on Max's collar.

"Max. With me." He stayed by Mandy's side, looking at the house, then at her and whining.

"No, buddy," she said, scratching his ears. "Not yet. We'll go soon." He sat, looking at the house.

The men came out of the house. They stood on the porch for a moment. Then one of them went over to Michael's truck. He looked inside, tried the door, then went back to the truck bed. Someone on the porch said something and the guy near the truck picked up a rock, arm drawn back as if to throw the rock through the passenger window. At just that moment, Michael hit the "Horn" button. Not only did the horn go off but the lights started flashing. The guy dropped the rock and looked all around, expecting to see someone come from the barn or somewhere else. Then they all ran for the Charger and left. They were almost to the road before the horn and lights stopped.

Mandy looked at Michael and grinned. "Smart ass. You kept your finger on the button."

Michael laughed. "Yea, well, this far away and no gun, it was all I could do. I just got the windshield replaced from a log truck throwing gravel and it would really piss me off to have to do it again."

"Hey. Whatever works."

They ran to the house. Max took off ahead of them and pushed his way through the door into the house. He was running through every room, looking to see if anyone was left in the house. Michael pulled out his phone.

"We need to stay out of the house. Don't touch anything. If there's prints here, the sheriff will need to go through it." Mandy nodded and called Max. They went back outside as Michael called the sheriff.

"Sheriff Waters, please. Michael Johnson. Hank? You might want to come out to Mandy Leed's place. I'm sure we can get you some finger prints. Yea, we'll be here, a big dog and us. No. He won't hurt anyone unless he feels Mandy's threatened. See ya in a bit."

"This all seems so surreal," Mandy said quietly.

"I know. It must seem part of a bad nightmare."

Michael covered her hand with his and gently rubbed the back of her hand with his thumb. Such a small gesture but so comforting.

"Yea. But it's real. It's really happening all over again and I don't want to do it again. I do believe one violent traumatic event is enough for one lifetime."

"None would be better for the average person."

"Some of us don't get to be that lucky. You being in the military are more than aware of that. I know that being in such an elite team, you saw more than regular military personnel did and they saw and see enough. There's no telling what you've seen." Or what he'd had to be involved in. Mandy knew orders were carried out whatever way possible. Just as long as the job got done.

"This isn't about me," Michael commented quietly.

"But you can relate to all of it. You've been here before, know the procedure and can give an educated guess as to what could happen." Mandy's voice was low and her look intense. She only had her one experience to draw on. She needed some direction and Michael was the only one who could give her any at all.

"Let's see what Hank says when he gets here and what information we get from my guys when they call back. I need more than what we've got before I guess at anything."

"He's a monster."

Michael squeezed her hand.

"And monsters can die. We both know there's more to this than what it appears. Maybe we can hit him from another direction or several at once." He paused. "What were you going to show me?"

Just then, his cell phone rang. He looked at Caller ID.

"Hey, buddy. What ya got for me?" Michael went quiet. He kept his gaze on Mandy. He motioned for paper and pen, pointing towards the truck. Mandy ran to it and Michael hit the UNLOCK on the key fob. She found everything in the console.

"Okay. Let me know." He hung up but before he could finish writing, the phone rang again, only this time, Caller ID said "unavailable." His brow wrinkled as he answered.

"Hello?" Mandy saw a fleeting shadow cross Michael's face. It was only there for a moment, then gone.

"Oh, yea?" His tone was guarded, edgy. "So, I guess congratulations are in order. When do you plan on being here? We'll see ya then." He hung up.

Mandy was leaning against the railing, waiting.

"Which do you want first?"

"How about the order of the calls?'

"Okay. First. A buddy of mine returned my call. He said Jim is involved with the Contrereas Cartel out of Bolivia. There's been some major drug busts all over the southwest. Jim has been doing some smuggling. He's smuggling it in building supplies and pottery he's getting in Mexico then he brings it across the border. He's also trying to setup another office in Arizona." There was something Michael wasn't saying. Mandy could feel it, see it in his face. She waited.

"Just tell me.

"He's got a $2,000,000.00 life insurance policy on you and he needs the money for the business and legal fees."

Mandy's face drained. She grabbed hold of the railing and took several deep breaths.

"What else?'

"The other call was Allison. She still works for the attorney general. She says she's remarried and wants to see the kids. She wants them to meet her husband."

"What timing." Mandy moved back to her chair and sat down. "It all makes sense now. The behavior, the abuse. I wonder if he was sampling his product. He used to say how he hated addicts – that they were worthless people who only took and gave nothing back. Guess he should know. But, damn! Two million dollars? I had no idea he had any life insurance me. There used to be one on him for a million dollars. I was the beneficiary, at least until the kids got through school. I imagine he had me taken off that. There was another one. It was for the business so people could be paid until they found another job. That's all I know." She looked up at Michael. "How is he getting it across the border without being detected? The dogs could smell it."

Michael stood up, pulling Mandy up with him. She leaned her head against his chest, listening to his heart beat. Solid. Strong. Things were starting to fall into place. She just needed to stay alive to figure out the rest of it.

"I don't know, babe. They have to be pretty inventive to get so much into the US."

They heard a vehicle coming in the drive. Mandy reached for her gun in her pocket. An SUV pulled up. Max walked downs the steps. He just stood there, not growling but not wagging his tail. A young woman got out of the passenger side. Mandy instantly relaxed and ran down the steps.

"Hey, mom."

Marie was beautiful. She resembled Mandy in the face. Her smile was definitely Mandy's as were the brown eyes. She had the same olive complexion with a hint of copper and that slender frame. Her hair was more dark brown with gold highlights. She was a beautiful as her mother. Mandy hugged her hard.

Brad had pulled the bags out of the back of the SUV before coming completely around to his mother. He grabbed her and hugged her off her feet, up to his 6'3" height. You could tell these were Mandy's kids. Brad's smile was a bit different and he had aqua blue eyes but the shape of his eyes were the same as Mandy's. And the dark brown hair. With his copper skin tone, his eyes jumped out at you. Mandy stood looking at them, tears running down her face as she looked at Michael with a smile. He walked down the steps to stand next to her, smiling because he hadn't seen her really smile since last night.

"Michael, these are my kids, Brad and Marie." Both shook Michael's hand. Both had a strong grip and friendly faces but he also picked up caution radiating from both of them. Good. They needed to be.

"And," Mandy said as Max pressed against her leg, tail wagging and a smile on his face, "this is Max. He showed up a couple of weeks ago and has moved in." Max sniffed both hands and licked them, his way of saying they were accepted.

Brad put the bags on the deck and sat down. Mandy explained what had just happened and that they were waiting for the sheriff. Michael was aware of them appraising the situation. They were quiet, letting Mandy talk.

"I know you must be hungry. As soon as the sheriff gets here and does whatever he needs to do, we can make dinner."

"I'm good for now, mom. Just thirsty."

"Here." Mandy handed Marie her tea. Marie smiled her thanks and finished the rest.

"So, mom, what all has happened since last night. I'm trying to organize everything in my brain and it's not working. I don't have the right sequence of everything." This was from Brad. He leaned back in his chair and stretched out his long legs. He folded his hands across his belly and gave the impression of being totally relaxed. Michael knew better. He could feel it.

Mandy leaned back in her chair.

"Can I tell you the same time I tell the sheriff? That way I only have to say it once."

"Sure. My brain can handle a while longer," Brad grinned.

"Smart ass."

"I know. Got it from my mom." That eased the tension as everyone chuckled, knowing it was true.

"Now," Mandy said. "What are you doing here? You know how ugly this could get."

Marie leaned forward and took Mandy's hand.

"Mom. We're here. We're staying 'til this bullshit is done. Dad has to stop. I don't even know who he is anymore. He's like a completely different person from who we knew growing up. He's become this psycho bastard from hell. Why do you think Brad's kept tabs on him all these years? I have a file over six inches thick on my desk full of memos, letters, emails, you name it, that have come across my desk in the last four years alone on our illustrious father. Brad knows more on a personal level than I do because he's monitored him. He has a stronger stomach for that crap than I do. I'll fight face to face but what Dad's doing makes me sick."

Mandy looked at her daughter. She was no longer a baby. She was a woman grown and could handle herself. She was strong. Mandy was so grateful for that. Brad leaned forward.

"We're here. We're staying. He deals with all of us."

"You guys have your own lives. I don't want them interrupted again because of your father and me."

"Mom. You did nothing wrong. Remember, we were there. We saw more than you think. As far as we're concerned, he's not our father. He just happened to be the donor. The man we knew as Dad is gone and not coming back. So," he smiled, "calm down and let us be here. We're family. We stand together. And I, for one need a shower so I hope the sheriff hurries up."

Mandy smiled. Just then, they heard a car coming in the drive. The county sheriff's SUV pulled in.

Hank Waters was a big man. He stood 6'4" and weighed 235 lbs that was solid muscle. He was average looking with dark brown hair and chocolate brown eyes. His square jaw could give him a stubborn look, at times, but what was so intriguing about him was the fact of how dedicated and compassionate he was. He believed in what he did and would always follow the law, though he had been known to let it be bent from time to time. He didn't allow it to be broken blatantly but understood that not everybody knew everything. He was 38 and had been a widower for about five years, his wife being killed by a drunk driver. That was one area he had zero tolerance for. Who could blame him?

"Hi, Mandy. Michael. Glad to see you again but sorry it because of these circumstances"

"You, too, Hank," Mandy answered. "Let me introduce my son and daughter, Brad and Marie. This is Sheriff Waters."

With pleasantries aside, Hank leaned against the railing on the deck. Mandy took a deep breath. Hank had brought out a small notebook and had a pen ready.

"I know this is tough, so just take your time. I understand that this whole thing started eight years ago. Is that right?"

With that question, Mandy started the whole story. She left out the part about Brad monitoring Jim's phone. That could get him in some serious trouble, regardless of the reason why. She knew that it should be healing since she'd kept everything to herself and the kids for so long. But at the moment, it just made her tired.

Hank had been given a very condensed version before he got to the house. Michael had only told him so much as he felt it should be coming from Mandy. He had known Michael for most of his life. Their families had been some of the some of the first ranchers in the area. He had only met Mandy a few times in town. She had always given him the impression of someone fighting a lethal battle. Now he knew he'd been dead on. He listened. Took notes. Asked questions when something wasn't clear to him. Studied faces. Brad seemed to be a straight shooter. There was no love lost for his father. Marie resembled her mother, same built, same dark brown eyes. She was an attorney. Interesting. He wouldn't hold that against her. So was Alex. He'd bet they would be a tough team together. Marie didn't try to control the situation. She sat and listened. It was obvious that her and Brad's only concern was for Mandy's safety.

"I know you can't do anything until a crime has been committed," Mandy was saying. "I also know he will try to kill me again. I think the one guy I saw in Matt's is who tried to kill me the last time. I know him from somewhere and that's where I really do believe it is. I got this feeling in the pit of my stomach and that's the only thing that seems to fit."

"Let me see what I can come up with. I may not be able to arrest anyone 'til something happens but that doesn't mean I'll let you be a target." Hank turned to Michael. "And you have some buddies coming?"

"What makes you think that?"

"Well, maybe because I've known you in some capacity most of my life."

"Don't let it get around, but, yea, I do. I made a few calls. Thought we might need some help if you couldn't."

"Who said I couldn't?"

"You have to wait 'til something happens, a law is broken. We don't."

"Not always. Let me see what's up. I'm waiting for some call backs. Okay if I go through the house and check for finger prints?" When Mandy nodded, Hank continued, "I'll have to take all your prints so we can eliminate those. Mandy, do you have any idea how you were found?"

"I've been asking myself that all night. It makes no sense to me. I'm good at hiding my tracks but maybe I slipped up somewhere. Maybe I blew it because I settled in one spot."

Hank was thoughtful. He made a few more notes in his little book.

"You need to check out Mandy's truck in the garage," Michael said. "There's a clear, full hand print on her right rear quarter panel." Hank nodded and pushed away from the railing, taking his finger print kit with him as he headed to the house.

After Hank dusted the house, Mandy's truck, checked the barn and pens, he left. He had his own calls to make and back up of his own to get in place. Plus, he wanted to find out more about these guys who were out and about in his county. He had a bad feeling about this one and he learned a long time ago to go with his gut. He was right 99.9% of the time.

It took about an hour to clean all the finger print dust off everything. Mandy started dinner. She would enjoy tonight's dinner because she could and also because she needed something to do that would take her mind off all this, even for a minute. She kept looking out the kitchen window above the sink. As it grew dark, she listened for any noise that wasn't familiar. Every nerve was on alert. Now she knew why she'd been so edgy lately. Something was coming. Well, it was here. Phoenix had felt it, pacing and not eating yesterday. She looked at Max. He was laying with his head on his paws, under the dining table where she usually sat. He raised his head to look at her, sensing she needed his support. Then he laid his head back down on his paws. If Max was okay, she'd trust him. He's let her know if anything was wrong.

Marie came into the kitchen and helped with dinner. She enjoyed cooking and it gave her and her mom some time together. They talked about her job and how things were going in general. Brad was quiet for a while and then started asking Michael about ranching, cattle, machinery and the business end of it. That surprised Mandy. Both of them did. They were city people. They needed the high energy of the city. Brad was always interested in business and how things worked. She just didn't know he'd be interested in ranching.

"You'd be proud, mom. I learned to ride."

Mandy looked at Marie. Horses were something neither of them had ever been interested in. They liked them but they weren't born with the "fever". Only Mandy had been. The surprise must have shown on her face.

"What brought this on?"

"Brad and I decided that since you were going to be in the country and raise horses, we at least needed to know the basics so we wouldn't be a pain in your ass when we came to visit and it's something we can do together. Your old trainer made some calls for both of us as to who to go to where we live. It was weird. Both of us started to love it once we started to understand the language of horses. We've been having a blast! We decided that it was a repressed gene in us. Didn't come out 'til we made it!" Brad turned around and looked at them from his conversation with Michael. He looked like a little boy who'd gotten and A on his test.

"I knew that would blow you away!" He started laughing.

Mandy looked at Michael with the same shocked look on her face. When she had started riding, she had wanted them involved but they were teenagers back then and were only interested in cars... boys, girls. Clothes...boys, girls. Sports... boys, girls. They lived in Southern

California and wanted that fast pace. Mandy finally gave up and enjoyed her horses by herself.

"Mom, Brad's learning to ride cutting horses. I've been taking lessons from a reining trainer. We're just trying different things. We've taught each other what we've learned by ourselves. Just trying to see what fits us." She put her arm around her mother.

"We rock, mom!"

Mandy would have never guessed they had been up to this. They continually surprised her. Always had. She just smiled.

"Guess you don't have complete "city kids" anymore," Michael grinned.

"I guess not. Weren't you saying you needed some more help moving cattle from the summer to the winter pastures?"

"Yes, I did. Are you volunteering?"

Mandy looked at her kids. They were just grinning. If they were acting like that, they had some confidence in their abilities.

"I think I'm volunteering all of us."

"Great. It will be one big family affair!"

Dinner was placed on the table and questions started flying about what was all involved moving a large herd of cattle. Michael explained how they were split up and what pastures were used. He always moved the cattle closer to the houses in the winter. Easier to get to when calving season came and safer from predators. The topics slowly changed to what was facing them now. They threw around ideas but everything was a guess at this point. They didn't know anything for sure. After dinner, with dishes done and everyone having a glass of wine, Mandy was suddenly exhausted. She couldn't think anymore. But before she completely shut down, she need to ask Brad what had been bothering her.

"Brad, could yours or Marie's phones been monitored?"

"I've been thinking the same thing, mom. That's the only thing that makes sense. We don't have any information on you written down or stored. We always cover our tracks when we come to visit. We change our phones constantly. It would have to be someone who really knew their stuff and had access to the equipment. I know private people can't get the security clearance for it and few companies can. The feds don't clear many. That doesn't mean it can't be done. I found a way to work around it and monitor Jim. Someone else could do what I've done."

"Okay. I'm just trying to figure this out. I can't think anymore. I'm going to bed." She paused and looked at the three of them. "Thank you for being here. All of you." She stood. Marie came and gave her a hug, as did Brad. As she walked past Michael, he grabbed her hand and squeezed it. She smiled at him and squeezed back.

She called Max and let him outside. He was back in a few minutes and stayed by her as she started down the hall.

"You have a body guard," Michael said.

"Appears so. Just to be on the safe side, if you need me, knock first and call his name. That should save you, I think."

Max was lying by the door when Mandy got to her room. She stopped and loved on him for a few minutes before heading into the shower. As the warm water ran down her neck and shoulders, the stress of the day eased. She tried to think of a way for everyone to get out of this without being hurt. But her brain was mush. Too much stress in a short period of time. She'd think about it tomorrow. She dried her hair and literally crawled into bed. She was asleep before her head hit the pillow.

Chapter 5

Mandy woke the next morning to the smell of coffee. She got dressed and went into the kitchen where Marie was filling two coffee mugs. Max was lying under the table.

"I figured you'd be up soon," Marie said as she handed Mandy her coffee.

"The coffee woke me up. Yummmm. This is good. Thank you." Mandy paused, savoring that first sip. "You make good coffee."

"Thanks, mom."

"Where are the guys?"

"Michael got a call and said he'd be back shortly. He slept on the couch all night, I think. I got bedding out for him. He and Brad were still talking when I went to bed. Brad's still asleep. You were out cold. Max let me in and when I crawled into bed, you didn't even move."

"That bed is big enough for several people," Mandy chuckled. "I wouldn't have known if a bomb went off last night. I woke in the same position I fell asleep in."

"That could make for a nice smut headline in the tabloids... *"Daughter 30 Still Sleeps With Mom.""*

Mandy laughed, almost spitting out her coffee. "You are so sick."

"Yea, well, what d'ya expect? Humor's gotten us through all this crap."

They were quiet for a few minutes. Marie broke the silence.

"Mom, we need to figure out a game plan. Any ideas? Know what you want to do?"

Mandy sat with her hands wrapped around her coffee mug.

"I want Jim to leave me alone," she said quietly. "That's all. I don't know where all this is coming from after all these years. Part of me wants to understand what I did for all this to come about and the other part just wants the bastard gone. I don't care where." She looked directly at Marie. "I don't want anymore damage to us that what's already been done. No matter how old you two are, you're my children. Nothing will ever change that and I will do whatever it takes to protect you 'til the day I die. That's what parents do, even if it means protecting against the other parent."

Marie looked at her mother. She was the bravest person she knew. Not many people could have endured the years of abuse and humiliation that Mandy had. Not only had she survived, she had grown into a new and more complete person. She would stand by her and protect her, too. It was a family thing.

"I was just going to say you're not old," Marie said with a completely straight face.

"Smart ass," Mandy said and they both laughed.

"Mom, I hear ya. I know what you're saying. Both of us know. But you have to realize something, too. You're our mother. We love no one more than you. Dad is no longer dad. He's just some thug. The same thug that tried to kill you. We can handle ourselves. Trust us."

Mandy sat, looking at her daughter with tears in her eyes. Just then, Brad came in the dining room. With messed up hair, a tee shirt and jeans, he kissed Mandy on the top of her head and walked into the kitchen.

"Yea, mom. What she said."

Michael came in the back door just then and Brad handed him coffee and poured another mug for himself.

"We've got some help that's arrived. They know who to look out for and who's good to go. And thank you," he said, nodding to Brad.

"So how about going to your place? I could use a horse fix."

"I know you could. Let's go."

"Well, let's wait 'til we finish coffee. I don't think any of us are going to do well without it." Mandy took a sip of coffee. "Who's here?"

"My friend Marty. We were in Delta Force together and retired at the same time. He brought a couple of guys with him and more will be here today. They're around your property. Someone will be guarding at all times. When the other men come in, we'll put them where they'll be needed."

As they headed out to Michael's, Mandy could only keep thinking that something more was coming. She could feel it. Max had been on alert in the house just before they left. He wasn't happy about being left behind. Michael kept checking all mirrors, as he had two nights ago. Maybe he was just always so aware. Mandy didn't think so. She felt the tension radiating off him. It would be interesting to see how Phoenix was acting today.

Mandy was out of the truck before Michael could shut it off. She opened the gate and walked through. The horses were at the far end of the pasture. They looked up when they heard the chain rattle on the gate, saw Mandy and came running. Michael, Brad and Marie stood at the gate and watched as all four horses came up to Mandy. They had slowed about ten feet out but still came directly to her, nickering as they came. She petted and spoke to each of them, giving all kisses on their soft, velvet noses. She turned and walked to the fence, smiling all the while.

When she go to the fence, she had Brad and Marie come up. They had been around the horses before but never with the intent on riding them or working them in any capacity. Mandy was still blown away that they could ride.

Brad and Phoenix seemed to get along well. Phoenix kept looking to Mandy as he couldn't figure out why Brad was asking him to do anything. He did what was asked and by the time they were done with the ground games, Phoenix kept his full attention on Brad. Mandy wasn't worried that Phoenix would accept Brad as a rider or as the leader in their little herd of two. Brad was calm and focused. Kona really liked Marie. She did all that was asked without any question. Mandy was pretty impressed as both horses were a liberty, with no halter on their heads. She knew her kids were safe with the horses and the horses were safe with them.

Michael had been leaning on the fence, watching. Mandy walked over to him with Chico and Cheyenne following.

"What d'ya think?"

"I think their pretty good. Both are very calm, stay on task. It doesn't appear to be much of a transition for the horses, from you to them. I think Marie may have a mare whether she was planning on one or not. Kona seems to have found her person. But I think Phoenix is only accepting Brad for the moment. He keeps looking at you. Whoever they trained with, their style is enough like yours. But, hey, I really like you so what the hell do I know?"

Mandy laughed. "You're such a goof."

Michael came into the pasture and introduce himself to the younger horses. Chico would have nothing to do with him. He smelled his outstretched hand and walked over behind Mandy. Cheyenne couldn't get enough of Michael. She smelled his hair, his face, nuzzled his neck. She let him rub her face, her ears, her neck and her belly. She lifted every hoof he asked for.

"I think you have a new mare," Mandy commented. She loved that Cheyenne was so accepting of Michael. She hadn't been around many men and Mandy was the one who had trained her.

"I like her," Michael said. "She's got a good heart. Is she very cowy?"

"I haven't worked cattle with her so I really don't know. She thinks it's fun when they're on the other side of the fence and they move when she lays her ears back. Other than that, I don't know. She doesn't get upset about much. The only time she ever really fussed at me was when I wasn't clear about what I was asking. I thought I was. She let me know otherwise."

"Well, let's see how well we work together."

They all tacked up. Michael had extra saddles in the barn. Mandy threw a bareback pad on Chico. He was very well trained under saddle so she thought she'd give him something else to think about. She took him over to the fence and climbed up. Chico just looked at her. When she was up on the rail she wanted to mount from, she gently swung one rein at his outside hip. Chico moved his hind legs over and lined up parallel to the fence, close enough for Mandy to mount. She leaned her body against him and Chico stood. She rubbed his neck and threw her leg over him. He still stood. She got her seat and sat there for a few minutes, until Chico dropped his head and let out a big sigh. She rubbed his neck again and gently squeezed her legs, the que to move out. When

Chico took a step, he immediately knew that this was just like with the saddle on. He kept an ear turned to Mandy. He was very aware of where she was on his back and listened to what she said.

Michael watched Mandy work Chico. He'd tacked up Cheyenne and was standing, watching. Cheyenne wasn't concerned with anything. She was standing with her head to Michael's shoulder, waiting. When Mandy moved out, Michael mounted.

They played for about two hours in the pasture, working figure eights, stopping, starting into different gaits. As they walked to cool down, Phoenix kept looking towards Michael's house. He still responded to Brad but the bond wasn't there. The more Brad tried to bring back him back, the more Phoenix disconnected. Mandy noticed, easing back on the reins for Chico to stop. Phoenix was acting as he had yesterday morning. Something's up, she thought.

Just then, Kenny rode out from behind the barn. His big bay gelding seemed to float over the ground at his easy trot. He rode to the fence and asked Michael if he'd seen anything. Michael answered no and Mandy thought of Phoenix's behavior.

"I saw tire tracks up behind the house. They were car tires, not truck or SUV. They stopped short of Grams' and Gramps' fence line, turned around and headed out. I let them know and Gramps thought it would be great fun. He got the rifle out and Grams was rolling her eyes as she headed to the closet to get the 410 shotgun. Jo rode over to tell David and Carmen to keep an eye out and then she was going to Larry's. I'll meet her back at the barn." Michael's mother was known for being very protective over every living thing on her ranch. "I imagine they're sitting in the rocking chairs, watching TV with the guns across their laps."

"Sounds about right to me," Michael said. His parents were in their late 70s and still very involved in the ranch. God help anyone who threatened them. They were like a tornado together.

"Will they be okay?" Mandy asked.

"They'll be fine. They're in better shape than most people their age and a lot who are younger. They ride all day when we're moving cattle and this is Wyoming. It's not easy but they can handle their own, trust me."

"I wanted to let you know as soon as I could. Dustin and I are keeping an eye on things. We'll let you know if we see anything else." Kenny let Michael know about a few ranch issues and headed back out.

They decided to end the play time. As soon as saddles came off and horses were brushed, they were all sent back out to the pasture. Phoenix came over to Mandy. She rubbed his ears, spoke softly to him and gave him a final rub on the neck before she pointed out to the pasture and clicked. He took all the horses to the back of the pasture. Halfway there, he turned back to Mandy and neighed, loud.

That gave Mandy just enough time to hit the dirt before a shot rang out and hit the fence post she had been standing next to. Another shot rang out and she heard the truck engine. Michael drove over so the truck was between her and whoever was shooting. He threw open the passenger door and yelled, "Get in!" She rolled over to the truck and climbed in, staying low. She saw Brad and Marie in the backseat, riding lower than the top of the seat. The minute Mandy was in, Michael slammed on the gas and headed out, hitting the speed dial on his phone.

"Kenny. We just got shot at. From the hill behind my house. No. I'm pretty sure they're gone. Let the folks know and your uncles and make sure Caitlyn and Dustin know. No one goes out alone. Keep all the dogs close. We're going to the line shack on the north side." He hung up.

They followed a deer trail once they got past the knoll behind the barn. Michael was driving faster than he should have in the terrain they were in, but adrenaline was keeping everyone on high. Mandy sat up in the seat and looked in the back. Brad nodded to her and Marie gave a slight grin. Michael could handle his truck. He knew exactly what it would do and pressed it hard. The terrain didn't bother him as much as being shot at and no way to defend anyone. That would stop as of now. No more going anywhere without a gun on him. His gun had been left in the truck. In all reality, it wouldn't have done much good. A 9mil against a rifle wasn't much of a fight. They had thought they were safe at Michael's. Obviously, they knew about him. No more thoughts of being safe anywhere. He went into military guard mode. Seemed odd to feel that way now, after so many years. Stranger still, it felt familiar after all this time.

They drove perhaps for an hour, driving up a steeper incline than the previous ones. At the bottom of the hill, there was a grove of evergreens and aspens. There was a huge pond. As they drove closer, the cabin was seen, nestled in the grove of trees. Michael drove around to the back of the cabin. The truck couldn't be seen if someone came down the hill.

They walked to the cabin. It was used for checking cattle and the fence line. If coming on horseback, the horses could be turned lose. There was plenty of grass and water. They wouldn't go far and could easily be caught. It wasn't a smart idea to ride out here after dark.

The cabin was small. There was a kitchen area with a camp stove and a small sitting area with a couch and two straight back chairs. There were two small bedrooms, each with two twin beds and a bathroom with a commode and sink. Michael opened a window to get some air in and walked back outside. Mandy heard him on the phone.

"We're here. Not sure. This son of a bitch is serious. No. Call Hank. Okay. I'll call Marty. Oh, yea? Good. He will. You too, son." He walked further away from the cabin, dialing another number. Mandy couldn't hear his conversation.

Mandy sat on the couch. She had finally stopped shaking. She'd drawn her legs up to her chest like she did when she was little. It was a while before she realized how cramped her legs were and stretched them out. She was trying hard to wrap her head around all of it. The last time, she'd been unconscious for three weeks and when she woke, she'd been in a fog for several days. She'd had time to mentally adjust. This was different. She was coherent. Dear Lord, she prayed, please help us.

Marie and Brad were talking in low tones and checking things out. Marie found some bedding and made up two of the beds. Brad went outside. Marie sat on the edge of the bed she had just made. She had seen some incredibly horrible people as an attorney. There had been a few cases she had turned down because she knew the client was guilty as sin and she refused to represent anyone she couldn't believe in. This was different. This was up close and personal. It was so much more devastating when the violence was aimed at you or yours. And it was different from the last time. This time, other people could be hurt or killed. She knew how that ate at her mother. Her legal mind was spinning. She knew Jim was involved in something major. Brad had kept her informed of all that he found out. They weren't petty crimes. They were felonies that could put him in jail for the rest of his life. She didn't know if Mandy had known before. With what Michael had found out, there was no doubt she knew now.

Michael walked in and sat on the couch next to Mandy. He reached for her hand. He took as much comfort from the touch as she did.

"Hank's checking my place. Marty's leaving people there and will be on his way up."

"What about your parents?"

"Marty'll talk to them and leave guys at all the houses and the property surrounding them."

"Could you ask Marty to bring my gun? It's in my bag in my room."

"He will. I thought you might want it. He's bringing up all our stuff and supplies. We might be here awhile."

"How the hell to they keep finding me? Brad, have you found out anything?"

"Not yet. Still workin' on it." His phone rang and he went outside, taking the queue from Michael that the reception was better out there.

They settled in, not saying much and waiting for Marty. Mandy walked outside, sat in the chair, paced, sat back down and paced some more, trying hard to work through this.

Marty showed up. Before he could get out of the truck, Max leaped out of the window and ran for Mandy. He jumped up with his paws on her shoulders and licked her face, making little noises like puppies make when they nurse. She hugged him hard and buried her face in the thick fur around his neck. Then he dropped to her side and sat there, telling the world he was there to protect her.

Marty and Michael watch the reunion and then talked at length by the truck. Brad joined them. When they walked up to the cabin, Michael made the introductions. Marty was a bit shorter than Michael, leaner with salt and pepper hair. He had a copper complexion and dark brown eyes. His humor showed in his eyes when he smiled, though this smiled was tight. After shaking Mandy's hand, he handed over her bag, which she immediately took her gun out of the side compartment, checked the safety and put it in her jacket pocket.

"Every lady needs a security blanket," Marty said with a grin.

"Thank you and you have no idea how true that is right now. Seems I have a few of them."

"I see that. When I was at the house and getting ready to leave, Max jumped in the truck. Before I could say no, he was parked himself in the front seat. He's a little large to argue with so here we are."

"I'm glad you did. I think we'll all sleep easier with him here. Are Michael's parents okay?"

"Yea, they're fine. We put people around all the houses and the property. I had to talk Michael's parents into letting me put someone in their house. I finally said that Michael would kill me if anything happened to them. His mom then said okay. Said it would be good to have someone in the house besides Mr. Crabby Pants. Guess dad is being a pain."

"Yea," Michael said. "He gets like that when he doesn't have control over who is on his property."

"Oh. I almost forgot. Kenny said to tell you that Alex in on her way home and not to start the fun without her."

Michael laughed. That sounded like Alex.

They unloaded supplies. There was enough food there for a week. Mandy hoped she'd be home by then, this nightmare over with.

They all went into the cabin. Five people filled up the small space. Mandy got drinks out of the supplies and handed them out.

"What do we do now, Michael? Wait?" Mandy felt so out of place with so many people involved. She didn't like feeling like a target and she couldn't shake the feeling since that first shot hit the post.

"How do you want to handle this? We need to figure out where and when with all the details so we have as much control as possible."

"I don't want him at my house. He doesn't get to go there. Where else could we set something up? I figure he won't come to an office. He'd feel it's a trap. It'd have to be somewhere more secluded."

"You're probably right. There's a building we use for the auctions on the ranch. It's about two miles from the house, just over the next ridge."

"Would anyone be there? Are there any auctions coming up?"

"Not that I know of. There could be but Kenny would know for sure. That might be the way to go. Jim would have his guys check it out. He'd be stupid not to. We can set up our own security. Let me call Kenny."

"Mom," Brad began as Michael walked outside, "do you think it's such a good idea to confront him?"

"Honey, I don't know what else to do. He finds me no matter where or what I do. There are people here that could get hurt or killed, including you. That's not acceptable. This whole thing is so senseless. If it's just him and me, it will end. And he doesn't know me anymore. He won't recognize me and has no clue what to expect from me. He won't expect me to stand against him." She paused. "Have you found out anything?"

"Nothing definite. My buddy says he doesn't like where it appears to be leading and is double checking. He'll let me know tomorrow. He'd been at for about 30 hours. I told him to go to bed."

"You're a good friend. And son. Thank you."

"Only 'cause of you, cutie," Brad grinned. He had called his mom "cutie" since he was little. He couldn't remember where he got it from but knew it fit at the time.

Marie looked at her mother. Dark circles were under her eyes. The last few days were beginning to show. Last night's sleep seemed years ago. It didn't take much for the full amount of stress to return. Marie silently prayed this would be over for good. Whatever way it ended, Mandy deserved peace.

"Mom, it's your call. This will be handled the way you want. We'll do whatever we need to do. It stays simple, easy." Brad wanted to ease the stress level, if he could. He also saw how it was affecting Mandy and could tell Marie was also starting to feel it. He felt so helpless to take care of his family. He had ever since this had begun. He'd gone up against Jim one time, when Jim had hit Mandy across the room. He'd been 15. He'd also gone flying across the room but Jim never hit Mandy again. He'd always thought when he was little that he and Marie would get married and have Sunday dinners with their spouses and kids at their parents. He never expected for them to be career people with no one significant in their lives or going up against their father to protect their mother. Life had a way of surprising you. He was sure Mandy never expected her life to play out as it had.

Mandy had been quiet, thinking over the scenarios of meeting Jim. She looked up as Michael came in.

"Kenny says there's nothing going on at the building. There's some construction so that could be to our advantage. I caught Marty before he got out of cell range. He'll meet me there. He's got good eyes."

Michael didn't like using Mandy as bait. He also knew it would be the only way to draw Jim out. Years of military intelligence stays with a person. It's not used every day but it stays in the back of your mind, offering support when needed. It did now.

"Well, there ya go," Mandy said with a tired grin. "What more could we need?"

"I thought you'd like that. We'll check stuff out tonight. You be okay here?"

"We'll be fine."

"Would you mind if I went with you?" Brad asked.

"Not at all," Michael replied. "Glad for the company."

After they left, Max lay down in front of the door, clearly stating no one would get through. He put his head on his massive paws and closed his eyes.

After doing the small amount of dishes and getting supplies put away, the cabin seemed so quiet with just Mandy and Marie there. It was as much peace as Mandy had had in the last few days. Life at her place seemed a million years ago.

The camping lantern gave off enough light to dimly see and a small amount of heat. All the windows had been closed. Mandy and Marie sat on opposite ends of the couch, sharing a blanket Marie had found in with the bedding. Mandy's gun was on the small table next to the couch.

"You okay?" Mandy asked. "I know this isn't the visit we'd been planning."

Marie gave a smirk.

"No. This will be better. All this bullshit will be ended and we'll all be together, as we're supposed to be. Just the three of us. I really don't care how dad's stopped at this point."

Mandy took Marie's hand and just held it.'

"Remember when we were kids? You used to tell us that the world may kick us when we were alone but together, we'd take on the world."

"Funny what you remember, huh?"

"You have no idea how many times I've hung onto that saying, especially when you were in the hospital."

"I still don't remember a lot about that. I wonder if I ever will."

"I'd be really surprised if you did, mom. You were either in surgery or unconscious. I was scared but glad you were sleeping. I knew you were trying to heal. I just stayed and held your hand. When I wasn't there, Brad was. We never left you alone, even with the guard outside your door. We were too scared to."

"Thank God that part is over. I was in a fog most of that year. It wasn't until about two months before I left rehab that my brain started to clear and work again – at least to where I felt it should be working." They were both quiet, remembering.

"I want you to think about something. I think it's something we all need to think about and work on." Mandy paused, looking at their interlocked hands. "We all need to forgive Jim. Before you protest, just think about this. Forgiveness isn't for Jim. It's for us. We aren't free until we do forgive him. That's a huge weight for all of us to carry around, all that anger and hate. I've been trying to. I thought I'd done a pretty good job until this came up. I feel like I'm back at square one. I think it would take a lot of weight off all our shoulders if we could."

Marie was quiet for a few moments.

"I know we need to, mom. It's just so hard. I was beginning to be able to detach myself from all of it. I could go over anything that came across my desk and really look at it from a legal point of view. Then this. All I want to do now is slap the shit outa him." She paused before going on. "That says a lot for the attorney in the family, huh?"

"I think it says you're human and hurt like everyone else. Sucks not being Wonder Woman, huh?"

Marie chuckled. She could always count on her mom to lighten the most difficult of issues. Mandy could see the bright side of anything. Sometimes it just took a few more minutes than others.

"Maybe it'll be easier when we don't have to look over our shoulders anymore."

"Yea, Mom, maybe"

Chapter 6

As Michael and Brad headed out to the auction building, Michael called Marty. He'd meet them at the turn off to the ranch.

"Thanks for letting me ride with you," Brad said. "I need to see the layout."

"No problem. I'd feel the same way."

"I don't know how much mom has told you. She's always been pretty quiet about this mess. "

"We had a long talk that first night. She told me the basics. I'm quite sure the reality was worse than what she told me."

Brad was quiet for a moment. "I don't mean any disrespect but I gotta ask what your intentions are."

Michael smiled. "Ya know, I've wanted to ask your mom out to dinner for the last four years. I knew she was working through some pretty tough issues. I've watched her pull herself together and start a whole new life for herself but it never felt like the right time. I'd come by once a week and check on her. We share that fence line to the east so I could ride fence any other time. I never wanted to push her. We would see each other in town, might have coffee and go our separate ways. I just kinda kept an eye on her. She's my neighbor and we watch out for each other out here." He paused. "I've always felt that with anyone, you just let whatever happen, happen. When it's right, it works itself out. Asking her out the other day was just a spur of the moment. I hadn't planned that." He chuckled. "Sure made my day. Anyway, to answer your question. Whatever happens, happens. I won't do anything to hurt her. She's a very special woman and I'll be there in any capacity we decide on. It's just not a decision that's going to be made until this is over. She doesn't need any distractions. None of us do. And no disrespect taken."

They came up on the turn off and Mary fell in behind. They drove about to the auction yard. It was dusk by then. The headlights showed the pens and then the building. It looked like a huge warehouse. Michael pulled flashlights for all of them from the toolbox. The door to the building was unlocked and when they stepped through the doorway, they could see where construction had been going on.

They scanned the building with their flashlights, looking for the electrical switch. Marty found it on the wall by the office. He flipped it and the lights came on.

"That's part of the new construction. There were no lights before."

Michael walked to the door of the office. Inside, he flipped the lights on. Parts of insulation were all over the floor and there were gaps in the ceiling where the tiles hadn't been replaced. There was a desk, four chairs and a coffee stand. His phone rang.

"Hey, Hank." Michael was quiet while Hank talked. Brad glanced at him as he walked around the room. He was looking where he could hide a video cam and some microphones. He knew Mandy could wear an ear piece that wouldn't show with her long hair. The cams could be seen. He knew Jim would have the office searched and he wanted to be sure to have one that couldn't be found. He looked at Michael. Michael's face gave nothing away so Brad had no idea about the call. The only time he's seen any expression at all was when he looked at Mandy or talked about her. That was okay. They'd had their talk. He knew where Michael stood and that was good with him.

Michael talked for a few more moments with Hank and disconnected. Before he could put his phone away, it rang again. He listened for a few moments and clicked it off.

"Change of plans"

"What's up?" Marty asked.

"Allison will be here tomorrow. Seems she got remarried and wants the kids to meet her new husband."

"Oh, really. Who'd she marry?"

"I don't know. I don't know what she's thinkin'. I couldn't tell her no without raising her curiosity. I don't know if her office is involved but we've got enough on our plates without the feds comin' in."

Brad continued to look around the office. He had decided where to put the electronics. He knew Jim's people wouldn't find the ones that counted. He'd give them a few when they scanned the area so they'd think they'd found them all. Marty checked out the rest of the building while Michael had gone outside.

"I'll get all the equipment in here and hide it," Brad said when Marty came back into the office. "They'll find a few of them but not the ones we'll be monitoring. That should make them happy. Plus, mom will be wearing an ear piece."

Marty was looking at Brad.

"How are you going to hide them from a scanner?"

"There's a new material out, or rather in the final stages of experiment, that can block the reading from a scanner. I have some and can it here with the rest of the equipment overnight. I'll place three video and three audio devices and wrap one of each. They'll only find the four and think they've found them all."

"Damn. That stuff would be worth a fortune. Where'd ya get it?"

"I have a friend who's an inventor. I try out his stuff and he splits the profits with me when he gets it patented and sold."

"Great to have friends like that. Who does he sell to?"

"Mainly the government. Keeps us half a step ahead of the bad guys."

"I bet sometimes not that far."

Brad let him know where he was going to place the equipment. Marty agreed with him. By the time they were done, it was pitch black outside. No stars. No moon. They found Michael by the light on in the truck. He'd had another call. This one was from Alex, letting him know she'd made it to the ranch. They headed out. Michael and Brad to the ranch and Marty to check on his men.

"Your ex is with the Attorney General's office, right?" Brad asked.

"Yea, she is. She's an attorney who prosecutes federal drug cases, big ones."

"Think she has anything to do with Jim's case?"

"I don't know. I think it's a bit strange that she's showing up now but I don't know if she knows anything about this. I haven't spoken to her in years and she hasn't seen the kids longer than we haven't spoken. She's never met Kenny or Dustin's wives. She's never known Alex. I think the last time she saw her, Alex wasn't even in kindergarten. I really don't know what this is about but I don't believe in coincidence." He waited for a moment then asked, "Why wouldn't Jim let Mandy in on any of the business dealings?"

"Ya know, I would love to say that I thought it was to protect us from whatever crap he'd gotten himself into but I know that's not true. Early on, mom called him on cutting corners. I remember that fight. I thought he was going to tear the house down. She quit saying anything after that. They didn't speak about business and barely spoke about anything else."

By then, they were at the ranch. Brad was curious about Alex. As they got out of the truck, a young woman came down the steps. She appeared to be about Marie's age. She wore jeans and a flannel shirt with boots. She had long dark brown hair, almost black and a tan complexion. She gave Michael a big hug and kiss.

"Hi, Dad! How are ya?" she asked, grinning up at him.

"I've had better days, baby-girl," he replied as he hugged her fiercely and kissed her cheek, "but it sure is good to see you." He gave her a squeeze before he released her. "I want you to meet Mandy's son, Brad. Brad, this is my daughter, Alex."

Alex released her dad and took Brad's hand. Her handshake was strong, solid.

"Nice to meet you," Brad said. The light from the house was behind her so her face was in shadow. Still, Brad knew she had dark eyes and would be surprised if you could see her pupils.

"You too, Brad. I really am sorry it's under these circumstances." She turned back to her dad. "Kenny said you're up at the line shack. Do you have time for some coffee before heading back up?"

Michael looked at Brad. "Okay with you?"

"Absolutely."

They went inside and sat at the island in Michael's kitchen.

"So, dad, what the hell is going on? I called Kenny as your phone wouldn't go through and he's telling me we have guards around the house and someone is trying to kill the lady who bought the twenty acres."

So over coffee, Michael gave Alex a shortened version of what had been happening. It had only been two days. It seemed like a week had past. He needed some sleep.

"So now you know almost as much as we do. I don't know why Allison is coming. Time seems a bit incredible to me."

"Thinks she knows Mandy is Jim's ex?"

"I don't know. I hadn't talked to her in years before she called yesterday. I was surprised she still had the number. I don't like it, though. I can tell you that."

"I bet you don't. She must have forgotten who you are."

"Oh, yea. Super Man."

"No, I didn't mean that. I just meant that you protect those that you care about and, obviously, you care about Mandy."

"Speaking of….who's staying with you?'

"No one. The guys aren't that far away and I can take care of myself. Dad. I'm a ranch kid. I'll be okay."

"Regardless, missy, I have to go back up to the cabin. Mandy and Marie are up there alone with no vehicle or horses to get out. These people know about me and the ranch. That was proven today. Why don't you stay with Larry?"

"Larry's at Amy's. I'm okay, dad. Honest."

"I can stay here, if that works for you," Brad offered. "They might think twice before doing anything to Alex if someone's with her. Maybe not. It might not matter but there's not much room for all of us at the cabin, plus Max."

"Who's Max?"

"Mandy's dog. He's huge and very protective of her. He just puts up with the rest of us."

"Dad, Brad can stay here. The guest room is already made up. Anyway, it will give "mom" something to wonder about when she gets here." Alex had a grin on her face and a twinkle in her eye. "I'll show Brad where the guns are and we'll be fine. And we'll give Allison something else to think about if she gets here before you do."

"Lord help us," Michael said, grinning as he got up and put his mug in the sink. He turned to Brad. "We'll bring your bag down tomorrow. I know you won't want to be out of communication with your mom for long. And, thank you. I feel better with you here."

"No problem. You're helping my mom. I can help your daughter."

Michael walked to the door and hugged Alex.

"We'll be down tomorrow. I'll call you when we're on our way."

Michael got back up to the cabin about midnight. He was tired to his soul. He walked up to the door and softly called Max's name. He heard the big dog get up from blocking the door and heard his tail thumping on the floor. It was safe to go in. The room was dim and he could see Mandy and Marie both asleep at opposite ends of the couch. Max shoved his head under Michael's hand. Michael rubbed his ears.

"Good boy," he whispered. He gently woke up Mandy and had her and Marie go into the bedroom. They'd sleep better in the beds. He and Max could guard, though right now, he would let Max guard. He'd be better at it. It had been a few years since he'd had to deal with anything like this. Hank would be here first thing in the morning with any information he had found out. Then they all could deal with Allison. That made tomorrow sound about as much fun as getting shot at today.

Chapter 7

Michael was up before dawn. He'd only slept about 6 hours but the quiet and peace of the line shack was like having slept 12 hours. He was making coffee on the old camp stove with an old- fashioned coffee pot when Mandy emerged from the bedroom.

"Hey, bedhead," he grinned at her.

Mandy grinned. "I must look like something the cat drug in."

"But you're still cute."

"And you're still a goof."

"That's okay."

The coffee started to percolate and soon the smell of coffee was strong in the small cabin. Michael poured three cups of coffee, giving one to Mandy and keeping one on the wooden counter for Marie. He figured she's be up any minute.

Mandy sipped her coffee. "This is perfect. You're good at this."

"And other things, but you're not awake yet."

"Give me a minute."

"You can have all the time you need"

They stood in the little makeshift kitchen, drinking coffee and enjoying just being comfortable with each other. It amazed Mandy. Her ex was trying to kill her and she and Michael were bantering back and forth as if they'd been together for years. Maybe it was the stress of the situation or maybe, just maybe, Michael was her soulmate. Yea. Right.

Marie came out of the small bedroom. Michael handed her some coffee that she gratefully accepted and nodded her thanks. As they slowly woke up with the caffeine in their systems, Michael filled them in on what happened the previous night. Both Mandy and Marie were curious about Alex. Not just because she was Michael's daughter but because Brad didn't put himself in situations unless he knew the whole story or the people involved. For him to offer to stay at the ranch with Alex after just meeting her was interesting. Marie wanted to see what kind of attorney Alex was. What was her legal mind like? What did she think of this whole mess, both on the legal level and the fact that her whole family was involved now. Would she be looking at it legally from the prosecution or defense side?

They were all outside in the early morning sun when Hank arrived. He let them know of the information Sally had shared with him. Jim's business was on the verge of collapse because of all the investigations. It wasn't just the connection with the drug cartel but he was also being investigated by the IRS. People were scared to do business with someone who was watched so closely. Mandy knew all that was in order. At least it had been. Jim was adamant about bookkeeping. Every month had to balance. She knew he'd never be caught that way. Sally was part of the team investigating him in California. She would let Hank know what she found out.

"He must be desperate," Mandy said. "He must still have that life insurance policy on me and that, plus the alimony back in his pocket, would be real good incentive to kill me."

Marie was sitting next to her mother. Her mind was racing. What could Jim be thinking? She saw him spending the rest of his life in prison but it appeared that didn't matter to him. That just felt wrong. She didn't really care where he spent his life, as long as he left them alone. She knew Brad had more memories of him than she did just because he was older. Her bad memories of her father outweighed the good and she refused to even think this situation could get any worse, though she knew it could. She looked at Michael. He appeared to be relaxed, leaning against one of the beams that held up the overhang of the porch. He would glance at Mandy from time to time as he talked with Hank. Marie knew he was anything but relaxed. He reminded her of Max-always alert. She glanced at Hank. His intense expression as he listened to Michael was intriguing. He really was a good looking man when you got to know him a bit. But she put him out of her mind. There was too much going on.

Alex and Brad were standing on the porch when they drove up. Marie had ridden with Hank at Mandy's insistence. If anyone was going to take another shot at her, she didn't want Marie close. Michael there was bad enough.

They were all pretty cautious getting out. Everyone was looking all around. Max didn't seem to be too concerned. He was sniffing a new place, marking every bush he could find, keeping his people in sight.

"Hey, Dad, Hank." Alex came down the steps, giving both Michael and Hank hugs as she came. She held her hand out to both Mandy and Marie.

"You must be Mandy and Marie. Brad has told me so much about you, I think I know you already. I'm glad to meet you. I only wish it could be under different circumstances." They all walked into the house.

"The guys are up in the upper pasture, Dad. About twenty cows decided to go visiting John Marshall's new bull. They won't be back before dark. Kenny said to tell you Caitlyn was with them and he had the radio." Radio contact would be the only way to reach them. They were out of cell range.

"And Allison should be here in about a half hour." Alex had saved the best for last. There was a note of disgust in her voice but she tried to hide it. Michael only nodded. This should prove to be interesting.

Brad was pouring coffee and handing out mugs all around. As he handed Mandy hers, he asked, "How are you? How'd you sleep?"

"I think I got some good sleep. We fell asleep on the couch and Michael had to wake us up when he came in. Max being there was a huge help."

"I'll bet." He looked at his sister. "Com'on. You look like you could use some sunshine." They walked outside. Mandy knew Brad had seen something in Marie's face. They could always read each other. She knew Marie was upset over the news that Hank brought. Maybe Brad could ease her mind.

Suddenly Max growled and walked to the door. A new Ford 350 pickup had pulled into the drive behind Hank's. Two people got out, a man and a woman. The woman was petite with highlighted brown hair. The man was about 6 ft, medium built with graying hair. Though they both wore jeans, they were dressed expensively and carried themselves with an air of authority.

Michael opened the door and stepped out with Alex right behind him.

"Hello, Allison."

"Hi, Michael. How're you?"

"We're doin' good." Until you showed up, he thought.

"Hello, Allison." Alex chose that moment to stand beside her father.

Allison stood there, staring at her daughter. As she hadn't seen her in years, she'd had no idea of the woman she'd become. Her eyes teared up and she so wanted to hug her. But she didn't have that right. She gave up that right years ago. What she hadn't known then was that it would hurt so bad now.

"Hi, Alex. You have grown into a beautiful woman."

"Thank you."

Allison turned to the man beside her.

"Michael, this is my husband, Alan Stewart. Alan, this is my ex-husband Michael Johnson and my daughter Alex."

Michael gave Alan a nod as he shook his hand. Alan nodded to Alex.

"Let's go in," Michael said. "No sense standing out here." And making targets of ourselves was the thought going through Michael's head.

When everyone was seated at the dining room table, Allison asked where Kenny and Dustin were. Alex explained they were repairing a broken fence line. She refused to tell Allison anything about her brothers. Michael nodded slightly. He knew what she was doing.

"How'd you meet?" Alex asked. She was playing the curious daughter to the max. She really didn't care how they met or where. She just wanted the conversation to hurry up and end so they'd leave. She didn't realize how little use she actually had for Allison until just this moment.

"Alan was the lead investigator on a case. We worked on it on and off for several years, getting nowhere. We started it up again a few years ago and reconnected. We've been married for two years." She looked at Alan and smiled. He reached for her hand.

Mandy sat across from Allison. She studied the woman who had been married to Michael and who had left him and three wonderful babies for a career. Alan was staring intently at Mandy.

"May I ask you something?"

"Sure."

"Are you the Mandy Thompson who was married to Jim Thompson from LA? Thompson Construction?"

Mandy stared at him. She hadn't been prepared for that.

"What does that have to do with anything?" Michael was quick to intercede.

"Are you?" Alan repeated, ignoring Michael.

"Why?"

"Because your name and your kid's names aren't all that common together and because he's under federal investigation."

"Yes."

"Son of a bitch," Alan muttered.

Mandy's mind raced. This was too much of a coincidence and, like Michael, she really didn't believe in them. She stared at Alan. After all this crap, she was going to jail behind the bastard. She looked at Michael and then back at Alan. The leak. It had to be the feds.

"Do you have a leak in your office?"

"What are you talking about?" Allison demanded.

"I've been found. No one has ever found me before. I know there's a leak. I know where it didn't come from so that leaves your office. That means you knew I was here and you came to find me. So?"

"There are matters we aren't at liberty to discuss as this is an ongoing investigation," Allison replied.

Mandy looked her dead in the eye. "Cut the bullshit. We're talking about my life and the lives of my family and people I care about. How did you find me?" Her voice has a steel quality to it.

"We had Brad and Marie's phones monitored," Allison said, looking down at her hands.

Mandy looked at Michael. There was fear on her face but also pure rage. Was that how Jim found her? Had someone on Allison's team leaked information or were they able to monitor the phones on their own?

Mandy stood. "You need to leave. Now."

Allison looked at her.

"I need some information from you." She said it quietly, with determination in her voice.

"I don't care what you need. You've crossed the line. For all I know, someone on your team gave information to the bastards who are trying to kill me. I don't want anything to do with you. I don't care who you are or who you're with." Every inch of her body was tense. Michael was at her back. Brad and Marie on either side.

"We need to have this conversation," Allison said as both she and Alan rose from the table. "I can arrest you as a material witness."

Mandy laughed. "Oh, that's choice. Where were you eight years ago? Tell ya what. I will say this only once. I know nothing of Jim's business. Deal with it."

The tension in the room was thick. Hank had not said a word. Now he stood next to Marie, Max was standing between Marie and Mandy, ready to protect. He could feel the air. It didn't feel good.

"You'd better go," Michael said. "If you don't know who piggybacked your system, you better find out before we do." Michael walked towards the door. Allison and Alan followed. Allison stopped next to Mandy before walking outside.

"I'm truly sorry for what's happened to you. I promise to find out what's going on."

"Excuse me if I don't believe you. I've been safe all these years because of myself, not you. You need to know this. He may get me this time. But I won't be going down alone. He will go with me and to hell with your investigation."

"What do you plan on doing?"

"Keeping us alive and safe. Just like I've always done."

Allison turned to Alex. "Please give your brothers my best."

Alex nodded. "I'll be sure to let them know." She took the card Allison offered.

"On the back is my home and cell numbers. Please feel free to use them." She looked like she wanted to hug Alex but again, refrained. Instead, she touched her arm and followed Alan and Michael out the door.

"Will she be safe?" she asked when came up to them.

Michael looked at her.

"As safe as we can be. You need to find the leak. It has to be your team."

"I will. Please call me if I can do anything to help." Michael nodded then headed back to the house as the Ford headed out.

"That was a surprise," Alex said to Michael. He didn't say anything, waiting for her to elaborate.

"I wasn't expecting any sort of warmth from her or any compassion. I thought Mandy was going to rip her face off." She smiled. "I wouldn't blame her at all. I haven't seen her since I was what four, five? And I've talked to her maybe five time since then. She's not what I expected."

"She seems to have grown up a bit," Michael said. "What were you expecting?"

"I don't know. Maybe someone harder."

"I don't know her anymore, baby, so I know I'm not much help. I don't know if the old Allison exists anymore or if that was the real Allison. Guess we'll just have to wait and see."

"Think she'll want to be in contact with any of us?"

"I don't know."

They walked back into the dining room. Michael leaned against the door frame.

"We need to make a plan." He looked at Mandy. "Your idea of meeting Jim is dangerous but I understand the necessity. I think the auction office is a good choice, especially since Brad can hide all the electronics and we have a bit more control."

"I think he should come to the house."

"I thought you didn't want him there."

"I don't but in all reality, it's the best place. I know the house. I know where all my weapons are and so will everyone else concerned. I know where someone would come in from, the hiding places. I know how to defend myself there."

"Okay. If that where you want to do this."

"It's not but I think it's the best place. The house is being watched. We know that. I'm going to ride over there. They won't expect that. They'll expect a vehicle from the from, not a rider from the back. Marty can take care of who comes in from the front. I can come in from the grove in the back."

"I'll come with you. We can move some cows to that pasture next to yours. No one will think anything about it."

"Mom, we're coming." Brad's tone left no room for argument.

"Okay." Mandy was thinking. This could get complicated but she wasn't going to tell them they couldn't come with her. They had earned the right.

"It'll look odd with just a few cows and so many riders. Even someone from LA could see that. So, how about this? Michael and I ride two of his horses. Forget the cows. You guys wait about 15minutes, ride Phoenix and Kona, pony Chico and Cheyenne. We should still be in sight when you leave. You'll be able to see the gate from the pasture. Since Jim and his people know nothing of ranch life, it will just look like two riders taking two horses wherever. Put on baseball caps, hats, different jackets. That should be good enough for anyone who's watching my house. You'll be far enough away that you shouldn't be recognized." She looked at Michael. "Think that would work?" Michael just nodded. "What's wrong? Bad idea?"

"No, it's a good idea. There's just something not right about Alan Stewart. I don't know what it is but something's off. For someone involved in this investigation, this whole situation, he offered nothing to the conversation or of any plan to keep you safe. It felt like he was checking you out and I don't know why. Hank, can you find out anything about him? I'll see if Marty can find out anything, too."

Hank hadn't said a word this whole time. He had on jeans, a tee shirt and a fleece lined jean jacket. Nothing that said sheriff. Allison and Alan had no idea who he was other than "Hank". Because he had been so quiet, they hadn't paid much attention to him. He had blended in with the wall, which is what he intended. He watched everyone and Marie had watched him.

"I remember a friend of mine with the DEA talking about an "Alan" regarding a meth case out of Nashville a few months ago. It was just a passing remark but let me see what I can find out."

"Hank, was that the case that involved the Colombians?" Alex asked. Marie looked at her. Obviously, they both had heard about that bust.

"Yea. The one with so many feds on the cartel's payroll."

Hank left and Marie and Alex got on their phones. They would have information soon.

"I think we all had the same feeling. There's something off there. It scares me that all of us are supposed to trust people that we have no idea of who they are. It's like because they say they're a Fed, that makes everything right. It doesn't. I know Allison was brought in because of her connection to you and they thought that would be their "in". LA county has all the information they want. They could have gotten it from them." Mandy continued to look at Michael. "I meant what I said."

"I know you did. Let's hope it doesn't come to that."

Mandy went outside to the pastures. She was so much on overload, she didn't care if someone was watching her. She walked farther than where she had been yesterday. Hopefully it was out of rifle range. She just needed a few minutes to herself to clear her head so she could think. She walked out to the horses. All of them started walking towards her, Phoenix in the lead. He dropped his head so he could get his ears scratched. He brought up his head and Mandy gently rubbed his nose and face. She kissed his velvet nose and he leaned his head against her chest. He knew she needed to give him her stress and he was willing to take it. Then he moved off so everyone could have some attention. She wanted to jump on his back and ride anywhere, be anywhere but where she was. Suddenly Phoenix's head came up, ears pointed to the gate behind her. Mandy turned and saw Brad and Michael coming across the pasture. Oh, great. Now what?

Chapter 8

"Jim called." Brad watched Mandy's face for any reaction. There was none. "He wants to talk to you but he didn't ask for your number. Just asked to have you call him."

"And you said?"

"I'd give you the message. I don't know if he knows we're here. I wasn't going to give him any information."

"He'll know as soon as I call him back. Your number will show."

"I'll show you how to block it."

"Guess he beat me to the punch, huh?"

Mandy held out her hand as they started walking back to the house. Brad had dialed the numbers and handed the phone to her. The screen showed "blocked." She walked and looked at Michael. He said nothing, just held her gaze.

"Jim. It's Mandy." She had stopped at the gate and was leaning against the fence. Her stomach was in knots. There was only silence on the end of the phone.

"I didn't think you'd call."

"I almost didn't. But this has to end. What the hell do you want from me? Wasn't almost killing me once good enough for you?" Mandy was breathing hard. She hadn't realized how angry she still was at him until she heard his voice. Right now, she wanted to bash his face in.

"I can't ever tell you how sorry I am. You wouldn't believe me anyway and you shouldn't. But I don't want to kill you. I never have. I want to talk to you. I can't make any of this right but I can at least explain it."

"Jim, you're full of shit. I've had your wonderful guys at my house, shoot at me and try to intimidate me into seeing you. You've got to be crazy. The only way I'll see you is in a public place with snipers on the rooftops, all aiming at you."

Jim was silent. He had expected her anger. He hadn't expected her hatred.

"Mandy, I didn't try to kill you. I didn't the first time and I'm not now. But I know who is. And it wasn't my men who came to your house. I don't know where you live."

"Yea, right. And I'm supposed to believe that. Not gonna happen."

"I know. I don't expect you to believe anything I say. Don't take my word for it. Do you still have your grandmother's trunk?'

"Yes."

"Turn it over and take off the bottom. It's fake. Call me after you find what's there." The line went dead.

Mandy tried to breathe but couldn't. She knew she was having a panic attack but that didn't help the fact she couldn't get enough air. She knew she had to calm down or it would get worse. She leaned her head on her arms, on the top rail of the fence. Michael kept rubbing her back in small circles and murmuring "relax". She focused on his voice. Soon she could draw full breaths. She stood up.

"I'm okay. Thank you."

Michael gave her a quick hug.

"Anytime," he smiled.

"Does that happen often, mom?" Brad stood there, concern written on his face and feeling completely helpless.

"Not anymore."

"That's good to know."

They started walking back towards the house.

"He said he didn't try to kill me but he knew who was. He said there's something underneath my grandmother's trunk."

"Where is it?"

"At the house. At the foot of my bed."

"Let's tack up. As soon as we get over the hill, we'll be able to see anyone else out there." Michael turned to Brad. "It's pretty open from here to your mom's. The trees are along the road but just keep your eyes open. If something feels funny, move away from it."

Brad nodded.

They headed out to Mandy's. Michael rode his big chestnut gelding, Milo. She was riding Lena, a beautiful dark bay mare. She was very willing and very responsive and had a gentle trot that felt like a rocking chair. Mandy sat back in her saddle, legs relaxed. She could ride all day.

They were coming to the end of the trees before moving out to the more open pastures, when Mandy caught movement out of the side of her eye. Michael noticed it at the same time and they moved farther out, watching the tree line. A cow and her new calf appeared, the baby not being more than a few days old. They stood watching them ride by.

"Think we're a bit jumpy?"

"No joke. I was wondering where that cow went. I didn't think she was bred this year."

"Maybe she went to visit your neighbors' bull."

"No. That baby is out of one ours. He's got his daddy's face."

Mandy's grove came into view about 45 minutes later. They slowed to a walk to cool out the horses. As they came up to the gate, Mandy could see the driveway and the turn around. The house looked peaceful and quiet. Suddenly, they both heard a growl and turned around to see Max about 10 feet behind them. He was looking at the house.

"I didn't know he was with us." Mandy dismounted and went to Max, rubbing his ears and talking to him. As glad as he was for her attention, he didn't take his focus from the house. She looked at Michael.

"We need to know if anyone is in the house."

"I know. It scares me."

"Do you still have water in the back pasture?"

"Yea. The stream runs all year."

They saw to the horses and started towards the house. Leaving the security of the trees made Mandy feel unprotected. She kept walking. Max was intent but no longer growling. Both of them pulled their guns out as they came up to the side of the barn, held down to their sides. Max trotted into the yard. There was no sound or movement from anywhere. Michael checked the barn. Max sniffed around the barn and the pens, then started towards the house. He was on the deck when they heard a pickup come down the drive. Mandy ran the rest of the way to the house, opened the door and rushed in. Michael slid to the side of the barn. Hank's truck came into view and everyone relaxed. Just as Hank and Alex stepped from the truck, Brad and Marie came walking from the trees.

Max had checked the house thoroughly, making sure no one was hiding anywhere. Satisfied, he went to his bed in the living room and stretched out, keep any eye on everyone. For now, his job was done.

Between Hank, Marie and Alex, the news about Alan Stewart was pretty iffy. He was involved in most of the high-profile drug cases in the country. As each one had been closer examined, they showed deaths of innocent people. These people had been family, friends and coworkers of supposedly legitimate business people who did business with the drug dealers. These people hadn't been involved in the drug business itself. The attitude of law enforcement was that they were casualties of the drug war. That information came from Alex's office. As Marie's family was involved, she had a bit more personal information on him. His background showed he had come from a very closeknit family in Chicago. When his parents were out to dinner for their 25th wedding anniversary, the restaurant had been blown up by a bomb placed under one of the tables. It was found out later, the table was reserved for the head of one of the cartels who was in Chicago doing business. It was the beginning of the cartel wars. Alan had been a junior in college at the time. He quit school and joined the Marines, needing to do something constructive and physical after the death of his parents. He served for eight years. At the end of his second enlistment, he had been approached to join the investigation team for the federal attorney general's office. From there, his track record showed 90% conviction rate on the cases he worked. Digging deeper found several offshore bank accounts with over $10,000,000.00 totaled.

Marie sat, going through her notes.

"We can't get a trace on where the money's coming from. It's either from drugs or payment from somewhere to kill some of the cartel leaders, is the general feeling. It's not believed that he's had anything to do with the deaths of the innocents. It's still being worked on. He does appear to have a code, though, not like he's a gun for hire and uses his position as a cover. From what we can find out, he believes in what he's doing. As to Allison's involvement, it's not known at this time. We don't know if she's part of it or in the dark. I don't see how she couldn't know, personally. Or at least suspect something. The money hits a rough spot. Either he's on the take or undercover."

"That's good information," Alex said. "How'd you come by it?"

Marie gave a small smirk. "I've got file cabinets in my office on anyone who has anything to do with this case. I only have part of them copied to a disk. We have an investigator that is amazing. He gives me anything he finds. Some of it has been by accident. A lot of it, he's worked on in between cases. I'd just been hired on as a law clerk the summer mom got hurt and we became good friends. His wife is like a sister to me."

"Ya know," Brad said thoughtfully, "this could be making some sense. There've been conversations where Jim wasn't looking like the bad guy. What's interesting is that if I can get these conversations, others can."

"What do you mean?" Mandy asked.

"There were a few times that Jim would be talking to someone and would make comments like "keep her safe", "send them in another direction", "don't let them near them." With all this coming up, I'm wondering if he was trying to protect us. At the time, I couldn't figure out who he was talking about. It never occurred to me that he was talking about us. The thought never crossed my mind."

"It's be a cold day in hell before I believe that." Mandy's eyes showed her anger. "I need a hell of a lot more proof."

"I know, mom. I'm not saying that. I'm only saying it's interesting. I don't know who he was talking about. Anyone who has anything to do with him, knows he has two kids and an ex-wife that has disappeared, literally. I know his behavior has changed the last couple of years. I'm just trying to put it all together. That's all. I've done what I've done to keep us all as safe as possible. Just looks like it could be going in a different direction than what we anticipated." He had been looking Mandy straight in the eye as he spoke. She nodded her acknowledgment of what he was saying. This was hard on all of them. They all had been thinking one line of thought and now it could be something completely different. It would take a bit to adjust to any other possibility.

"I didn't get much else," Hank put in. "He has been questioned regarding some deaths. He was a sniper in the Marines and still has some connections. He's incredibly intelligent, has good instincts and seems to be above board. The only thing showing against him as solid evidence is the money. If it was legit, why an offshore account?"

Michael hadn't said a word during all this. At that moment, his cell rang. Mandy could tell from his response, it was Marty.

"Marty got the same info. He's put everyone on high alert that we may be dealing with military professionals."

Mandy got up. She needed to look at the trunk. This was harder than she thought it would be. For some reason, she didn't want to find whatever it was that Jim wanted her to see. It made no sense to her logical mind. But, that's what she was feeling at the moment. She shook it off. Now was not the time for this. She still felt like walking down the hall was like walking down a long tunnel with no end. When she got to her room, she realized Max had come with her. Standing in her doorway, he looked up at her with eyes filled with love and loyalty. He wouldn't let her do whatever she had to without him. Whether she knew it or not, she needed him. He knew it.

She stared at the trunk for several minutes, wishing she'd never been found and dreading what she was about to see. This is stupid, she thought. What if things weren't the way we thought? Jim had done nothing in the previous years to have his family think any different. There had been no acknowledgment of or apology for the pain caused. She realized why she was so scared to see what the trunk had to show. It felt like he was controlling her life again. With that fear, he was. Enough. I'm done with this bullshit. She walked to the truck and turned it over.

There were holes along the underside. The bottom had been replaced with the screws placed differently. She got a screwdriver from the mudroom. Michael found her and Max on the floor, taking the bottom off. It was a false bottom, a piece of plywood screwed up against the original piece. There was a manila envelope taped to the bottom. The tape was yellow with age, cracked and peeling in places. Michael leaned against the door frame with his hands in his pockets.

Mandy's hands were shaking as she opened the envelope. She pulled out pictures and a letter. The pictures had been taken outside and looked as if were taken from some distance away. There were several pictures of Jim with a Hispanic man. They appeared to be having some sort of discussion. One picture showed the man pointing a finger into Jim's chest and from the look on Jim's face, he was beyond angry. There were other pictures of the same man with Alan Stewart and a few of another Hispanic man. A picture of Alan and Allison.

Mandy picked up the letter and started to read. No mistake. It was Jim's handwriting.

September 15, 2012

Dear Mandy,

If you're reading this letter, you have also found the pictures. That will mean that everything has gone from worse to right straight to hell.

First of all, I did not try to kill you. I know all the evidence pointed to me. But I didn't send anyone to your apartment that day. At that point, I didn't know where you were. That being said, let me start at the beginning. You may not want to read any of this and you may not believe it. But, I swear to you, what I am writing now is the truth. As I don't know what's going to happen, I wanted you to know. No. I need you to know the truth. I have been a complete and total bastard as a husband and father. But I did not try to kill you. I am taping this to the bottom of your grandmother's trunk. Brad called and said he was coming to pick it up tomorrow. I know you wouldn't talk to me, even if I tried to contact you. I'm glad you won't. It may keep all of you safe a little while longer.

I abused and hurt you beyond belief. To say I'm sorry sounds so trite, even to me. At the time all this began, I was young, dumb and had this distorted notion of what life was to be. Reality bit me hard and fast. Before I knew, I had put my family, myself and my business in jeopardy.

It started with the strip mall. My first big job on my own, that I under bid. Everything you said about that job was true.

I'd been to Mexico the previous month. I'd been looking for a Mexican builder down there as I'd been approached to build the strip-mall. The owners wanted something different, along the lines of the old haciendas. I wanted to do everything right, as authentic as possible. I found a guy who was an incredible architect. We got along well. He knew of a factory that still did the stone work and pottery by hand. I felt we were set. I contacted the owners, gave them our ideas and the bid. He went for it and we signed the paperwork. Then all hell broke loose.

I learned I'd signed on with the Juarez drug cartel. They are part of the Contrereas Cartel. The guy I signed with was the brother-in-law of the head of the cartel. They wanted me to bring in the pottery and bricks as there would be cocaine and later meth in the shipments. I have no idea how they were getting it past DEA without it being detected. It was brought into the warehouse, broke open for the drug packages and distributed to the dealers. The pottery was then ground back into the clay and remolded. Same for the bricks. During this time, they decided they wanted me to build a new sub-division along the same line as the strip mall, only the houses were to be very high end. We hit a snag with the environmental laws and that was put on hold as we didn't know how long before we could break ground. It was at this point our marriage fell apart.

I have no excuse for the abuse. No one should ever treat the person they vowed to love, honor, cherish and protect forever the way I treated you. The kids should never have seen any of it. Saying I'm sorry sounds so cheap. You were my stress relief. Instead of trusting you to help, I shut you out because I was terrified of you and the kids being hurt. In the end, that's exactly what happened and I was the one to cause it to all of you.

The one guy with me in the pictures is Juan Alphonso Garcia. He's the brother-in-law of Jorge Miguel Contrereas. He's the head of the Contrereas drug cartel. Garcia runs the Juarez cartel. There's also a picture of Garcia with Contrereas. The American is Alan Stewart. He's a fed but I don't know in what capacity. I do know he's in bed with the cartel. The other picture is of him and a woman who, I think, is with the Attorney General's office. I believe she's a prosecutor. I don't know if she's involved or not.

About ten years ago, I got tired of all of it. I'd lost you, even if we weren't divorced yet. The kids barely spoke to me, the company wasn't what I intended and I was tired. The stress level was insane. Garcia told me he would kill my family. I believed him and went along for another few years. Then you left and I didn't know where you were. No matter how hard I tried to find you, you had disappeared. You were found completely by accident by one of Garcia's men when you were coming out of a grocery store. He followed you home. The attack came a few days later. When I got the news, I thought you were dead. I was beyond anything. The kids wouldn't have anything to do with me as they honestly felt I had tried to have you killed. I knew they were lost to me. I couldn't think, couldn't function. My two lead guys were handling the business as I couldn't. By the grace of God, you survived. When I saw them wheel you into the courtroom with all the bandages, casts, IVs, I died. At that point, I didn't care what happened to me as long as you lived. My attorney was hired by the cartel to represent me as they didn't trust anyone I hired. He knew I hadn't done anything to you but he knew who did. He was devastated by the viciousness of what had been done to you. I was found not guilty but I was and am guilty. If not for my own stupidity, none of this would have happened.

Jim

Mandy sat with the letter in her hand. She was completely drained. She looked at Michael for the first time. He was still leaning against the door frame. He saw the anguish in her eyes, on her face. She handed him the letter. He read it and handed it back. Then she handed him the pictures.

"Do you believe him?"

"I don't know. It doesn't change anything. Someone's still trying to kill me. I think if it's not Jim, it has to be Garcia and/or Contrereas."

"Are you going to see him?"

"I don't know how to avoid it," Mandy sighed as she got up from the floor. "Things have changed since that letter was written. He must be an incredible source for them to keep him this long. It still feels like there's something more to this." She paused. "What do you think about Allison and Alan?"

"Allison always loved the law. Her being involved with someone who deals drugs or murders people doesn't make sense to me. But we were a long time ago and who knows how she's changed. As for Alan, there's two ways for this. Either he's a dirty fed or he's undercover. Nothing else makes any sense."

Mandy walked up to him.

"Both our families and friends are involved in this because of trying to help me."

Michael reached for her and hugged her. "It'll be okay, babe. We've got an incredible team on our side."

They walked back out to the kitchen. Everyone was at the island. Mandy put the letter and the pictures on the counter and gave a brief description of the contents. Both Brad and Marie read the letter, reviewed the pictures.

"Do you believe him, mom?"

"I don't know. I have to rearrange my whole thought process."

"According to this picture, Allison has known Alan a long time," Alex said.

"She'd said they'd worked together a long time," Michael said, sitting on one of the stools. He sat rolling his empty coffee mug in his hands.

Mandy had taken the letter and pictures into her office. She came back out and handed copies to Hank.

"I don't know what to do with these except give them to you. I'll have the originals when you need them." Hank nodded. He was going to take everything in and contact the state police and the FBI. It was time to bring them all in. He knew this was going to escalate and he needed more back up than what he had. He stood up.

"I'm going to the office and get things started." He turned to Marie. "Would you like to come with me?"

"Sure." She looked at Mandy and leaned in to give her a kiss. "I'll be back in a bit."

In the living room with her legs drawn up and her arms wrapped around them, Mandy tried to slow down her thoughts. So many memories, both good and bad, went through her head. The attack, the look of fear on her daughter's face, anger on her son's. Jim's awe when Brad was born and total happiness when he held Marie for the first time. She replayed the conversations with the doctors, facing reconstructive surgery and not knowing what all that meant. Of the joy on the surgeon's face when he told her the damage wasn't as extensive as they had first thought. The courtroom, Sally beside her, holding her hand to try and ease the shaking that was throughout Mandy's body. She had thought she'd faced it all but the letter brought everything back. Not with the same crippling intensity but still with incredible power. Damn. She was so tired.

She woke to Michael gently shaking her.

"Why don't you go in and lie down? We'll be here."

Mandy looked at him, completely disoriented. Then she remembered.

"Good idea." She unfolded her legs and found they had gone to sleep. It took a few minutes for the circulation to return. She went to her room. It has always been her sanctuary. It felt so safe now.

Chapter 9

Mandy didn't know how long she slept. It was dark when she woke. Max had gotten off the bed at some point and was on the floor. Mandy heard quiet voices coming from the kitchen and smelled food. Someone was cooking chicken. She chuckled. She'd been thinking about chicken. Seriously?

After refreshing a bit, Mandy went into the kitchen. Alex, Brad and Marie were making dinner. Brad was making homemade biscuits, Marie was making dessert and Alex was making salad and frying chicken. Hank and Michael at the table, talking in low voices.

"Hey," Michael smiled, standing up. "You look a lot better. How ya feelin'?"

"I think some of the cobwebs are gone," Mandy grinned back. "Dinner woke me up. It smells wonderful."

"Good," Marie said. "We decided to give the law and you a break tonight. You slept for four hours."

Mandy stared in disbelief. She hadn't taken a four- hour nap since she was in the hospital. "Seriously?"

"Yes, mam'm. Figured if you slept that hard, you'd need someone to make you dinner. And Brad volunteered his famous biscuits, Alex is doing her dangerous fried chicken and toss salad and I am making key lime pie."

"Whoa," Mandy said. "Maybe I should take more four -hour naps!"

Mandy sat at the table, across from Hank.

"Hey, Hank. How was your afternoon?"

"Pretty good. I heard from Sally and she wants you to call her after we have dinner. There's a 'no talk shop' rule tonight at the dinner table."

"Oh, yea?"

"Yea. Marie said we all need a break."

"She's pretty smart that way."

"So I'm finding out," Hank grinned.

Dinner was wonderful. There was a slight tension in the air but everyone tried to ignore it. They talked about anything except what was staring them in the face. The coming winter, cattle, horses, ranching in general. The huge white elephant stayed in the background. Towards the end of the meal, it leaned towards the law. As Mandy cleared the table and brought out a bottle of white wine, the conversation became about Jim and the discoveries made that afternoon.

Hank had contacted Sally with the information he had. She shared hers. She found a guy who was undercover but was willing to meet with her tomorrow night.

Mandy sipped her wine.

"I need to set up a meeting with Jim. Home isn't a big secret anymore since so many people have already been here."

"Are you sure that's what you want to do?" Michael asked.

"No. I want this over with but I don't see another way to accomplish that. If that letter is true, then Jim's more of a target than I am. Does anyone have a better idea?" No one had any suggestions. "Guess we roll with that, then,"

They discussed time, where to position people, who would be in the house. Mandy let everyone know about her escape door and how to operate everything. She showed them all where the guns were hidden. Even if Jim was a victim, it didn't mean they wouldn't come after him here. They needed all bases covered and everyone to have as much information as possible.

Morning came. As Mandy got out of bed, she looked out her window and wondered if these were the last mornings she would see this view. Can't go there, she thought as she pulled on her jeans. The circles under her eyes weren't as bad as she thought they'd be but they were still there. I'd probably look like a raccoon if I hadn't taken that four-hour nap yesterday. The strange thoughts kept popping through her head. She knew she was avoiding the issue but she couldn't stop. Oh, well. Admission is half the battle. Maybe she could win this war.

Everyone was pretty quiet as she made the call.

"I found the pictures and your letter."

"Do you believe them?"

"I don't know. But regardless, we need to talk to end this. Either one of us kills the other or someone else does."

"I don't want you dead. Or hurt anymore than what's been done. I can't change that. Where do you want to meet?"

"My house."

"Your house?" The surprise in Jim's voice was unmistakable.

"Your men have already been here. Don't take this as a friendly invitation."

"It wasn't my men who've been at your house. I won't take it that way. I'll bring two people with me. They can validate what I say."

"Like I'd believe 'em. When will you be here?"

"I'll make arrangements and call you back."

"Call Brad."

"Okay. I'll call him in few hours." Jim hung up.

Mandy put the phone down. She was having trouble breathing. Michael was next to her and reached for her hand. Immediately, breathing was easier. In a time of crisis and I react to Michael, Mandy thought. How flamin' ironic. She looked at Brad.

"He'll call you in a few hours."

Brad nodded.

Marie handed Mandy a cup of coffee. She took it gratefully.

"I'm going to give Marty an update." Michael stood. He gave Mandy's shoulder a squeeze. "I'll be back in a bit."

Mandy went out on the back porch. She needed to be outside and feel the fall sun on her face. The pens looked so empty with the horses still in the back pasture. They were safer there.

Michael came up the steps.

"You okay?"

Mandy smiled at him. "As well as I can be. You?"

"I'm good." He reached for her hand. "Want to go check on the horses?"

"How'd you know?"

"That's what you do."

Mandy let Marie know where they were going and Max followed her out the back door. They were both quiet, just walking through the pens to get to the back pasture. They knew this could be the last time they spend together. Not knowing what tomorrow would bring was nothing new in anyone's life. No one ever did know but when dealing with what could be a violent confrontation, you had a tendency to contemplate. Mandy wondered if people in war zones felt like this or if they just kept their mind on the mission at hand. Scenes flashed through her head. The kids when they were little, birthday parties, vacations, BBQs at the house, graduations. The happiness they once all shared seemed like a million years ago.

They reached the grove of trees. Mandy immediately felt safer. She walked the trail to the tack shed she had put back there and checked the tack. Michael was behind her. He'd been in this position many, many times before. He realized how used he'd gotten to his life. No stress of day to day survival as out in the field, on a mission. The nightmares had stopped on a nightly basis. He still had them occasionally. This made him wonder if they'd be coming back.

The trail widened behind the shed so two people could walk side by side. Michael stepped up beside Mandy and took her hand. She stopped and looked at him with a question on her face.

"I want you to know that I think you are the most amazing woman."

"This coming from the combat vet?"

"Yea. I've known a lot of people who've gone into combat with a lot less courage than you."

"I don't know about all that," Mandy replied. "I don't know about courage. I do know that if God brings us to it, He'll get us through it. It's that simple. I trust that."

"He doesn't make mistakes."

"He got me through surgery, rehab and all the fear that was included. He'll get us through this. He hasn't brought us this far for nothing."

Michael leaned down and kissed her. It started out as a gentle little kiss but turned into a hungry kiss of passion. Mandy's arm slid around his neck, his around her waist.

"I've been wanting to do that for several years," Michael grinned, still holding her close.

"The thought crossed my mind several times," Mandy smiled. "I'm surprised I remember how."

"If you can get back on a horse, you can remember how to kiss."

"Is that your phenomenal insight?"

"No," Michael laughed. "Experience."

"Ahh. I see."

They continued walking through the trees and came to the fence line. The horses ran across the pasture when Mandy called. They were like little kids, all vying for attention at the same time. For the next half hour, it was all about the horses. Michael and Mandy laughed at their antics to get attention. Milo reached Michael and turned to kick out at anyone who got to close. Michael sent him back out to the pasture, letting him know that wasn't allowed. Milo came back, head dropped, licking and chewing. Michael called him over. All was forgiven. Too soon they had to get back. Final rubs and soft words.

"Look."

Max was waiting for them. He'd been lying in the grass, patiently waiting. He'd never tried to divide their attention. Now, he got up and went to the fence. Phoenix and Kona both dropped their heads and Max sniffed noses with them. The other four didn't know what to make of this big dog. He looked like a predator to them. Chico snorted and backed up. Milo was curious. He cautiously stepped forward. Max laid down, telling Milo he wasn't a threat. Milo came up and sniffed him. Max didn't move. Milo moved away. It was okay with him. Lena didn't seem to care, neither did Cheyenne. They weren't bothered. Maybe because they could smell Mandy on Max and just figured he was okay. Chico was going to take some convincing.

Max came over to Mandy when all the horses moved back out to the pasture. She crouched down and hugged the big dog.

"You are such a special guy," she said as she hugged him. Max licked her face and Mandy laughed. "You know it, too."

"He's pretty obvious in how much he adores you," Michael said as they started walking back. "What were you going to show me the other day before we were so rudely interrupted with unexpected visitors?"

"Come on. I'll show you now."

They walked to the trees but instead of going towards the house, Mandy led them off to the right. They had gone about 25 feet when they came to a small clearing. There were a couple of chairs and a small table made from a tree stump. It was small area where you could rest and just enjoy being out in the grove, which is what Michael thought Mandy had in mind when she set it up.

"This is nice," Michael said, looking around. He went to one of the wooden chairs and sat down. It was very comfortable. He thought of what a reprieve this would be on a hot summer day. "What made you think of setting something up back here?"

"I was tightening the fence one day, not long after I moved in. I'd been out here for several hours and was going back to the house. I was tired and wanted just to sit for a minute. Since there was nothing here, I decided to put something here."

"Good idea."

They started back to the house, Max leading the way. Suddenly, he stopped. He looked back at Mandy and then ahead but didn't move. They came up on either side of him and heard footsteps on the trail. As Max wasn't growling, they weren't too concerned. In a moment, Brad came into view.

"Hey," he said as he rubbed Max's ears. "Jim called. Said he'll be here in about 3:00." Mandy's face went white. "It'll be okay"

"I know. We'll get through this. First, I need to talk to you and Marie, before he gets here."

Michael and Alex went outside to check in with Marty. He had no idea what she wanted to talk to her kids about. He felt she'd tell him if she wanted him to know. Some things were private. Some things could be left until a later date. And their relationship hadn't progressed that far.

As they sat at the table, Mandy let them know what she wanted done with the property and the horses if she didn't make it through this. She'd had a will drawn up and let them know where it was. It was in her safe, in her office closet. That was where the original of Jim's letter and the pictures were and any important papers, like the deed to the property plus her cash that she always kept on hand.

Marie looked at her mother. "We'll do whatever you want. Your place won't be sold, neither will the horses. We'll figure it out. BUT you're coming out of this alive and well. We all are." Decision made.

Mandy got her .32 and put it in the pocket of her sweatshirt. She couldn't get warm the last few days. Over stressed and over tired kept her cold. She just hoped she wouldn't make any mistakes.

With the conversation done, they started moving. Guns were checked. Ammunition boxes and clips were double checked. Everyone kept extra everything on them. Furniture was rearranged. Everything could be fixed or replaced if damage. As long as everyone stayed safe. That's all Mandy cared about.

A car pulled into the drive. Mandy went to the door, Michael beside her and Max in front to guard. He could feel the tension. She stepped out onto the porch with her hand in her pocket.

Jim got out of the car with two men. One looked like the guy in the restaurant but not exactly. Jim looked the same to her. A bit older, a bit heavier. His hair was gray now, He had dark circles under his eyes and she could see the strain on his face. He stood beside the car, staring at her.

"If you have any weapons, they need to be handed over now," Mandy's voice was low and commanding. Jim nodded to his companions and they handed over their guns to Michael. They walked into the house, into the dining room where Brad and Marie were standing. Alex was behind Brad, off to the side. The look on Jim's face said it all.

"You'll have to excuse me if I'm not the perfect hostess," Mandy said with a hint of sarcasm. "You can sit down."

"I wouldn't have recognized you," Jim said as he pulled out a chair.

"Lucky for me."

"I didn't try to kill you."

"Let's say for the moment, I give you the benefit of the doubt. Why the hell have you kept the insurance policy on me if not to kill me to get your ass out of the mess you've put yourself in?" Mandy was leaning across the table from Jim. Her eyes were blazing with anger. That was the one thing that stayed the same, Jim thought. Whatever she was feeling always showed in her eyes.

"I didn't know about the insurance money until just a few months ago. When we got divorced, the policy was automatically canceled because we were no longer married. I've also learned there's policies on Brad and Marie with me as the beneficiary. All three policies were written in Columbia through an American insurance company. I'm trying to get copies of all of them now. Garcia reinstated yours. I don't know how and I don't know how he got the ones on Brad and Marie. He's holding them all over my head so that I'd keep transporting the drugs. If I don't, he kills all of you and I go down for with the perfect motive. Contrereas has connections everywhere and into everything. I have been trying to find you but haven't been able to. All I could think of to keep you safe, was to keep you with me. He'd never suspect that."

Mandy looked at him, completely dumbfounded. He had to be crazy.

"What the hell have you been smokin'? Have you lost your mind? I won't go anywhere with you or anyone connected with you. I don't want anything to do with you. I haven't for eight years - over eight years. For me to have anything to do with you will be when hell freezes over. Am I making myself clear or do you need further explanation?"

"No, you've made yourself perfectly clear. I only hope I can keep Brad and Marie safe." Jim stood.

Brad looked at his father. Marie stood still beside him.

"We have, can and will take care of ourselves and mom." Brad spoke low.

"Obviously, this was a waste of time. I hope that someday you can forgive me." Jim started for the door.

The door opened and Max moved in front of Mandy as she turned. Michael had been leaning against the wall and quickly moved to the kitchen, gun at his side. Hank came through the door. He wasn't in uniform but in jeans. He nodded to Michael and came to the table.

"You scared us to death," Mandy said, pulling her hand out of her pocket.

"Sorry. I wanted to give you time to say what you needed to say before I came in."

"Nothing settled."

Hank nodded and looked at Jim.

"I'm Hank Waters, County Sheriff." He held out his hand to Jim, who looked like he was ready to bolt. "Don't be alarmed. I'm here to help you figure a way out of the mess you've created for yourself." Jim slowly took his hand. Jim's two men stood behind him.

"Let's sit down and see if we can figure this out."

Mandy started into the kitchen, relief written on her face.

"Did you set me up?" Jim asked from the table.

"I didn't think you were wanted for anything or I might have thought about it if you were."

Jim smiled a tired smile.

"Fair enough." He turned to Hank. "There's no way in hell you can help me. I've dug myself a hole so deep, I can see no way out. Except one. These two guys," he indicated both men on either side of him, "have been with me since the beginning. We started on the same construction crew together. They know everything as it involves them and their families. If you have some plan, let's hear it 'cause we've gone over every scenario every way we can think of for over 20 years."

Hank settled in his chair. Marie brought out the coffee and Mandy stayed in the kitchen. She needed to distance herself and get herself in control. She had to breathe and it was getting pretty tight in the dining room. She didn't need another panic attack now. She leaned against the doorway, listening. She breathed deeply the aroma of coffee. It always had such a calming effect. She looked up to see Michael watching her from where he stood behind Hank. He winked at her. Mandy smiled into her coffee.

"Mr. Thompson, have you ever considered turning states evidence against Garcia and Contrereas?"

"Call me Jim. These two men with are Rafe and Julio. And yes, we have. I was approached several years ago. At that time, they wouldn't or couldn't guarantee the safety of our families. I told them I didn't know where Mandy was and if I said anything like that to my kids, they wouldn't believe me as they felt I had tried to kill their mother. Without knowing my family and Rafe's and Julio's would be protected and safe, we all said no. When I refused, they threatened to leak information that we were cooperating anyway. I told them if they did that, we'd end up dead and they wouldn't have a case."

"Who approached you?"

"The first time, it was Craig West. I believe he is or was with the FBI. That was about 10 years ago. The last time was two years ago and that was Alan Stewart. I believe he's with the Attorney General's office."

Mandy looked at Michael. He showed nothing on his face.

"Would you be willing to now with all your families in protective custody?"

"I know Mandy and Brad and Marie won't go. This decision isn't about including them. If they were going to be protected, it should have been done years ago when Mandy was attacked. Let's not go there as it has left a very sour taste in my mouth for law enforcement." Jim looked at his companions. They were all exhausted. "Can you give us a few minutes? This isn't just my decision. We've been together in this all these years and their families are also at risk."

Hank nodded and got up from the table. Everyone moved back into the kitchen, giving Jim and his companions room and space to talk this out. There was hope on their faces, but not a lot. They had so much fear for wives, children, parents, siblings.

Mandy leaned against the counter at the far end of the kitchen. Michael came and stood beside her. She could see into the dining room. Jim was standing, leaning against the far wall with his hands in his pockets. Mandy watched him. She was still angry at him but not nearly what she had been. That was confusing as she hadn't known how angry she was until she heard his voice and then seeing him. For that anger to dissipate to any degree was confusing and felt strange. She'd have to figure this out at a later date. Psych 101.

"Did you know about the offer?" she asked Michael, keeping her voice low.

"I thought something like this would come up. Hank plays his cards pretty close to his vest. Since he's been in contact with Sally, I wasn't sure."

"What do you make of Alan approaching him?"

"Seems there's a lot about Alan we don't know."

"No joke. It feels like a million different surprises are hitting us all at once. We don't a get chance to figure one out before we get hit with another. But I suppose that's what they want, to keep us unbalanced."

"Exactly," Michael replied.

Jim and his men came into the kitchen.

"We have to be sure our families in California are safe. Then we'll talk."

"I don't blame you in the least," Hank replied. "Do you remember Detective Sally Shore with LA County Sheriff office?"

"Yea, she was with Mandy from the beginning 'til Mandy left rehab."

"She is more than willing to get your families to safety. Would you trust her?"

Both Rafe and Julio nodded.

"When you get it set up, we need to contact them on a clean cell. None of them will go anywhere unless Rafe and Julio say it's okay."

"No problem," Hank replied. He took out his phone and dialed Sally. She was on speed dial.

"Hey, Sally. You ready to help with this mess? We need some on your end." With that, names and addresses were given. Code words set up so people would know that Sally was sent from their loved one. Julio and Rafe made phone calls. Meetings were set. When people were safe, Sally would call back. She was doing all this on her own. Had set up the safe houses and would get the families there. She trusted no one as she didn't know if anyone in the department was also working for the cartel. She wouldn't take the chance with anyone's life. Jim and his men would go with Hank when all was in place.

"So where does this leave us?" Jim asked when Hank hung up from Sally.

"We may not be as sophisticated as California but we're good at what we do. Our State Attorney General's office may be willing to step in once they know the whole story. We'll keep you out of sight until then. I know you're in a tough spot. Will you trust me one step at a time?"

Jim looked at Hank. He studied him for a few minutes. Hank withstood the scrutiny and didn't falter. Jim slowly nodded.

"Good. As soon as Sally calls back, we'll get you outa here."

"Wait a minute," Mandy said."I know you from somewhere." She was looking at Rafe. "I know it could have been years ago at one of the functions but it feels more recent. I can't place you. Did we meet anywhere other than anything associated with the company?"

"No, I don't believe so," Rafe replied. He looked down at his hands and then back up at Mandy. "I look familiar because it was my brother Miguel that attacked you."

Mandy stared at him, all color drained from her face and she started to shake. Brad immediately was at her side, easing her into a chair.

"Your brother tried to kill me?" She looked at Jim. "Who the hell did you bring into my house?"

"Mandy." Jim came to her side, reaching for her hand. Mandy snatched it away. "Rafe's brother Miguel has been with the cartel since he was 10 years old. Rafe has always worked for me when he was in Mexico or with me when he came to the states. He tried to warn me years ago but I was already in too deep. Miguel was ordered to kill you so they could have more control over me and bringing in the drugs."

Just then, Max growled and the sound of a pickup was heard pulling in the drive. Alex looked out the window.

"It's Allison and Alan." She turned to Michael. "How'd they know about Mandy's place?"

"Good question."

Mandy looked at Jim. She had a split moment to make a decision.

"Come with me." They moved down the hallway to her bedroom. She showed them the closet and the hidden hallway.

"Stay here til I come and get you. Don't say a word." She closed the hidden door, resetting everything in the closet. She stood for a moment, breathing deep.

Allison and Alan were just coming in the mudroom when Mandy returned.

"We understand Jim's on his way to see you," Allison began. "We thought you might want to leave. We came to help."

"I'll be fine here. If I leave, no one will know where I'm going."

"You don't seem to understand what you're up against," Alan stated. Before he could continue, Mandy's temper exploded. She'd had enough of his crap.

"No," she said in a very controlled voice. "YOU don't understand. I'm done with this fuckin' bullshit. I've been shot at, stabbed, beaten, spent a couple of years rebuilding my body and my mind and six years in hiding. Would you like to tell me where the hell you were during that time? Why didn't you nail the bastard back then? Did you protect my kids? Do you think you can use me as bait to get to the cartel? Hope you can get them before they get me?" Her brown eyes had turned coal black. She was in Alan's face. "I seriously doubt you have any idea about me but I can guarantee you WILL if you keep pushing me and I can also guarantee you won't like me." Alan's eyes never left her face. Mandy glared back at him. Allison looked at Michael for help. He gave none.

"You should go." It was Alex who spoke. "We'll take care of things here."

Allison was saying something to Mandy about calling her if she needed anything but Mandy couldn't hear her. Her temper and adrenaline were too high. Allison tried to put her card in Mandy's hand but it fell to the floor. Mandy was fighting to regain control. She hated losing her temper. It took everything she had out of her and usually a couple of days to come back to normal. She didn't have that luxury now. She was going to have get it together NOW, not in a few days.

"You okay?" Michael's concern was in his voice. He made no attempt to touch her. Now wasn't the time.

"No. I just want to beat the shit outa someone. Preferably one of the fucking assholes trying to kill me or maybe the jackass that just left." She was shaking. She felt like a trapped animal. Flight or fight response. She wanted to fight. "Why couldn't the bastards just leave me alone? Damn it." She paused. "I better get the guys out of the closet."

"Let me do it," Michael offered with a grin. "You might deck one of them."

She looked up at him.

"You could be right."

As Michael moved down the hallway, Marie grabbed Mandy and pulled her into the kitchen. She hugged her hard. Alex came in.

"Just so you know, "Marie said, with her arm still around Mandy, "when mom starts cussin', get out of her way. She will kick ass, show no mercy and take no prisoners."

"I got that," Alex said. "I thought you did really well. I probably WOULD have hit him." That got as chuckle from all three of them.

"Mom, we're gonna be okay."

"I know. I'm so thankful for you."

"Back atcha."

"And I'm thankful for being able to know this incredible family." Alex was standing on the other side of Mandy. She reached for Mandy's hand. "You all are incredible."

"Especially Brad," Marie joked.

"That's beside the point," Alex said, grinning. "I've never known such a close family. You three have been through hell and still stand strong. And just so you know," she said, leaning in and kissing Mandy's cheek," my dad's a good guy, too."

"I know," Mandy grinned, squeezing her hand.

Jim came into the dining room. Sorrow was all over his face and he looked at Mandy. He had heard the exchange between her and Alan. In all the years they were married, he'd never heard heard so much anger from her. It bothered him that he was the cause of all this pain. Even though he wasn't who had done it, he was the cause of it. So much pain for his family to endure. He would be spending the rest of his life trying to make up for it.

Dinner was made in record time. Steaks were grabbed out of the freezer, thawed in the microwave, then potatoes set up to cook in there. Salad was thrown into a bowl with any fresh vegetables that could be found in the fridge. Rolls were brought from the freezer, wrapped in foil and placed in the oven. Cooking was a distraction for everyone, as was eating. They could forget the drama of the day. Mandy was drained. She did her best to keep up her end of the conversation going. Everyone was trying but soon the dinner table was quiet.

They sat around the table, everyone with a glass of wine or a beer and waited for Sally to call. Until then, they were just passing time.

Chapter 10

It was nine o'clock when Sally called. Both families were hidden and safe. Only she knew where they were. In most aspects, it made it easier. A few were harder but that was okay. Hank spoke to her and then handed the phone to Mandy.

"Hey, girlfriend. How ya holdin' up?"

"Let's say I've had better days. I thought I'd handle this stress a lot better than what I have been. I'm sorry I didn't call you back last night. I was whooped."

"I have no doubt. No worries. I talked to Hank and knew you were okay. It's going to be okay, Mandy. This nightmare is going to be over with. We just have to take it one step at a time."

"Yea, I know. Life is one big 12 Step Program."

Sally laughed. "When this is over, we need to have a girl's night out."

"You got it. If we decide to get together here, I know this great steak house." Mandy looked at Michael and smiled.

"Great. Consider it a done deal. See? The universe knows we have plans. We're good."

Mandy laughed. "Well, there ya go. Who would dare interrupt our plans?"

"Exactly. No one with a brain would dare." Sally paused. "I'll talk to you in a few days. You take care."

"I will. You, too, Sal."

Hank stood up and looked at Jim.

"Ready?"

Jim, Rafe and Julio nodded.

"Where are you taking them?" Mandy asked.

"Somewhere only I know. There's too many odd coincidences going on and too many unknown agendas. We'll be safe, Mandy. I promise." He started for the door and looked at Marie. "I'll call you." Marie smiled and nodded.

After they left, Mandy cleared off the table, putting dishes in the dishwasher. She came back and sat at the table with Brad, who'd been quiet all night.

"You okay?"

"Yea. I'm fine. Just so strange to see Jim. He seems a bit deflated from the last time I saw him, like all the wind's been knocked out of his sails."

"I know. I'm thinking maybe he wasn't behind all this. I don't hate him, honey, if that's what you're wondering. I thought I did but I don't. I just wanted him to leave me alone. I still do. As for caring about him, he's right there along with anyone else we share breathing space with. That's all. I'm still angry but I don't hate him. He's a mess. His bad choices have screwed up all our lives and he's feelin' it. And I really do need to control my temper."

"Maybe when all this done, Mom, you'll finally have some peace. I know these years have been hell on you. As for losing your temper, anyone who pushes a person when they know what you've been through, deserves what they get. Too bad." He paused. "But I really thought I was going to have to pull you off the jackass."

"Me, too. And these years have been just as hard on you guys."

"Yea, but it hasn't been 24/7, in our face like for you. It's been 24/7 but over our shoulder, like an extra 30 lbs. You've been living it. Somehow, that doesn't compare."

Mandy smiled at him. "No worries, honey. I'm tougher than I look. Especially when someone pisses me off."

"Like I said. I think you're allowed."

"Thanks."

"Figured you were long overdue. Anyway, you only directed it at who deserved it. I'd have held you back from going totally postal." Brad ginned. "Any idea what's going to happen to Jim now?"

"No. I don't think we'll get any answers 'til Hank feels he can trust someone. He's too concerned about the leak. That's okay because I think it keeps all of us safer."

"Yea, that's what I thought."

Marie and Alex came in and sat down.

"Hank just called, Mom."

Mandy gave her a questioning look. Michael came in from outside.

"He said they were where they were going to be and he'll call tomorrow."

Mandy nodded. She was scared to think this may really be coming to an end but hope was beginning to form in her heart. Oh, Lord, please.

"Dad, I'm gonna go home." Alex stood. "What's the plan for tomorrow?"

"There isn't one. We're playin' it by ear at this point. With Jim and his guys with Hank, we don't know what going to happen or what to expect. We can only try to be prepared for anything."

"But you're good here? Your guys are still playing camp-out?'

"Yes, honey. They're still here. Who's going with you?"

"Dad. Didn't we just have this discussion? I'm not in any danger. I'm a big girl."

"We don't know that."

"What? That I'm a big girl?" Alex was trying to lighten the air and Mandy couldn't help but smirk. That was funny.

"Brad and I will go with her," Marie volunteered. "I'm not worried about mom with you, Max and the place surrounded by an army. We'll be okay. And besides, isn't your house being watched, too?"

"Yea, it is. But call when you get there and've checked out the house."

Alex kissed her dad. "You're so cute."

The three of them left. Mandy felt better with them gone, felt they were safe away from her. She got both Michael and her a cup of coffee and brought them into the living room as Michael had moved to the couch. Max went to his bed under the window. Mandy sat at the opposite end of the couch from Michael.

"You've been awfully quiet tonight."

"Yea."

"What're you thinking about?"

"What do you think Jim will do from here?"

"I have no idea." Mandy swung her legs up onto the coffee table and took a sip of coffee. "I really don't care as long as it doesn't involve us. I'm really beginning to have some hope this might be ending."

"So do we still have a future?"

Mandy smiled at him. "I thought we were going to take is slow and see where it leads."

"Well, doesn't that have to mean a future?" Michael's voice had that sexy tease to it that Mandy loved. He put his legs up on the coffee table and rubbed her feet with his own. He looked at her over his coffee mug. Even stressed as she was, she still made his heart skip a beat. He knew more about their relationship than he was letting on. Now wasn't the time. She had enough on her plate.

"Yea, it does mean that. Why you asking?"

"Just askin'. Just wanted to know if anything'd changed."

Mandy was thoughtful for a moment. "What do you want from me?"

"Do I have to want anything from you?"

Mandy looked at him. He looked so relaxed, leaning back in the corner of the couch with his stocking feet on the table, still rubbing hers.

"I'm not good at this."

He laughed. "Oh. And I am?"

Mandy chuckled as she sipped coffee.

"Guess we're both a bit out of practice."

"To say the least."

They were both quiet for a moment. Then Michael put his hand out to Mandy. She took it and he pulled her close to him. He kissed the top of her head as she snuggled in.

"I would love to wake up next to you in the morning."

"Really?" She looked up at him. His face didn't have it's customary grin as he held her face with one hand.

"Really."

Michael's phone rang. It was Alex. They were at the house and it had been cleared. They snuggled back together, enjoying the closeness of each other and the quiet of the house. Mandy slipped into sleep, listening to the steady beat of Michael's heart.

Mandy woke to Max. He was pushing her arm with his nose and whining. Mandy stirred, trying to get her bearings.

Michael lay still, his arm around her.

"Someone's outside." He spoke low. The only light on was over the dining room table and it was on low dim. The living room was almost pitch black. "I'm going to slide off the couch and get the gun in the end table." Just then, his phone vibrated.

"Yea."

"You got company." Marty was on the line.

"How many?"

"Two in the front. We got them. Probably two more out back."

"Meet in the back."

Mandy was on the floor. She started crawling to the hallway, staying as close to furniture as she could. Michael grabbed the gun and followed. Mandy stood when she got in the hallway and moved as quickly and silently as she could, grabbing the 9mil with 2 clips in her dresser. As they were going through the closet door, they heard the crash of the back door. Someone was in. They moved to the concealed door, Mandy getting Michael and Max ahead of her so she could close it. They stood leaning against the wall, breathing hard through their mouths and praying no one heard them. Max stood between them and started his low rumble when he heard someone in Mandy's room. A hand on his head quieted him instantly. Mandy's heart was racing. She looked at Michael. He nodded towards the backdoor and she moved towards it. Silently, she slid open the hidden door and stepped onto the back deck. The door slid shut. She moved close to the house, staying in the shadows. There was movement to her right and Mandy hugged in closer to the house, deeper into the protection of the shadows. Michael rushed silently into the dark. Suddenly, Max lunged in front of her and knocked someone to the ground. He stood on their chest, growling in their face.

"Max! Off!" Michael commanded. Max stepped off the person he'd been standing on. Michael grabbed the guy by the shirt and hauled him up. He didn't say a word, just shoved him forward. Mandy went in the back door, or what was left of it as it was split in two and hanging by one hinge. She turned on the outside light. Five of the intruders had been caught and were leaned against Michael's truck, their hands zipped tied behind their backs. They looked a bit worse for wear.

"The counties sending a couple of units."

Marty looked at Michael. "Good. I'd hate to have to beat info outa 'em."

Michael smirked. "I bet you would."

"How'd they get past you?" Mandy asked.

"I'd say luck. I'd just had everybody check in when I saw the two guys in the back. I tried to raise my guy back there and he didn't respond. I had everybody close ranks and come in. We caught a few on the way in."

"What happened to your guy in the back?"

"He got hit from behind." Just then, two men came from the side of the barn, one almost carrying the other. Marty ran to them and helped bring the one guy up on the deck. They sat him in a chair. He had a large lump on the back of his head and a gash on the side that was still bleeding. Mandy ran into the house for towels. Michael applied pressure while Marty ran for his truck. They got him inside and Marty took off for the hospital. As he was driving out, the sheriff's cruisers were coming in. He stopped, told them he had an injured man and would be at the hospital. After statements were taken, Marty's guys faded back into the dark, knowing how real the threat was now that one of their own had been injured. They'd be extra vigilante now. Tonight felt like they had failed and that wasn't acceptable to anyone.

As they were walking into the house, Michael's phone vibrated. Mandy was already in the house as he took the call. She was exhausted. She sat on the couch, Max at her feet.

"That was Hank. Jim said since an attempt was make so fast, they'll get reinforcements and hit us again to keep us unbalanced. Pretty typical. I told Hank we're leaving."

"Where are we going?"

"To the first place I suggested. My cabin. Only the kids know where it's at. My brothers know and so does Dad but they haven't been up there in years. The only way in is by horseback or hike. I know you'll be safe there."

"Guess it's good we never unpacked."

By now, the sun was starting to hint about coming up. It was just turning pink on the top of the mountains. They couldn't leave yet so Mandy started making breakfast. She knew it was going to be a tough ride. Even though she rode almost every day, most of the day, this was going to be different. This would be steady riding with few breaks. Given the fact they were both exhausted to begin with, they would need all their strength for the concentration this journey would take. She made two pots of coffee, one for now, one to take with them. She made it strong. They'd need it.

Michael hated doing this to her. He knew how tired she was. He was beat as well but he knew their best chance of getting out of there was now. The cartel was short-handed. Her safety had been compromised and she wasn't safe here anymore. May not be safe at the cabin for very long. They would eventually find it but hopefully it would take a bit. It was built into the side of a hill surrounded by trees. It was easy to defend.

They talked about supplies while they ate omelets and toast. By the time they were done, the sun was up enough so they could tack up the horses. Michael tacked up at the pasture as his tack was in the shed there. Then they brought the horses up to the barn so Mandy could tack up. Her own saddle would be a lot more comfortable. She brought two bags with her, one for clothes, one for guns and ammo. She carried her shotgun and put it in the rifle boot of her saddle. She wondered how far away she'd have to be from Phoenix before she could fire. She'd have to ask Michael, if she remembered. As she walked out of the barn with Phoenix, she felt like she was back in the 1800s. It seemed funny that she would be safer doing something so old fashioned when life had made such progress. But then, maybe not so much. People were still greedy and selfish. Too bad the saying "It's all about the love" hadn't engulfed the world.

Mounted, they headed to the ranch. Max ran ahead, leading the way. He settled into that dog trot that ate up the miles, horses behind him. Mandy wondered at the incredible ability of the horses and Max. There she went again. Thinking of anything except what was right in her face.

It was a beautiful morning, though no one noticed it. Getting to Michael's took less time than previously, or it just seemed that way. There was an urgency in the air and everyone was responding to it. When they got to the ranch and told everyone what they were doing, everyone wanted to come with them, not feeling that Mandy would be safe out of their sight. Michael calmly explained they could travel faster and be less conspicuous being only the two of them. Also, it would be easier to hide two horses and two people. Michael won the argument. Alex knew where the cabin was. She or Kenny or Dustin could take any of them up there if needed. Michael grabbed two sleeping bags. Mandy had rolled her two together along with a bag of dog food and tide it down to the back of her saddle. Both of them had packed their saddle bags with supplies. Hugs were given with the unspoken fear it would the last ones any of them would receive. They headed out through the same pasture the horses had been in. As they crested the rise, they turned to look back. Everybody was still on the front porch. Smoke was coming from the chimneys of Michael's, his parents and farther away, his brother David's. They raised their hands in a wave, turned and headed down the back side of the rise, went through a small meadow and began the climb through the tree line.

The ride to Michael's had taken the edge off the horses and they settled in to a gentle trot, following Max. They rode steadily upwards for about three hours before stopping for a short rest. There was as a small stream and some grass. The horses drank and grazed. Max had some water and flopped down on a bed of pine needles. He would rest while he could. Mandy and Michael shared coffee and trail mix. Not much was said.

They made two more stops before they got to the cabin. It was starting to get dark when they came out of the woods. They turned the horses out in the corral next to the house. Saddles and saddle blankets went on the fence rail. Horses were fed from the hay kept in the small shed. Michael kept it stocked as he was here several times a year. Summer pasture wasn't far. He pumped fresh water into the trough. When the horses were seen to, they headed to the cabin.

Mandy was surprised when she went in. She'd never been in a burm cabin before and really didn't know what to expect. Max snooped all through it and made his place by the door, laying down and blocking it. The front part looked like any other cabin. There was a porch with two front windows. The inside was nothing lavish but there were a couple of comfortable chairs in the small living room and a small pot-bellied stove in the corner. There was a stack of kindling and another of logs against the wall by the stove. A small area to cook had a sink made from a metal water pan with a hand pump. The counter was made from a wood plank and had a camp stove on with an old coffee pot along the side. Several shelves were along the wall with canned goods and coffee. A cooler was on the floor. The back of the cabin was what had been built into the side of the hill. The one bedroom was back there. It had a platform bed frame in the middle of it and Michael pulled an air mattress from a box in the corner with two pillows. The air pump filled the mattress in a matter of minutes. Two sleeping bags were zipped together and laid on the mattress then the other two were zipped together and laid on top. Michael threw the two pillows. Home sweet home.

The was an outhouse on the side of the cabin and a make shift shower on the porch. The outhouse was quite a distance from the cabin, at least in the dark. I'm definitely taking Max with me, Mandy thought as she looked outside.

"Okay. What's the secret to the shower?"

Michael grinned.

"See the pan under the kitchen counter? We heat water in that and pour it into a plastic container that's above the shower. Then we alternate cold and hot until it's full. Takes longer the first time because it's empty but after that, it takes a less."

"Okay to take the lantern to the outhouse?"

"Absolutely. And take that tin can with the rocks in it. Bears don't like loud noises."

"Along with Max and my gun."

"Those, too."

"Cool. I got this."

While Mandy was outside, Michael made a fire, put the water on the camp stove to heat and grabbed towels. He'd tried to stock it with a few essentials but had never had to stay here for an extended period of time. He knew there was enough food for about a week. He didn't know where they'd be in a week. Hopefully still there or home.

"I thought this would really be roughin' it but this is pretty nice," Mandy said when she came back in. She moved around Michael and started to unload saddle bags.

"Thanks. I usually keep it stocked for a few days, at least. I've been caught up here in a freak snowstorm, bringing cattle down. That happens only once. You wise up real fast."

"You done good, bubba."

"Bubba?"

"Yea. I have a few nicknames for people. You get used to it."

Michael laughed. "Yea, I guess I will." He reached for her, pulling her to him and gently kissed her. "I may just come up with a few for you."

"That could be fun," she murmured as she kissed him back. She really didn't care what they faced right then. It felt so good to be held and to hold someone who cared as much about her as she did him. It had been long time. Way before her marriage had ended.

"Oh, yea." Michael continued with his gentle kisses along her jaw, down her neck. "Driving you crazy would be fun." Just then, the water boiled.

"Guess we better pay attention to the shower water," Mandy giggled as she moved to grab the pan.

"Yea. I'll just have to make you crazy later," Michael said as he took the pan from Mandy and moved to the outside shower container. He poured the water into the container. They filled it two more times with hot water and then cold.

"There. Not like home but it'll get you clean."

"Works for me." Mandy grabbed her towel and the lantern. This shower would feel wonderful, regardless. After riding all day under the tension they were feeling, the hot water felt like heaven. She quickly learned to shut off the water when she was soaping up, on to rinse. Same to wash her hair. It was cold when she shut off the shower. She wrapped up in the big towel and grabbed her clothes. She'd get dressed inside.

Michael was walking through the door with more water for the shower. He stopped and stared at her.

"God, you're beautiful."

Mandy laughed. "Oh, yea. Just flamin' gorgeous!"

Michael leaned in and kissed her. "Yes, you are."

Mandy stepped aside as Michael went out the door. She went into the bedroom. It was warm, even without the stove in there. It must be because the room was insulated from the ground. She quickly put on lotion, sweats and combed her wet hair. Even her thick hair was drying fast in the warm room.

Michael was back in when she came out of the bedroom.

"Feel better?"

"Much. That's a great shower. I wasn't expecting anything in a cabin, let alone a shower. What can I do to help?"

"Would you put dinner in some boiling water while I get in the shower?"

"Absolutely. Anything specific you want?"

"Whatever's in there."

By the time dinner was done, Michael was out of the shower. He'd brought in a bottle of wine, grabbed a wine opener and two small mason jars.

"You're just full of surprises," Mandy said as she took a sip of the Chardonnay. "I love your wine glasses."

"Ya' all know how we country folk is," Michael said in a southern drawl. "We come up with anythin' for the occasion." Mandy laughed.

Dinner ended up being chicken, vegetables and potatoes. It hit the spot after such a long day. Max had eaten and was sleeping in front of the wood stove, gently snoring and whimpering. He was dreaming.

"What's around here?"

"Trails, some caves. There's a valley not far from here. We'll go out tomorrow so you at least have an idea of the area. If, by chance, they come up here and we get separated, you'll need an idea of where to go. The caves would be good to hide in and the valley has another way out. You can't see it from this end. You have to know where the trail is even when you're close to it." He reached for her hand and gently rubbed the top. "We're gonna get through this. Remember that."

"I know. I'm trying."

"I know, babe. It really is going to be okay. I'm not saying they will or won't find us here. I know it will be lot harder for them if they do and we have a little time to prepare. It's not like your place or the ranch where they can show up any time they want to."

"I know. It's just so different this time. More people are involved and at risk and it's more complicated than it was. It was simple before. I ran to stay alive and keep everyone I cared about safe. I learned to hide my tracks. Now, it's no matter what I do, they find me."

"Well, we hadn't gone far from your place. It really wouldn't have taken much to find you. Just a little patience."

"I hadn't thought about that." Mandy had responded to Michael's touch, rubbing the side of his hand. He had a way of putting things in a logical perspective. "Too many things've happened. I'm not thinking right. I'm feel like a hysterical female and I hate that."

Michael smiled. "You're not a hysterical female. Your whole reaction seems pretty normal to me. And I'm here this time. You're not alone in this."

"I think you're here for more than that."

"I hope so."

Mandy smiled. She did, too.

Michael looked at her.

"What're you thinking?"

"A future with you. Wondering."

"That," he said as he stood and pulled Mandy up next to him, "sounds like a great thought." He kissed her with a passion Mandy didn't know existed, leaving her breathless for more. She stepped back and looked up at him. At that moment, she didn't care about a future. She cared about now.

Michael smiled his slow, sexy smile and reached for her hand.

"Come on. Let's see if I can make you crazy."

Chapter 11

Mandy woke to the smell of coffee. She stretched lazily and couldn't remember feeling so relaxed. Damn. She couldn't remember when she'd made love for most of the night. She was still surprised at the passion they ignited together. She never expected that at this time in her life. But she never expected her life to turn out has it had so a positive surprise was wonderful. And being with Michael felt so right, so natural. The connection was complete and after not feeling connected to anyone except Marie and Brad for so long, it was a very welcomed feeling.

She got up and put on her sweats, brushing her hair before she went into the kitchen. Michael was standing with his back to her with only a pair of sweats on. She saw where he had been injured on his right shoulder. The bullet wound she felt last night. Between the military and ranch life, the muscles in his back were amazing. He turned and smiled, leaning down to kiss her while handing her coffee.

"Hi, sleepy." He tasted of coffee and toothpaste. "Sleep okay?"

"More than okay. I don't know when I ever slept that hard." Mandy sipped her coffee. Perfect.

"You were out when I got up. I thought I'd let you sleep."

"You had another thought?" she asked, looking over the rim of her mug.

"Oh, yea," he grinned. "Lots of them but seeing as we only got about four hours sleep, I thought I'd give you a break."

Mandy chuckled. "What time is it?"

"A bit after ten."

"Damn! The horses, Max! They've gotta be fed!" She started running for the door.

"Hold on. It's all done. Everybody's been fed and watered. Max even went outside with me to feed, though he sat on the porch. We handled it. No worries. I'm here. I know how. Trust me."

Mandy looked at him a bit sheepishly.

"I'm sorry. I didn't mean it that way. I'm just not use to having any help. I learned real quick to depend on myself." She paused. "Max must really like you to go outside with you."

"He sniffed around a bit. Not very far, just the front of the cabin. I think he wanted to keep any eye on the door and me. When he was done snoopin', he just sat there and waited for me to be done." He kissed the top of her head as he placed two bowls of oatmeal on the small table.

"I could get use to this," Mandy said, taking a bite of oatmeal.

"Use to what?" Michael was trying to keep the grin off his face.

"Sleeping late, coffee, breakfast. Driven crazy half the night. You."

"I must be off my game. It should have been all night."

"We did need some sleep."

"True. Guess we'll just have to practice more."

Mandy smiled at the thought of that. The sexual tension was still there, though not as strong at the moment. Last night had eased it a bit. Mandy hoped it would never dissipate completely. She could think of nothing better than to spend a lifetime with someone like that. Lord! What was she thinking? One night and she was thinking long term. Damn, girl! You have literally lost your mind!

They finished breakfast and cleaned up. Getting dressed brought playful kisses and thoughts of staying in bed the rest of the day. Practicality won out. Mandy had to know the area, just in case they were found.

After checking the horses, Michael showed the different paths from the cabin and where the three paths joined into one towards the valley. They hiked for a couple of hours, Max investigating but never very far from them. The caves that were close to the cabin were pretty good size. In one, the back had branches that blocked it. Michael moved them and showed Mandy the short cut to get to the other side of the hill.

"That could come in handy."

"Yea. It has in the past. Got chased by a bear once. He was too big to get through."

Mandy stopped and stared at him.

"How could you even think? I'd have been so scared, I wouldn't have been able to think of what to do."

"It was weird. It was like in combat. My whole emotional system shut down and survival kicked in. You don't think about it 'til later." He held his hand out to her. "And then you grab the closet beer."

"No shit. I'd be grabbin' the whole bottle of wine!"

They walked back out and continued on towards the valley. They came around a bend to find Max sitting in the middle of the trail, waiting for them. As soon as he saw them, he bounded into the trees, barking. He came back and did the same thing. They followed him to another cave.

"Good boy!" Michael said, rubbing his ears and patting his side. He looked in the cave and walked in. Small trees and bushes hid it. If you didn't know it was there, you'd walk right by. Michael had never known about it in all the years he had been in these mountains. He found a tree branch and put it in the cave.

"If we have to run up here, hopefully we'll be far enough ahead to wipe out any prints."

The cave wasn't that deep and you had to stoop in the back as it was shorter in height. The flashlight didn't reveal any bones or debris. It was surprisingly clean. It went back about 30 feet and a small opening was to the side, concealed in the shadows. Max had gone through the opening and come back.

"It must go back farther," Michael said. He studied the opening and all around the cave for a moment then started to crawling through the opening. Mandy followed Michael and they came to a cavern that was about 20 feet across. There was light coming from a hole in the top so it wasn't completely dark. It was as clean as the cave had been. Michael found that odd. There was no indication of any animal using it for shelter.

They crawled back out and proceeded down into the valley. As it was getting to be mid – afternoon, they didn't explore it. They could do that tomorrow, riding the horses in. Today had been for Mandy to get to safety if she had to and for them to figure out a meeting place if they got split up.

As they headed back, Mandy started thinking of different scenarios and what they could do in each one. Always have a backup plan. Nothing was full proof so it was better to have details figured out ahead of time. If all your plans fell through, your decisions would be made on the information you had on hand. If there was enough warning, Mandy knew she'd go into the valley. There was more room to run and more places to hide. Plus she could see who would be shooting at her. She still wasn't comfortable shooting someone. She knew she could injure someone and not feel real bad about that, but to kill someone......... That would take some more thinking. Michael was right. She was going to need to wrap her head around that. She thought if it came to protecting herself or someone else, she could do it but she also knew she could just as easily freeze and not be able to pull the trigger. The thought was hard to deal with. She never had been a person who believed in violence. Her dad had taught her that issues could be solved with communication. As she got older, she understood that was only if all people involved were willing to communicate.

They got back to the cabin just as the sun was setting. It was phenomenal to see it set over the mountain peaks. The pink blending in with the orange looked like a wave of fire setting. She looked to the east and saw a huge moon coming up over the mountains on the other side of the valley, deep yellow and so big you could actually see the craters that made up the Man in the Moon. It didn't seem that far away. It seemed more like she could reach out and touch it. Home was in the valley below, between the two mountain ranges and she saw this scene from her back deck all the time. It seemed so much closer and so much MORE. It took her breath away.

They fed the horses, refilled the water trough. When they got in the cabin, they fed Max and started to heat the water for showers, sitting at the table and talking about scenarios they could be facing. They both seemed to have thought along the same lines. They talked out everything they could think of so they would know what to expect from each other. It helped Mandy to know what Michael expected from her and what he'd be doing.

Dinner was repeat of last night. Dishes were done and Mandy got into the shower. As Mandy was soaping up, she felt a chill. She opened her eyes to see Michael in the small shower with her. He laughed as Mandy tried to get soap out of her eyes and move to give him room. His arm went around her so she wouldn't lose her balance, then he pulled the water cord on both of them, getting him wet and the soap off her. The space was small for one person and with two, there was no room to move. Trading places to soap and rinse off became a sensual movement with being so close. They grabbed towels and headed inside, only to drop them on the floor of the bedroom.

Michael stood looking at her in the dim light of the lantern. He ran his fingers through her damp hair, careful not to yank on any tangles. She ran her hands down his sides to his hips and back up.

"You have to be the most incredible woman I have ever met." His touch along with his body heat was taking her away from the reality of the situation. Her arms went around him to pull him close, skin to skin, heart to heart. "And I think it's time to see if I can make you crazy all night long."

"Then what would we have to practice at?" Mandy murmured against his lips.

"I can think of several things," came the reply and he eased her onto the bed. "I didn't say we'd get it perfect in one night."

Chapter 12

The pounding on the door woke Mandy with a start. Max was in the bedroom, facing the door, rumbling his deep rumble. Michael flew out of bed, grabbing his jeans and his gun. He was going towards the door, staying close to the wall.

"Dad, wake up! It's Dustin!" The tone was low and urgent.

Michael cracked the door then swung it open. Mandy had thrown on her sweats and a tee shirt and was standing against the wall, her gun at her side.

"What's wrong?" Michael knew that Dustin wouldn't have come unless something drastic had happened.

"Brad's been shot." Dustin looked at Mandy. "I'm sorry to come bargin' in like this. I came as soon as I knew he was stable and could get another horse saddled. They took him into Jackson."

Mandy's face had gone white. Her legs started to buckle and the room started to spin. She couldn't breathe. She started to slide down the wall, dropping her gun to the floor. Michael grabbed her and eased her into a chair, pressing her head to her knees.

"He's stable and gonna be okay."

Mandy started to sit up. She didn't need a damn panic attack now. Brad. Oh, God. Please, God, please. The room slowed down and she could breath. She nodded to Michael. He eased back.

"What happened?" Her voice was strained but she had to know the details.

"We were outside. We'd just come in from moving cattle this morning. Brad was at the gate and was closing it behind the last cows going into the south pasture when the shot rang out and he was down."

"Where'd it come from?" Michael was trying hard to stay focused. This was the second time people had been attacked at the ranch.

"I want to say from the trees but I'm not sure. Marty checked the area. He has no idea how they got past his guys and is not happy. The deputies were coming in as I was leaving. They wanted me to stick around but I figured you were a higher priority. Kirsten was home today. She jumped in before Brad hit the ground and started ordering everyone."

Michael looked at his youngest son. He was a lot like Michael, blood or not. He didn't get upset easily and tended to play down situations. He saw no sense in exacerbating anything, no matter how dire. He just dealt with whatever it was.

"I don't imagine Marty's happy. Neither am I. What about Brad?"

"Kristen got pressure on his leg, we loaded him into the truck and took him in. It was a through and through shot. There's a lot of stitches but he's going to be okay. No main artery was hit. As soon as I knew he'd be okay, I went home and saddled a fresh horse and headed up."

Mandy had been holding onto Michael's jeans. She released them and stood. Brad was stable. That's all that mattered.

"Was anyone else hurt?" The fear was in her voice. She'd been scared of this happening. Now it had.

"No. We all hit the ground. There were no other shots. Marie and Alex are at the hospital with him. Kirsten's still there. Kenny and Jo are back at the ranch with Marty. They're seein' if they can find anything. Kenny doesn't handle waiting well."

Michael nodded. Kenny did have a few of Allison's traits. As solid and steady as he was, he hated sitting and waiting. He'd rather be doing something, anything, even if was doing something that had already been done.

"We can't do anything tonight. We'll leave a dawn." Michael was already planning the ride down. They weren't going down the same way they came up. He looked at Dustin. "Did you put your horse in the corral?"

"No. I need to take care of him. Hay still in the shed?"

"Yea. Throw some to Milo and Phoenix. They should leave your horse alone as long as they have something to eat." He paused as Dustin headed to the door. "Have you eaten?"

"No".

"We'll have something for you when you come back in."

"Dustin?" Mandy stepped up to him and put her hand on his arm. He stopped and looked at her with a question in his eyes.

"Thank you for coming up here."

He patted her hand.

"No problem. I know if it's been one of us, Brad or Marie would have come to find Dad. Just so you know. Marie wanted to come. Alex gave me that look and asked her to stay. I think Alex is trying to keep her safe. She's scared Marie may also be a target." She dropped her hand as Dustin went out the door. Thank God for Alex. She was thinking even under stress. Bless her heart.

"They didn't waste any time." Michael's statement hit home. Mandy couldn't hide. If she did, they went after the people she loved. Why didn't this bastard leave her alone? What was driving him? What was this really all about? This just didn't make sense, no matter how you looked at it. There was more to it than drug smuggling.

"Yea. It's pretty extreme for smuggling. It feels more personal. We're missing something and don't have a clue as to what the hell it is."

Michael nodded. He knew the more attention that was drawn, the more dangerous this would get. He was trying to stay one step ahead of these bastards and they kept knocking him back three. They knew exactly what they were doing. The question was, who did they want? Did they want Mandy to draw Jim out or did they know Jim was here and were trying to draw him out?

Dustin came back in, ate dinner and then sat back, drinking a beer.

"I think I was followed up the mountain."

Michael and Mandy both looked at him.

"As I was heading up, I heard a plane. I was in the trees. I know they couldn't see me. I heard it for about a half hour, then it was gone. It was getting dark so I know they didn't want to fly in the mountains at night. At first, I thought it was hunters, scouting elk or deer. But it didn't feel right. Felt like Iraq."

"I'd bet they were looking for you."

"Yea. That's what I thought. Everyone was accounted for except me and it wouldn't take much to know I wasn't at the ranch. We may have company heading down."

"Heads up all the way down. I think we'll go down the back way. I was going to show Mandy that way tomorrow anyway. We'll end up at David's."

Dustin cleaned his dishes and laid his sleeping bag out on the floor, near the wood stove. Max went into the bedroom and laid on Mandy's side of the floor.

"Dad, have you got an extra pillow?"

"Sure." Michael grabbed one from the shelf in the bedroom and tossed it at him. "Thanks, son. I appreciate what you did today."

"No problem, Dad. Family's family." He snuggled down and was asleep instantly.

There was no door to the bedroom. The lantern gave off just enough light so no one tripped over anything in the dark. Mandy crawled under the covers and turned to face Michael.

"What are you thinking?" she whispered as she cuddled next to him.

"I'm wondering who the cartel is after, you or Jim. Did Brad get shot to draw out you or him? Do they know he's here? Do they know he's agreed to testify? If they get Jim, will they leave you alone or do they want you both and why?" He had pulled her close to him, her head in the crook of his shoulder, his hand running through her hair. The softness of it helped him relax and think.

"There's so many questions and no answers."

"Yet." They were quiet for several moments, settling in, waiting for sleep to come. "You okay?"

"Yea. Kinda. My heart stopped when Dustin first said Brad got shot but when he told us the rest, well, I'm as okay as I can be. I know he's young and strong but he's still my son. Just the thought of him being shot. Shit! Michael, my son was shot by the maniac who's trying to kill me." She was quiet for a moment. "Remember when you told me that I really needed to think long and hard about shooting a person and I had to try and think through every step of that process?" Michael nodded. "Right now, I'd have no problem pulling the trigger."

Mandy lay quiet, her head resting on Michael's chest, listening to the steady beat of his heart. It was a soothing sound. Steady, strong. It dissipated the fear that clutched her heart. She tried to think her way through it. She was certain they needed to leave the mountain. It felt right that Dustin had been followed. There was no reason for a plane to be up here now. No ranches were for sale in the area, all the cattle had already been brought down to winter pastures and hunting season didn't open for another month. Someone could be up here scouting hunting areas but that didn't feel right. Too soon after got Brad got shot and Dustin didn't feel right about it either. Right now, everyone was safe. What was the right move to make? Regardless of what was right, she needed to see Brad. She needed to see that he was alright for herself. Suddenly, the adrenaline rush crashed and she couldn't keep her eyes open any longer. She snuggled in closer to Michael. He pulled her closer and kissed the top of her head.

Chapter 13

They were tacked up by daylight. As soon as the sun came over the mountain and they had enough light to see, they headed down. Phoenix had been pacing again, grabbing mouthfuls of hay and kept looking towards the trail they came in on. He calmed a bit when they headed out the back way, through the valley. By the time they were through the valley and coming into the tree-line at the opposite end, he's settled into his trail walk. Mandy listened to him this time.

Once off the mountain, they would be coming in behind Michael's house and right through his brother David's pasture. David would know of anything new information since yesterday. He and his wife Carmen always knew of what happened anywhere within a hundred miles. His wife was Native American and what David didn't know, she always heard through the rez grapevine. Even though they were far from the reservation at Lander, Carmen's family kept in touch with everything on a daily basis. Michael was expecting their sons and their daughter to be home or on their way by now.

They had ridden for several hours. The sun was up and in the distance they heard the sound of a plane. Michael kept them in the trees. He very much doubted they would have people on the ground. They were city people. He doubted they could handle the terrain or horses it would take to get to the cabin. But the plane could give information. Not too much farther and they saw the plane. It was flying low. He knew how pilots maneuvered when they were searching. They stopped and let the plane pass. Michael knew they would be circling and coming back. He only hoped they'd be at David's by the time they did. When they left the trees, they would be crossing David's pasture and that would put them out in the open until they got to David's barn.

Several hours later, they came to the tree-line. It was higher on this side than on Michael's side. They dismounted and decided to rest. Mandy's legs were numb and it took a few minutes to get circulation back for everyone. They were going to have to cross 20 acres of pasture before getting to David's. Luckily, the cattle had been brought down to the winter pasture. They could possibly blend in as just moving cattle.

Smoke came out of the chimney of David's house. His house was situated much like Michael's, with a grove of trees on the west side. The house faced the road with the trees in the back. His barn was set back and to the north of the house with crossed fenced pastures in the back. Both horses and cattle dotted the postures at this distance.

They remounted and headed out of the trees. Phoenix had been calm all the way down. Now, Mandy could feel him tense the closer they got to the house. Mandy eased up closer to Michael. Dustin pulled up along her.

"Something's not right.

Michael looked at her. He'd felt it the minute they came out of the trees. Dustin was looking all around. He rode relaxed but his intensity was increasing.

"I know." Michael knew his brother. There should be activity outside this time of day. The place was too quiet. Michael eased Milo over to the right and headed to the barn. The cattle moved for them. They knew better than to argue with a horse. The horses in the other pasture had come up to the fence line and walked with them part of the way then moved back to grazing. Max had moved out in front, keeping his steady trot towards the barn. Suddenly, he shot forward, running low. He stopped and dropped to his belly at the corner of the barn, waiting. They rode up to the corner and dismounted. The large doors were in the front of the barn with an over- sized walk through door in the back. Michael had his gun in his hand as he quietly opened the door and listened. Max silently went past him, staying low and in the shadows. The barn was empty but you could feel a presence had been there.

"I swear he's part wolf," Michael muttered as he put his gun back in his shoulder holster. He went back and grabbed Milo's reins and walked back through the door. Mandy followed with her hand on Max's head, rubbing his ears. In the barn, it was silent except for the sounds of removing tack. Dustin had rubbed down his horse first and made sure all three horses had hay and water. They had worked hard today and deserved the rest. Suddenly, the big door slid open and David walked in, a rifle in his arm. Max was instantly in front of the stall Mandy and Phoenix were in, on alert. Michael and Dustin had spun around at the first sound from the door. Everyone relaxed when they realized who was there.

David was another Michael, a little older, a little grayer. Same built, same steel blue eyes, same olive complexion. He was an inch or two taller and maybe 20 pounds heavier. He shut the door and turned to look at his brother. He smiled and held out his hand. The handshake turned into a hug.

"Man, you know how to scare a person, don't ya?" He stood back and looked at Michael, hands back in the pockets of his jacket, his rifle balanced on his forearm. He walked over and gave Dustin a hug and turned to Mandy, who had walked up.

"And you must be Mandy. I think you must be made out of cast iron."

Mandy smiled up at this big man. "Not hardly. I just run on adrenaline and coffee."

"And there are positives to that," he smiled. "Come on, you guys. We got fresh coffee and a meal waiting for you. We need to talk while you eat."

Walking into the house from the back door, put them into the mud room. Jackets and boots came off and were hung up on hooks with the boots against the wall. It was an assault on the senses. The smell of chocolate and apples and cinnamon made them all realize how hungry they were. Clam chowder was in a big pot in the middle of the table with homemade biscuits, chocolate chip cookies and apple pie. A large pitcher of milk and a carafe of coffee was in everyone's easy reach.

David's wife Carmen was just putting the finishing filling coffee mugs. Dustin went over and hugged his aunt. She barely reached his shoulder. Her long hair was braided down her back. Her brown face and black eyes were smiling as she looked at her nephew.

"Hi, honey! Are you hungry, by any chance?"

"Auntie, you have no idea! We're more than starved! We've been riding since daylight."

"Come. Sit and eat. Then we can talk when your brains and your tummies have something to work with." She grabbed Mandy's arm, still smiling, and led her to the table. No one needed an invitation to sit. They were too hungry and too tired. The thick clam chowder and hot coffee brought all their spirits up. The conversation picked up when everyone had eaten for a few minutes.

"We had some visitors around here," David started. "They've pretty much stayed out of sight but the dogs have been on alert and the horses have been nervous. I think someone's been in the barn but I haven't been able to find any tracks. Just a feeling when you walk in. Today's the first day it's been a bit calm. I'm beginning to think you being here has something to do with that." He looked at Michael as if he could see the answers on his face.

"You're probably right," Michael said quietly. Exhaustion radiated off of him. "We were followed off the mountain. I don't think it was on foot or horseback but when they realize how we left the cabin, the only logical way down leads here."

"Same ones who shot Brad?"

"Most likely. We need to get to the hospital. Mandy needs to see Brad for herself. We just can't figure out what this is all about. Are they using Mandy to get to Jim? Do they know Jim's here and figure they can hit his family to bring him in?" He looked at Mandy and gave a tired grin. "Even ex-family members."

"So where do these guys come in who're following you?"

"That was my fault," Dustin said. "I was followed when I headed up the mountain to let Dad and Mandy know about Brad. It was a plane that was flying low so I was able to lose them in the trees but I heard that plane for awhile. We figured they'd be heading up at daylight so we headed out the back way."

"Through the back of the canyon." David made it a thoughtful statement. He knew that canyon as well as Michael. "Take my truck. I'll take care of the horses. Go find out about Brad."

Carmen reached over and placed her hand on Mandy's.

"I know you've been through hell," she said quietly. "But this will end and you will have your family back. Maybe more than what you bargained for." The was a mischievous glint in her eye.

Mandy smiled at her. "How could you possibly know that?"

"Oh, you know us natives. We believe a lot in sign. This morning I saw a red-tailed hawk flying above the pasture. I knew you were coming and I know all will be well."

Mandy squeezed her hand. "Thank you."

Max had been lying near the door. David and Carmen's dogs weren't sure about him so they just stayed away. He was ready to go as soon as he saw Mandy stand up. She motioned for him to come and hugged him when he got to her side. They had been through a lot in a short period of time. He had taught her a lot and so had Michael.

"Will you be alright?" Mandy said, looking at Carmen and David.

"We'll be fine. We've dealt with jerks before. No problem. You're the ones who need to be careful." David stood with his arm around his wife. They looked relaxed but Mandy knew they were far from it. She would hate to be someone to come up against them. It would not end pretty for the other guy.

They headed outside. It was just beginning to get dark. David's truck was a newer Chevy Silverado 3500. The diesel engine rumbled as they headed to the road. The cattle looked like little brown and black dots in the pastures.

Mandy was in the backseat with Max. He had stretched out with his head on her lap and had promptly fallen asleep. Mandy didn't know how Michael did it. She knew he was as tired as she was but he kept going. Like the Energizer Bunny. That thought made her smile in the dark. The last few days had taken their toll on her. She slouched down in the seat and leaned her head back, playing with Max's soft ears. Her eyes burned. Maybe if she closed them just for a minute, they'd stop hurting.

Chapter 14

Mandy woke as the truck slowed. She was confused as to where they were for a minute then realized they were at the hospital and had been stopped by the deputy in the parking lot. All cars were being stopped and searched. There were police cars everywhere. You could feel the tension in the air. As Michael pulled up to the check point, the deputy recognized him.

"Hey, Michael. Been expecting you." The deputy looked as if he's been around a few blocks, though he wasn't that old. Maybe 30, Mandy thought. Possible military.

"Yea. We've had a bit of a time getting here. Know what room Brad's in?"

"No. They've been moving him, as a precaution. They'll probably know at the nurse's station. That's all I know."

"Thanks. Be careful, Greg. These guys aren't playin'."

"I've heard. Watch your six."

Michael parked as close to the door as he could. There was more light there and the deputies would keep an eye on the truck. The entrance was brightly lit with lower lights once you got inside. Michael would feel a lot better once they were inside. He walked in solid strides with Mandy right beside him and Dustin bringing up the rear, looking everywhere. She was more determined than Michael to get in the hospital.

Mandy walked up to the nurse on duty. She looked up from the chart she was noting.

"May I help you?"

"Yes. Could you please let me know what room Brad Thompson is in?"

The nurse suddenly looked nervous. She stood.

"Just a moment. I'll be right back." She walked down the hallway and through the swinging doors. A moment later she came back with Hank. Mandy felt a huge sense of relief when she saw him.

"I knew you'd been here soon," Hank said, walking up. "How are you holding up?" He looked at all three of them. Dustin was fine, gave Hank a thumbs up. Michael and Mandy just nodded. Hank motioned towards the elevators. As they entered, he made sure no one else was wanting to get on and rapidly hit the "Close" button. Then he punched the floor. Mandy made note of it. At least she knew what floor he was on for the moment.

"I know no matter what I say, you'll need to see for yourself," Hank said. "I don't blame you. I would, too. But seriously, Mandy, he's doin' good." He nodded to the guard and stepped aside at the door to room 404, right across from the nurse's station. Mandy took a deep breath and walked inside.

Brad was hooked up to monitors and an IV bag. The monitors were beeping in a steady rhythm. Mandy knew he'd be monitored for a certain period of time after surgery so that didn't concern her. Marie looked up as the door opened. She got up and went to her mom, putting her arms around her. Mandy hung on to her, looking at Brad over Marie's shoulder. He was asleep, breathing steady. She watched the rise and fall of his chest.

"He's fine, Mom. Just still out from the anesthesia," Marie spoke quietly. She leaned back and kissed her mom's cheek and then hugged Michael and Dustin, whispering "Thank you" in Dustin's ear. He hugged her back and nodded.

Alex was asleep in a recliner on the other side of the bed. She was curled up on her side, facing Brad. The nurses had brought in a blanket and covered her. As Mandy was watching, she stirred and woke up, smiling a bit when she saw everyone. Rising and smoothing her hair as she walked over to her dad, hugging him and Mandy at the same time. Going up to her brother, she said, "Glad you made it up and back. Scared me when I heard the plane."

"No worries." Dustin hugged her.

"He was in surgery for about two hours," Marie began. "He's got some muscle damage and the doctor says he may have to have more surgery but it's a wait and see kinda thing. Depends on scar tissue and how well he heals. He has about 125 stitches in his leg that will dissolve. The incision is about eight inches long and has staples on the outside. He's pretty bruised but the doctor says he's in such good shape that he should be fine. Might hurt a bit more because his leg muscle is so developed but he seemed pretty optimistic. Brad should be waking up soon."

Mandy stood with her hands in her pockets. Her face was drained of all color as she stared at her son. Marie stood next to her, holding her hand in her pocket.

Brad stirred. He moaned a bit and opened his eyes.

"Hey, Mom," he slurred. "How are ya? What cha doin' here?"

"Just hangin' out with you. How ya feelin'?"

"Great, now. After the drugs wear off, it might be different."

"Yea, it might. Go back to sleep, honey."

"Okay." Brad closed his eyes and was immediately asleep.

Mandy straightened. It was such a relief to see him and to know for herself he would be okay. She walked out the door and went over to where Michael and Hank were talking with one of the deputies.

"Does Jim know?"

"Yea. He's pretty upset. He thinks if he contacts the cartel, he can make all of this stop."

"Bullshit," Mandy said. Her voice had a steel quality to it. "They'll keep after us to keep him in line, just like they've always done. They'll keep him alive for whatever sick reason this bastard feels he's justified in doing so. Can I see him?"

Hank looked at her then at Michael.

"Hank." Mandy said his name quietly. "This has nothing to do with Michael. I'm trying to avoid anyone else getting shot. I'm the best chance we have. Let me talk to him."

Hank looked at her and nodded. "Meet me out front."

"Mom, what are you gonna do?" Marie was standing next to Michael. Mandy hadn't even heard her come up.

"I'm going to talk to Jim. This idea about contacting the cartel is stupid. It will mean everything has been for nothing."

"What if he won't listen to you?"

She looked at Marie and grinned. "I'll have Max guard him."

Michael chuckled. "That'll do it."

Before anymore could be said, Kirsten came up. Dustin was standing next to the door and grinned when he saw his wife. She hugged him hard and they murmured for a few moments. She then hugged Michael and turned to Mandy with an out stretched hand.

"Hi. I'm Kirsten. I'm so glad to meet you. I've heard so much about you."

Mandy took her hand and hugged her. Kirsten was infectious. She had a gentle smile and a loving presence about her. There was a twinkle in her eye that Mandy suspected meant she had a wicked sense of humor. Her whole being radiated calm. Mandy was glad she'd been at the ranch. She was sure everyone benefited from her being there.

"I can't thank you enough for what you've done for my family." Mandy held onto Kirsten's hand.

"No problem. You're all family to me. You just never knew it!" Her smile lit up the room. Mandy glanced at Dustin. He adored her.

Dr. Kendricks came up. He was a tall man, almost as tall as Michael but lanky. Mandy imagined he played basketball in school. Somehow, he never quite grew into his arms and legs.

"Having a party without me?" he asked with a smile on his face. Mandy smiled. Thank God it was a doctor with a sense of humor.

Introductions were made and then the doctor turned serious.

"Let's go into the waiting room. I checked before I came down and no one is in there. I think it would be better than the hallway."

The waiting room was just across from the nurse's station. As they walked into the room, Mandy glanced back and was relieved to see the deputy standing by Brad's door. He was talking into his com line attached to his collar. He gave Mandy a nod and said "sheriff."

"Brad has a guardian angel looking out for him or someone's not a very good shot," Dr. Kendricks began. "The bullet missed the artery in his leg by a heartbeat, literally. There's no reason it didn't. It also didn't shatter the bone. It's like it took a life of it's own and veered away. I'm just thankful it moved, for whatever reason. There is some damage to the muscles and nerves in his thigh. We won't know to what extent until he starts moving it. He does have feeling so that's a good sign. Plus, he's in excellent physical shape. We'll just have to wait and see how his body heals. Most of the stitches are inside and will dissolve on their own in about a week to 10 days. He's has to come back in for the staples to be removed and I want to see how he's healing. I'll put him in a leg brace that will go from the top of his thigh to below his knee. Keeping the leg immobile for about a week will ensure everything on the inside stays stitched together. Then we'll get him in for physical therapy. He's going to be down for the next few days. As he feels better, he'll start moving more. We'll get him used to the crutches and make sure he knows he can't go hiking or jump on his horse for a while. I really don't foresee any issues at this point."

Mandy was thoughtful for a moment.

"When can he be released?"

"I'm thinking day after tomorrow or the next day. I just want to be sure he comes out of the anesthesia okay and can tolerate the pain meds. Because it's late now, I would rather be safe than sorry and not have him have to come back in. I've got him on iv antibiotics and will be sending some home with him." He smiled. "Before he went under, he said he'd be good with extra strength Tylenol. The first couple of days might need more than that."

Mandy gave a half grin. "He's got a high pain tolerance. Always has. I think this might be a bit out of his league this time."

Dr. Kendricks left and they discussed Brad's care with Kirsten. Marie and Alex were well aware of what he was going to need and with both of them with him, it made it a lot easier. Kirsten would help when she was off shift. Mandy felt another huge relief. These people were complete professionals when it came to patient care. He would be fine.

Dustin was going to stay at the hospital until Kirsten got off. He'd already called Kenny to come and pick them up. Tomorrow, they'd get the horses from David's and take them to Michael's. He really didn't want to leave Kirsten alone. He knew she could take care of herself. Dynamite came in small packages. He would just feel better knowing for himself that she was safe. Until this was over with, they all were presumed targets.

Michael grabbed Mandy's hand as they left the waiting room. They took the stairs down the four flights of stairs, Michael not letting go. It seemed so natural for them. Michael couldn't remember ever being this comfortable with Allison. This was such a completely new and so much "more" feeling.

As they walked through the glass doors, they saw Hank's truck parked behind David's. He was on the phone and motioned frantically to them. They started running. Mandy ran to David's truck, called Max and ran to Hank's, opening the back door and jumping in behind Max. She wasn't all the way in before Hank took off.

"There was a report of shots fired at the safe house." Hank maneuvered out of the parking lot, lights flashing. As soon as they cleared the parking lot, he hit the siren. Mandy didn't know how far they had to go but she had a bad feeling in the pit of her stomach. As if sensing her apprehension, Max leaned closer to her and put his nose on her cheek, offering comfort the only way he knew how. Mandy tightened her hold around him.

It took less than ten minutes to make the drive. The house was out of town on a ranch road, setting back about a mile between two hills. Hank had driven like a race car driver to get there and only slowed to take the turn onto the dirt road. He sped up to just before the bend about 50 feet from the house. Lights and siren had been turned off halfway there. There was no traffic this time of night and he didn't know if anyone was still around.

He parked in the turn- around in front of the house, jumping out as soon as he hit PARK. Mandy and Michael were right behind him.

All guns were drawn and everyone moved slowly towards the house, Hank taking the front, Mandy and Michael the back. Max went ahead of them. He wasn't barking or growling. As they came around the corner, Max came out of the house. He stood looking at them, then ran back inside. They ran after him, slowing when coming to the back door. Mandy figured no one was there. Max wouldn't have gone inside. They entered a kitchen. Max was looking into a living room where Hank was speaking urgently on the phone. He ended the call.

"My guys are down. Jim and his guys are gone."

Michael rushed in. Both men were in the living room, one unconscious in the middle of the floor with blood pooled under his head. Mandy could see he was still breathing, though it was labored. Hank grabbed a towel and gently turned him so he could see where the blood was coming from and applied pressure. He prayed the ambulance would hurry.

The other deputy was sitting on the floor, his back against the base of the couch. He was holding his side, blood gushing around his hand. Mandy grabbed another towel and applied pressure to his side.

"They blew in here before we knew they were even here. There was no sound at all. No warning, just the door blowin' open and them comin' in firing." He coughed. Mandy murmured to be quiet and concentrate on breathing. "I can't. I know I'm gonna pass out and you need info. There was four of 'em, Hispanic, all about 5'10" to 6", 170 to 190. One has a scar that runs from about the middle of his arm to the middle knuckle on the left hand. One has long hair, kinda messy." His voice was starting to fade.

"That's more information than we had coming in," Mandy said softly. The bleeding had slowed. The deputy leaned back. Mandy grabbed one of the pillows off the couch and put it behind his head to give him some support. His breathing came easier. "Don't talk anymore. You're going to need all your strength for the healing ahead." He smiled slowly and slipped in unconsciousness. Mandy looked up. The sirens were close. She hadn't heard them before now. Then, the EMTs were through the front door and taking over.

Michael and Max had disappeared. As soon as Michael saw Mandy and Hank taking care of the two deputies, he left out the back. Max was trying to catch a scent, circling off the back porch. Suddenly, he looked at Michael and took off to the grove of trees that was about 50 yards from the barn. Michael ran after him, trying not to fall in the dark. The lights from the house gave just enough light to barely see. The shadows could hide anyone.

The brush was thick in the grove. Michael had a small Mag-light and could see tire prints. It appeared a larger vehicle had parked there, probably an SUV or pickup. It made sense. With all this vegetation, noise wouldn't be heard in the house. They were caught completely by surprise. The question was, how? He knew no one knew of this safe house. He stood and looked around as far as the light could show him. The vehicle had come across the pasture on the opposite side of the trees. That's where the tire marks led. That would account for no sound. Someone had done their homework.

Michael headed back to the barn. Max was at the door, waiting for him. As he opened the door, Max crouched, looking straight ahead into the dark, rumbling in his chest. Someone was in there.

Michael slowly eased through the door. Max had crawled on his belly inside. Once inside, he stood and started sniffing. The barn had that musty barn smell but there was a faint trace of something else. It took Michael a moment to place it. Cologne. It was men's cologne. That's what Max had been reacting to. Michael stayed in the shadows. There were several bales of hay, a tractor and six stalls that had the gates shut but not latched.

Michael made his way around the whole barn, checked inside all the stalls. No one was there. There were footprints all over the barn but it only appeared to be two sets. At the back of the barn, the door had been opened twice from the dirt marks on the ground. The first time had been wider than the second. Coming in and going out. Max came over and nudged his hand. Michael followed him as he moved to the front of the barn. There, opposite from where Michael had come in, Max was sniffing. Michael looked around, careful to keep Max from the new set prints. It was clear this was where someone had watched the house.

Mandy opened the door. Michael held up his hand. She stopped with a questioning look on her face.

"There's footprints in the dirt."

"How many were in here?"

"From what I can see, I think two. Someone watched the house and someone watched the back."

"The EMTs just picked up the guys."

"What'd they say?"

"Both are in pretty bad shape. They had them stable enough to transport but I don't know anything else." She paused. "They took Jim."

"I know." He walked over to her. "You okay?"

Mandy looked at him and gave him a small tired smile.

"Of course."

Michael pulled her against him, felt her arms encircle his waist. Her hair smelled like wild flowers. How could anyone smell like wild flowers after they day they'd had?

They walked back to the house. Hank was just finishing a call.

"The FBI's on their way."

Michael nodded. Now it was official for Allison and Alan to be involved.

"I found where they watched the house from the barn and the back pasture. I know how they got here. They probably left the same way. I didn't see where any vehicle was close to the house."

Hank looked at him. "How old're the tracks?"

"No more than an hour or two."

"Let's go."

"What about the FBI?" Mandy asked as they jogged to the truck.

"We'll call 'em when we find Jim."

Michael told Hank where he found the tracks and they followed them to a dirt road that was a back way to town. It was easy to see where they went. Hank literally flew down the road until he came to the highway. He could see where they had swung wide to the right, towards Jackson. He did the same, taking the turn on two wheels. Mandy strained against her seat belt as she hung onto Max.

"Sorry," Hank yelled as he stepped on the gas as soon as all four tires were back on the road. He checked the rearview mirror. Mandy looked at him and nodded. He drove on, gaining speed. They came to the outskirts of town, the tougher side, with factories, warehouses and seedy motels. Hank slowed and came to a stop.

"We need to look for a black Charger with a rental sticker on it," Mandy said. She hoped they'd find another vehicle along with it.

Hank slowly drove down the street. Jackson Hole wasn't that big. There weren't that many cheap motels or warehouses but they checked them all on one side and then turned around to check the other. It was close to midnight. The town was quiet except for a few of the bars but they were at the other end of town. The ones on this end had closed a long time ago. As they were heading out of town, Michael noticed a building set back from the road. There were two dump trucks parked on the side. He saw a car parked in front of one of them. He pointed to the side and Hank drove in, slowly. He parked to the offside of the truck farthest from the building, hoping it could shield them if the need arose. They got out of the truck, Hank turning off the overhead light. Doors were only closed, not shut. Max jumped out and went around the back of Hank's truck, immediately on alert.

Everyone had pulled their guns when they exited the truck. The black Charger was in front of the first dump truck and Max was circling. When he got to the right rear passenger door, he looked at Mandy and whined. She placed her hand on his head.

"That's the side Jim got out on," she said softly. "Search, Max." He ran to the front of the car and then to the front of the building and dropped to the ground, hackles up. He didn't make a sound, just looked at Mandy then back at the door.

"There's someone on the other side," she whispered. Both Michael and Hank nodded. Hand signals kept Hank there at the front with Michael and Mandy going around the back. Hank would give hem 30 seconds to get in position and then he was going in.

They ran as quietly as possible. No one was outside the back door but you could hear voices. Suddenly the back door opened. Michael pushed Mandy behind him at the side of the building as he dropped behind a stack of tires. The guard came out holding a 357 in his hand. He looked all around and then started walking to the other end of the building. Michael jumped up and silently ran up behind the guard, throwing his arm around his neck. The gun fell to the ground as the guard reached for Michael's arm. In a minute, he was unconscious and dead weight. Michael drug him back to the other side of the tires, pulled zip ties from his back pocket and tied up the guard. He wrapped a gag around his mouth, tied to the back of his head just as the guy was coming to. He was confused for a moment then saw Mandy and hatred gleamed from his eyes. He was muttering in Spanish but nothing was clear. Mandy could make out only one word. Puta. Her blood boiled. She leaned down, close to his ear.

"Whore, huh? Let me tell you something. I'm the nastiest whore you will ever meet. God save your ass from me, you fucking bastard." She could tell by the look on his face that he understood everything she said. Max was standing next to her.

"Guard." Max immediately sat down. As the man tried to wiggle his hands and legs to test the ties, Max growled and showed his teeth.

"I wouldn't move if I were you, asshole. He might rip our face off."

Michael looked over at her and chuckled.

"What's so funny?"

"You. You're such a bad-ass."

"Thank you very much. Glad you think so."

They moved slowly to the door. Michael knew Hank was already inside. This was going to be a bit tricky. They didn't know the layout of the warehouse. When he opened that door, they wouldn't know what was on the other side. Michael opened it slowly. It opened into a hallway that was about 20 feet long. There were voices that appeared to be coming from the right of the hallway. Someone was yelling and someone was being hit. Hard.

They moved down the hallway. There were two offices in the left side. Michael listened at each door. Quiet. He opened the first door. Empty. No closet to check. Same with the second one. They crept down the rest of the hallway, guns drawn, careful not to make any sound. As they got closer to the front of the hallway, Michael looked up. There appeared to be a storage area above the same type of hallway on the other side of the warehouse. Above, there was a guard rail around the edge. There were some boxes up there. Michael was wondering if anyone was up there when Hank showed himself in a small opening between the storage boxes. He motioned there were four men. Jim was tied up. He motioned that on the count of three, they'd go in. Michael nodded. Hank's fingers showed one, two, three.

"Police!" Hank yelled. The men swung around, guns drawn, the one yelling in Spanish. They immediately started firing towards the door that Hank had entered. Michael launched himself around the corner, staying low. He saw the four men, Jim tied to a chair, beaten and bloody. He quickly fired, dropping two of them. Hank fired from his vantage point and dropped the other two. Slowly Michael stood. Mandy came running, stopped short of the open doorway. She saw Michael standing, looking up to where Hand was standing.

'I'm good," he yelled down. Michael nodded. He turned to look at Mandy.

"It's okay. Come on."

Mandy walked out. She still had her gun in her hand, though it was lowered. Hank was running across the warehouse. He made sure all the guns were kicked away from the downed men. He nodded to Mandy. She put the safety on her gun, shoved it into her pocket and ran to Jim. His face was beaten, his right eye swollen shut. His left eye was puffy and swelling, already bruising. His jaw looked crooked. There was blood all over his shirt and a bullet hole in his left shoulder.

"Jim, can you hear me?" She gently touched his face. He tried to bring his head up to look at her. It took too much effort.

"Check my guys," he said between clenched teeth. "They're in a room."

Mandy looked at Michael. He nodded and walked to the other side of the warehouse. Hank was on the phone, calling for back up and an ambulance. He also requested the county coroner. He wanted everyone there immediately. Before he hung up, the sirens could be heard and coming closer.

Michael came back with Rafe and Julio. Both had facial bruising and walked slow. Mandy looked at them.

"You guys look pretty rough. You okay?"

Both of them looked at her and nodded. They tried for small grins but it hurt too much.

"We could be worse," Rafe said in accented English. "We'll live, thanks to you. We cannot thank you enough. To say it, seems very...... weak? Mandy, please believe me that we had nothing to do with what happened to you." He coughed, spitting blood. "And all of us, our families included, are so sorry for all you have been through." His swollen black eyes pleaded with her.

Mandy reached for his arm, the one that wasn't holding his side.

"I'm beginning to," she smiled. "Just don't know why all this is continuing. These guys are seriously deranged. I don't know where all this is coming from."

"Neither do we," said Julio. Those were the first words that Mandy had heard him speak since she had met him. He was younger than Rafe and Jim, maybe early to middle thirties. He was taller than Roberto's stocky 5'9". Maybe 6". He was lighter complexed, dark brown hair instead of black and chocolate brown eyes. High cheek bones and an angular face, that was beginning to bruise around his jaw line. It was already swollen.

"The ambulance should be here any moment. Just hold on a few more minutes." Mandy walked back over to Jim and knelt in front of him. She touched his arm. Jim slowly opened his eye.

"They okay?" he whispered.

"Yea, they are. A bit beat up but they look better than you."

Jim tried to laugh, then quit. It hurt too much. "I don't think that would take much."

Mandy looked up as the EMTs entered the warehouse. They came in with stretchers, two stopped at Miguel and Juan and two more came to Jim. Hank had cut the ropes that had tied him to the chair and had placed his arms in his lap. It seemed to ease the stress on his shoulders. Mandy stepped back as they came forward. They were immediately busy, checking the bullet wound, taking vitals. The bleeding from his shoulder had stopped but Mandy knew it would start up again when they started to check it. They got him stable and radioed the hospital they were ready to transport. The ER would be ready for all of them. Within minutes, only the police and FBI were left.

Hank walked over to them with a guy to looked like a fed to Mandy. Black suit, white shirt, tie. Mandy stiffened. He could be the leak or part of it. Michael looked at her. He saw the tension around her eyes, felt it in her body. He squeezed her hand. She squeezed back, never taking her eyes off the fed.

Michael spoke before Mandy could think of what to say.

"There's a guard out back. He's gagged and tied up. Max is guarding."

Hank grinned. "Bet he loved that."

Hank made the introductions to Special Agent Craig West. Mandy didn't let any emotion cross her face that she recognized his name. She didn't say a word. Just waited.

"You're a hard woman to find." Agent West smiled at Mandy. She didn't smile back. Just looked at him. He wasn't bad looking. About 6'1", brown hair, brown eyes. He carried himself well. Must work out,

Mandy thought. Probably at a gym before work. Suddenly, she wanted to see him put in the kind of day both she and Michael did. Wondered if he could keep up. There I go again, she thought. Any thought except the here and now.

Mandy didn't trust him. All her instincts screamed "RUN…... NOW!" But she couldn't so she stood, facing him.

"That was the idea," she said.

"I've heard Sheriff Waters version of what's lead up to this. I'd like to hear yours."

"That will be no problem. Tomorrow."

"Today would be better."

"I really do understand you need information as soon as possible. You have Hank's information. Ours will be no different. We've been up since before sunrise, ridden down a mountain, seen my son who was shot, found Jim and dealt with the jerks who took him. Sorry. You have to wait. I can't think."

He turned to Michael.

"You're gonna have to wait. We're done. We can't give you anymore information. We need food, a shower and sleep. You can see us tomorrow."

"You need to let me put you and your family in protective custody."

Michael kept hold of Mandy's hand as he pulled her closer to him and started to walk out.

"Not in this lifetime. Hank?" he called. "Okay to take your truck?"

"Yea. I'll pick it up tomorrow."

"Just not before noon."

"Done."

Agent West looked t Hank.

"Do you always let witnesses tell you what they're going to do?"

"When it's Michael Johnson, I do. He's lived here all his life, is ex – military, and he's been involved since all this began here. He's been shot at, his family put in danger and he's stayed strong. If he says noon tomorrow, that's when it'll be."

"I wasn't talking about him."

"Mandy will come in as she said she would. She's been through too much not to. She'll keep her word."

"Guess I'm getting pretty cynical. Beautiful women seem to have another agenda in my business."

"Maybe it's time you looked into another aspect of your business." With that, Hank walked over to Greg, the deputy from the hospital. He had requested Greg when he called for backup. They talked softly as they walked out of the warehouse.

"Maybe he's right," Craig thought as he walked out. Reports wouldn't be due for at least 24 hours. All the reports had to be in and he had to have copies before he could write his. He was curious to see if the guard would talk. He was the only one alive. When the gag had been removed, he had been yelling in Spanish. Craig was pretty fluent in Spanish but he didn't know half of what the guy said. He did catch "redheaded whore." Mandy would love that one. Probably why the bastard got gagged in the first place.

Chapter 15

Max slept all the way home, stretched out in the backseat of Hank's truck. He had been asleep before they left the parking lot. Mandy settled in. She tried to relax but the tension in her neck and shoulders was too painful. It would take a bit. Michael was the picture of calm. The only thing that gave him away was the constant vigil in the mirrors.

"How do you do that?" Mandy asked.

"Do what?"

"Seem so calm. You act like all we did was move some cows."

Michael leaned on the console and reached for her hand. She immediately felt the calm. It went through her body like warm water. She clasped his hand and leaned back against the headrest. It felt so good to be with him.

"Better?" he asked.

"Much. But you didn't answer."

"I don't know the exact terminology. I learned in combat that the stress of survival can kill you so I had to come up something else. It's like putting your complete emotional system in a safe place and keeping it there until it's safe to bring it out. I learned to run on brain power and logic. Sometimes there was emotional baggage to deal with but it had to be done later. Under fire, you don't have time to feel. It takes all you have to survive."

"Kinda like going to your "happy place"."

Michael chuckled. "I never thought of it like that but, yea. That's exactly right. All I did was share with you."

"Oh, you can share with me anytime," Mandy smiled.

"And I hope to," he grinned back at her.

They were taking the back roads to Mandy's. It was past midnight. The stars were twinkling in the sky. Mandy held onto Michael's hand and looked for the moon. There were a few clouds and it was hidden at the moment. She wondered what animals were watching them drive by from the groves and pastures they were passing. Suddenly, Michael released her hand.

"What?" she asked, looking in the side mirror. There, she saw headlights rapidly gaining on them.

"Guess we have company."

"Craig?"

"Maybe. I know he wants answers from us."

Michael crested a hill and lost the lights for the moment on the downside. As before, he pulled off the road, turned the truck around and shut it off. A few minutes later, a dark sedan drove past. It was too dark to make out who was inside.

"Looks like a fed car. Feel like four- wheelin' to your house?"

"Anything so we don't have to go through an interrogation tonight," Mandy said wearily. "I'd probably fall asleep trying to answer questions."

"I hear ya, babe. Let's go on a cross country adventure." Michael started the big truck, put it four – wheel drive and headed down a literal trail. They drove through pastures, down ravines, up hills and finally made it to Mandy's from her back pasture. She got out to open the back gate and saw a flashlight in the window.

"Did you see that?" Mandy asked as she got back in the truck but Michael was already on the phone to Marty.

"Marty's got it. Said to wait a few minutes. He doesn't want us to get hit in a cross fire."

Mandy sat, watching her house. Max was on the console, crouched as he was to big to stand on it. He intently stared at the house. Michael rubbed his ears. Mandy had her hand on his shoulder.

Michael started the truck. His few minutes were up. He drove to the back of the barn, lights off.

They got out of the truck, Max staying close. Guns were drawn, safeties off. It was so quiet. How the truck wasn't heard in the still of the night was surprising. Mandy knew the barn and the distance would have blocked some of the noise but not all of it. Suddenly, Max shot forward. He was growling the deep rumble of attack as he ran towards the house. The back door was open. Whoever was in there has propped open the door from the deck. Max was in the house before Mandy could call him back. As they ran after him, there was a shot and glass shattering.

Michael went through the kitchen. Mandy went through the mudroom. One of them hit the lights.

Marty was standing with his gun drawn over a man who was bleeding from his shoulder. Max was standing on Special Agent Craig West's chest, teeth bared, in his face. The agent was reaching for his gun. It was too far away but just to be sure, Mandy kicked it farther.

"What the hell are you doing in my house?"

"Call off your dog and I'll tell ya."

"No. You tell me. THEN I'll call off my dog." Mandy was beyond angry. A calm had enveloped her. Her whole emotional system was in shut down. Michael saw the look in her eye. He knew she could shoot West and not think twice about it. Now was not the time to shoot a fed.

"Easy, babe. Give me your gun. I'll take care of him." Michael reached for Mandy's gun, slowly. She looked at him and realized what she was doing. She handed her gun over.

"Come 'ere, Max," she said. Max went to Mandy and stood in front of her, daring the agent to come close

Michael stood with his gun still aimed at Agent West.

"You never answered the question." His voice was low and commanding.

"I don't have to," West smirked as he got up. "Your friend will be charged with shooting a federal agent."

Michael looked at Marty who still held his gun on the injured agent.

"Oh, I hope you try," Marty remarked. "Seems breaking and entering, not identifying yourselves as law enforcement, let alone federal agents, intimidating a witness to begin with, should carry some weight. I'm quite sure I can come up with more. You see, AGENT West, I also have friends in high places, so bring it on. I would love to see your ass suspended or fired." West had the common sense to stay quiet.

Mandy had called 911 for an ambulance for the injured agent. She knew Hank would also show up. Looks like a shower and sleep would have to wait again, she thought as she went to grab a towel for the agent. Couldn't wait too much longer. None of them were going to be on their feet. They were beyond exhaustion.

She applied pressure to the agent's shoulder. He sucked in air through his teeth.

"It will ease the pain a bit if you breathe through it," Mandy said as she kept the pressure applied. He looked at her, held her eyes and slowly breathed. The pain did ease a bit. At least he didn't feel like he was going to pass out. He nodded to her and applied the pressure himself. Marty stepped back, lowering his gun. This guy wasn't going to do anything or try to go anywhere.

Agent West looked from Mandy to Michael. Michael hadn't holstered his gun, though he had lowered it. West knew if he made a wrong move, Michael would shoot him. He knew when he followed them, he was pushing his luck. He should have waited until tomorrow, which was today now, as they had said. His partner getting shot was on him and he knew it.

"Okay if I check my partner?" he asked.

Michael nodded, bringing his gun back up.

West kneeled down next to the man. His face was pale.

"You okay?"

"I've had better nights." The agent grimaced as another wave of pain hit. The sirens sounded in the background. Thank God. Just a few more minutes and he's get that blessed shot of morphine.

West grabbed his arm. "I'm sorry it got so outa hand. I should've listened not only to you but to these people."

"Just payback for when you got shot in Chicago. Now we're even."

West just shook his head as the EMTs came through the door. He backed away as they took over. He looked up. Mandy and that damn wolf-dog were gone but Michael and Marty were still in the room. Michael still hadn't holstered his gun.

"You gonna put that gun up or are you planning on shooting me?"

"I'll put it up when I figure you can be trusted not to have it out."

"Fair enough." West looked for his gun, then saw it stuck in Marty's waist band.

"You'll get it back when you leave, if you're not under arrest." Michael refused to give an inch.

Just then, Hank came through the door. One look and he knew all he needed to know. He checked on the agent and talked to the EMTs as they wheeled him out the door. He turned to Agent West.

"Couldn't leave it alone, could you? Couldn't give these people some desperately needed rest so they could think straight?" Hank was livid. These were his people, in his county that he had sworn to protect. It was a responsibility he didn't take lightly. He'd try to tell this jackass of an FBI agent that you didn't disrespect people here, especially ex – military. He was worried, stressed and more tired that he could ever remember being.

The agent had enough sense to look embarrassed.

"Let me tell you how this is gonna work. You are leaving here, now. You will not contact anyone or go to anyone's house except with my permission. And don't give me any shit about your superiors because I don't care. I will be calling Washington to whoever you answer to and will get your ass written up if not fired. Get the hell outa here before I arrest you."

"You can't arrest a federal agent."

"Watch me."

Marty handed Michael the agent's gun. Michael held onto it as he escorted him to the door. West looked in the kitchen where he saw Mandy sitting on the floor with that wolf-dog beside her, his head in her lap, watching him leave. Mandy didn't look up, just sat there playing with Max's ear. Michael waited until he heard the agent's car head out. He walked into the kitchen. Mandy looked up at him. She was a pasty color with massive dark circles under her eyes. He gently touched her head, then went into the living room where Marty was talking to Hank.

"Marty was just telling me what happened here. When the car pulled in and the alarm didn't go off, he thought it was okay"

"Yea, until we all saw the flashlight instead of the house light. I was outside the living room window and saw their silhouettes. I shot first, figured I'd ask questions later. Just my luck it was the feds."

"I'm just glad you were here," Michael said. "I just can't figure out why the alarm didn't go off."

"All I can figure out is they disarmed it by remote control. Damn. There's so many people involved in this. How has Mandy managed to stay hidden for so long?" Marty ran his hands through his hair, a habit he picked up overseas when he got frustrated. "I thought she could be exaggerating a bit, but she's not. That woman is dead on. And if Jim's not trying to kill her, the cartel is a lot more sophisticated than anyone has given them credit for."

"I agree with all you're saying," Michael said. "But seriously, I can't think anymore. Neither can Mandy. She's on the floor in the kitchen. We need sleep. I'm going to board up the window you so exquisitely put a bullet through and go to bed. How about we talk when we wake up?"

"Tell ya what. You guys go to bed. Marty and I'll board up the window."

"Done," Michael said. He started for the kitchen.

Hank and Marty went out the back door to the barn. Marty knew the plywood was there and there were some tools in the mudroom. He and Hank could get the window covered in about ten minutes. Hopefully, Michael and Mandy will be able to get some needed rest.

Michael knelt beside Mandy.

"Hey, babe. Can you stand up?"

Mandy looked up and tried to smile.

"Maybe."

She grabbed hold of his arm and Michael pulled her up. The room spun for a moment, then cleared. They walked back to the bedroom, arms around each other. Mandy sat on the bed and began pulling her boots off. Michael sat in the chair and leaned his head back. He was so tired, he thought about sleeping right there and then remembered he'd been in the same clothes for two days. No. Not acceptable. He got up and undressed. Mandy was already in the shower. He opened the door and stepped in. She looked up at him as water ran down her face and gave him a tired grin. He reached for the bar of soap and washed her back. Mandy closed her eyes and leaned her forehead against his chest. That felt so good.

They grabbed towels and dried off in record time. Mandy tried to blow dry her hair but couldn't hold up the hair dryer 'til her hair was completely dry so she gave up. It wasn't all the way wet.

Michael had walked out to the living room. The window was boarded up. Marty left a note on the table that he was going to be close all day. Good. But in reality, Michael was too tired to care. He grabbed his gun to put in the nightstand, made sure it had a full clip with a bullet in the chamber and put the safety on. He made his way back to the bedroom and crawled in beside Mandy. She was already asleep but snuggled in when she felt Michael beside her. He covered them both, made sure Max was asleep in his bed and was asleep before his head hit the pillow.

Chapter 16

Mandy woke confused. She knew she was home, in her bed but she was wrapped in someone's arms. Then she relaxed. Michael snuggled closer to her, pulling her tight against him. She dozed off again.

The next time Mandy woke up, Michael was gone. The bedroom door was open and she smelled coffee. She looked at the clock. Whoa! Four o'clock! She knew she fell asleep somewhere around dawn so she had slept all day. She got out of bed, got dressed, washed her face and brushed her teeth. She messed with her hair a bit. It'll do. She wanted some coffee.

Walking down the hall, she heard Michael and Marty speaking in low voices. They sat at the kitchen table. Michael looked up and smiled when he saw her.

"Hey, gorgeous." He came over and kissed her.

"Hey, handsome," she smiled as she kissed him back. She turned to Marty, the smile still on her face. "How are ya?"

"Good. You sure look better than when I saw you last," Marty replied. "Glad we had no further surprises."

"I hear ya." Mandy grabbed a mug of coffee and sat down. The silence was so peaceful.

Marty nodded towards Max. "He came out when I came in about six o'clock. He came up for his ears to be scratched and then went to his bed. I sure slept better knowing he was in here."

"He's a good guy," Michael agreed. "He sure takes care of Mandy."

"It's funny," Mandy said. "I was working horses one morning and I saw him in the trees at the side of the house. The size of him had me scared for a minute but he walked out real slow, tail wagging and this doggy smile on his face. He sat down outside the round pen and just waited for me. When I was taking my tack back to the barn, he followed me. He was thin. I knew he'd been running for a while. We got to know each other in the barn. I sat on a bale of hay and he came and sat in front of me and put his paw on my leg. When I put my hand out, he gave it one little sniff and licked my hand. That was it! I fell in love! He's been here ever since. I know he's been trained well, especially for only being about three. The vet was surprised that he wasn't chipped. He is now but he wasn't then. You'd think anyone who put so much training into him wouldn't want to lose him."

"That's true," Marty agreed. "Makes you wonder where he came from."

"Yea, but I'd like to see someone come and try to take him now. Where was he when we went to dinner that night? He wasn't here when we left."

"Up 'til then, he'd come and go. He's stayed since all this crap has started." Mandy had wondered where Max would go. He never stayed gone long. The longest had been about 36 hours. He obviously was there to stay now.

"Have you heard from Hank?" Mandy asked.

"No," Michael replied. "I think he's waiting to hear from us. He's gonna be needing his truck soon."

"I wonder if he'll let Agent West come back out here."

"I doubt it. He most likely called Washington this morning. No tellin' if West is still here or on his way back. If Hank had his way, the guy is on a plane. I've never seen him so mad in all the years I've known him."

"Seeing him that mad once was enough," Mandy agreed. "Just glad it wasn't at me." She got up from the table.

"Are you guys hungry?"

"Starved."

Just then Marty's phone rang. He looked at the number, then at Michael and answered.

"Yea, Josh. What's up?" Josh was one of the three guys on patrol in the front of the property. Marty quickly stood up, motioned for Michael to grab his gun and go with him.

"Lock the door and get a gun," Michael said as he left.

Mandy grabbed her 9mil out of the kitchen drawer, checked the clip and made sure there was a round in the chamber. She shut off the lights and stood by the window. It was getting dusk. The sun was almost down. She saw a shadow by the pasture, saw it go past the horse pens towards the barn. Max was at the door, growling that deep growl down in his chest. She was tempted to let him loose but knew whoever was out there most likely also had a gun and she wouldn't risk Max getting shot. So she waited.

A shot was fired, followed by two more but from a different caliber. Then quiet. Mandy was pacing when there was a knock at the door.

"Mandy, it's me," Michael said softly. She ran to the back door and let him in.

"What were those shots?"

"There was a sniper up in the trees. I saw him just as he fired and hit the ground. The last two shots were mine."

"Did you shoot him?"

"Yea. He's not dead, yet. Marty wasn't in all that big a hurry to call an ambulance."

"What about Josh? Is everybody okay?"

"Everybody's good. There's been a car driving up and down the road for about a half hour. Josh knew something was outa line. He called Marty when the guy passed the second time and started to slow down like he was going to turn in. Josh thought it was a set up. Seems the guy had dropped off the sniper just before the crest of the hill down the road. We got to Josh without any problem but by then, the other guy was up in the tree. He thought he could take out the three of us. That didn't happen. When the car came back, we were outa sight along with the wounded sniper. The car came in about 20 feet and the guy got out, looking for his buddy. Marty came up behind him and knocked him out. The other passenger got out of the car and ran down the road. Josh went after him. He thinks there's another car out there."

"I think he's in the barn."

"What?"

"I saw a shadow by the pens going towards the barn. I think he's still there. He wouldn't take off across country when it's getting dark and he doesn't know where he is."

"Stay here."

"Don't think so. My barn." She gave him that "Don't mess with me" look and Michael knew better than to push it.

They started out the back door. Max was ready to shoot past them.

"Max. With me," Mandy softly commanded. He stayed right by her side.

They got to the barn. Mandy touched Michael's arm and pointed to the sliding door. It was open just enough for someone to go through. That didn't feel right to Mandy. It was too obvious. These were people who could sneak up on elite soldiers. Michael looked at her. He didn't like it, either. Max wasn't concerned about what was in the barn, more what was behind it. They moved past the door. The window was to the tack room. That door was shut so they couldn't see inside. They moved on, slowly, quietly, listening for any movement, any noise. Suddenly, Max took off and headed straight for the back of the barn. Just as they came around the corner, Mandy saw a man with a gun pointed at Max just as he launched himself. The man fired and Max went down. She screamed and ran to Max just as Michael fired. He hit the guy in the right shoulder. His gun flew out of his hand and he hit the ground, screaming.

Michael ran up to him and kicked his gun farther from his body. He looked down at him, not seeing clearly with the only light was coming from the security light at the front corner of the barn.

"I suggest you shut up. That woman over there just might decide to shoot you for shooting her dog." The guy quieted to heavy gasps.

Michael ran to Mandy. She was holding Max in her arms. There was a deep gash along his side to his back leg. She'd taken off her sweatshirt and tied it around him as best she could to help stop the bleeding. She looked up at Michael, tears streaming down her face.

Marty came running up. He saw the whole scene in one glance. Josh was right behind him.

"Go get the truck. Keys will either be in the ignition or under the seat." Josh turned and ran as Marty went to Michael.

"Max got shot?" There was disbelief in Marty's voice. That huge doge seemed invincible.

"Yea. He went after that son of a bitch over there. He's shot in the right shoulder. Thought we might get some info outa him. Too bad I didn't kill the bastard."

"No shit."

Josh pulled around in Hank's truck. Mandy tied a handkerchief around Max's mouth and tied it behind his head.

"Just in case," she said as Michael picked him up. Mandy ran to the truck, opened the back door and slid in. She cradled Max's head and supported his shoulder as Michael slid him into the back seat. As he shut the door, he turned to Marty.

"Take care of that jerk. I know he needs medical like the other guy but see if you can get anything out of him. We'll be back as soon as we can." Marty nodded and went to the guy on the ground. Josh was at the corner of the barn with the wounded sniper. Hank was on the way and he could make the medical call. Right now, Michael didn't care if both of them died.

Mandy was just done talking to the vet as Michael started the engine. He would meet them at the clinic. She gently petted Max's head, playing with his ear. He was panting and Mandy knew he was going into shock. He looked up at her and then closed his eyes. Please, God, don't let him die, she prayed.

They got to the vet in record time. As they pulled into the driveway 10 minutes later, the whole team was waiting for them with a gurney. They gently eased Max on it and covered him with a blanket 'til they got him inside. Mandy walked with her hand on his head, his eyes never leaving her face. Her sweatshirt was drenched with his blood but the bleeding had slowed to a slight trickle.

"That's a pretty deep shot," Dr. Harrison said. "There doesn't seem to be damage to any major organs. Ripped the hell out of his muscle, though." He spoke quietly as his team brought in the portable x-ray machine and others prepared the surgical suite. "I want some x-rays but I'm pretty sure he got two broken ribs. Those we can tape. I'll shave him, stitch him up and keep an IV on him overnight. I gave him a slight sedation to ease the stress and it looks like it taken hold. That plus the

IV should help with the shock." He squeezed her shoulder. "Don't worry. We'll get him through this. Let me get those x-rays and I'll come and get you in a few minutes."

Mandy walked out to the waiting room. Michael had been pacing and stopped when he heard Mandy come in. She came and stood next to him, laying her head on his shoulder.

"The bullet went pretty deep," she said quietly. "He's probably got some broken ribs but they didn't think there's any damage to major organs. They gave him a sedative to help with the shock and started running an IV. They're taking x-rays before taking him into surgery." Michael had put his arm around her, pulling her close. He had also grown to love the big dog in a short period of time.

Dr. Harrison came into the waiting room.

"He does have two broken ribs and a cracked third. There are bone fragments that need to be cleaned up but there was no damage to any vital organs. The bullet is still in him. It lodged in his thigh muscle. I don't understand how it got there but you can see the path in the x-ray. I'm just glad it stopped when it did. That could have really torn up his hind leg."

They talked about recovery time and how long Max would have to stay. Dr. Harrison would call her as soon as he was out of surgery. She knew he'd take some time to come out of the anesthesia so she'd come back in the morning.

The drive back to the house was quiet. Michael could feel the anger radiate off Mandy. Her son had been shot and now her dog. He knew her brain was doing about 500 MPH. His was and so he knew they were in the same frame of mind. They were about half way back to the house when Mandy finally spoke.

"I hope that son of a bitch is still at the house and hasn't passed out."

"What's your plan, babe?" Michael was trying to remain calm but he was seething as much as Mandy was. He needed to stay in control for her as she was so close to losing it completely.

"I'm going to find out what this stupid-ass shit is all about. No pain, no gain. Time these bastards hurt."

"Well, okay then."

Mandy looked at him and grinned. The tension eased a bit.

"Guess that was a bit harsh, huh?"

"No, not at all. I thought it was pretty tame, myself. You did better than what I was thinking."

"Glad we're on the same page."

"We usually are."

They pulled into the drive and parked behind two ambulances that pulled out before they were out of the truck. Stepping up onto the deck to where Hank and Marty were standing, Mandy saw the look on Marty's face and raised her eyebrows in a questioning look.

"Hank wrecked all my fun."

"How did he do that?"

"Told him he couldn't leave any more marks on those guys," Hank answered. "He thought a few more bruises were in order."

"I was thinking a few more broken bones would be appropriate," Mandy answered. "They shot my son, shot my dog and I don't know who's going to be next. Not to mention Mary's guys that have been hurt. I'd just like to beat the shit outa one of them and I really don't care which one."

Hank nodded. "Can't blame you. I'd be feeling the same if I was you. Probably worse, to tell the truth."

"Maybe it's time for me to go hunting."

"Where do you want to hunt?"

"South America seems a good place to start."

"Go on the offensive instead of always being on the defensive?"

"Something like that."

"Mandy, I can't protect you there," Hank said, looking directly at her.

"I know that." She didn't falter in her gaze back at him. "I don't expect you to. I know what my strengths and weaknesses are. Right now, the people I love are targets. As much as they are my strength, they are my weak link this bastard is going after. I just wonder how the son of a bitch will like the tables turned."

Hank looked at her. "You'd go after his family?"

"No. But he wouldn't know that."

Hank laughed. "You're sneaky, aren't you?"

"No. Just tired of this crap."

"How's Max?" Marty asked.

Mandy gave the update. It was amazing to her how much these people cared, who, until a few days ago, were strangers. Being alone, even if it's to protect, makes you forget the heart of people. Guess it's because all you have to focus on is the ugly people, Mandy thought. Man. Do I need an attitude adjustment.

Mandy found several frozen pizzas in the freezer and got them in the oven. She was beat but knew the guys would be hungry even if she wasn't.

Her phone vibrated in her pocket. Dr. Harrison. Max was out of surgery. There had been damage to his muscles, two broken ribs and two more cracked ones. Max had 97 stitches, 65 would dissolve in about 7-10 days. He'd have to come back in 10 days to have the others taken out, which was when Dr. Harrison wanted to see him. He'd done well during the surgery but he thought he should stay an extra day just to be on the safe side. And, yes, Mandy could see him tomorrow. Dr. Harrison also had the bullet for Mandy and he would be staying with him tonight until he fully out of the anesthesia.

Mandy was so grateful. Hanging up the phone, she was laughing and crying at the same time. She was so relieved that he was going to be alright. That big dog had taken her heart. She had known that. She just didn't know how much of her heart until now. He had almost died protecting her. That thought brought her back to reality. Brad could have been killed and now Max. She looked around the room and tried not to think of Michael, Marty, Hank, Josh or any of the other guys being hurt. The ones that were in the hospital now were more than enough. God. She was so tired of this.

The timer went off and pizzas were done. As some came out, others went in. The guys outside took turns coming in for something to eat and them went back out to continue patrol. They wouldn't be caught by surprise again.

Chapter 17

Michael woke before dawn. The rest of the night had been quiet and both he and Mandy had slept. His internal clock usually wouldn't let him sleep past six o'clock and now that it was fall, it was still dark at that time. Mandy had slept hard until about two am and then the nightmare began. This time, she didn't wake up but responded to his quiet, soothing voice telling her everything would be alright. She was safe now, safe with him. "I've got ya, babe," he murmured over and over, all the while holding her against him so even in the midst of the nightmare, she'd feel his solid presence. It didn't last long nor did it have the strength it did before. Mandy never woke up but settled quietly in his arms. He didn't know when it happened but he knew he wanted to spend the rest of his life with this woman. He'd never really understood when people spoke of soulmates, of searching for that person a lifetime. He did now. It was crystal clear.

Mandy woke to Michael's blue eyes staring at her.

"Hey, big man."

"Hey yourself," he softly replied, gently kissing her forehead. "Feel better?"

"Yea," Mandy said. "I do."

"Good. Want to feel even better?"

"Absolutely."

Mandy was at the vet clinic at ten o'clock. Michael had stayed at the house with Marty. She parked her blue Silverado around the back. Might as well not advertise she was here.

Walking in, there were three dogs with their people. Two were puppies on leashes, playing in front of a big guy who appeared to be a local rancher. The third sat very quietly beside a petite lady. She appeared to be Hispanic with long black hair, loosely pulled back to the nap of her next. The only jewelry she wore were small gold hoop earrings. The dog was a mix. Looked to be shepherd and border collie.

As Mandy walked up to the desk, the receptionist looked up and smiled. Her name tag said Alana.

"I bet you're wondering how the big guy is doing."

"Yes, I am," Mandy smiled back. "Did he sleep well?"

"Oh, yea. He was still pretty groggy from the anesthesia and isn't fully out of it now but he's doing really well. He knows he has to be careful of his side. I would imagine it bites a bit when he moves. Come on back." She got up and opened the door leading down the hallway to the kennels.

"He's pretty smart," Mandy commented as she followed the woman down the hall. "I'm sure he won't move any faster than he has to."

Dr. Harrison met them walking down the hall, coming out of an exam room. He saw Mandy and smiled.

"Good morning! I know you're on your way to see Max." When Mandy smiled and nodded, he continued. "He slept pretty good. I was here until about five o'clock and went home to shower but he did well. I imagine he'll be happy to see you."

"That does my heart good. That big dog saved my life yesterday," Mandy said quietly with tears in her eyes.

Dr. Harrison put his hand on her arm.

"He's a very special guy. One of these days, you' re going to have to tell me the story behind him."

Mandy smiled. "It's be a long one. Will he still have to stay today?"

"Yea. I think that would be best. He seems pretty stable now but I want to see if he's able to tolerate the pain. I really don't want to load him up on pain meds."

"What about aspirin? Would that be okay?"

"That would work but let's see how he does first. When you take him home, I don't want you to have to bring him back in until we need to take out the stitches."

"Okay. And thank you. I really don't know what I would've done if we'd lost him."

"No problem, Mandy. I'm glad I was here to help."

They walked down the hall and Alana opened the door to the kennels. Max was in a bottom kennel, laying on his side. He barely fit.

Mandy opened the door. Max had lifted up his head when he saw her, wagging his tail. Mandy got on the floor and sat there, petting him and kissing that huge head. Max licked her hand and then laid back down, but still wagged his tail.

"Hey, buddy," Mandy spoke softly. "How are you feelin'? I can't take you home 'til tomorrow but I wanted to be sure you were okay." She murmured to him and looked at his side. Where he was taped, it was padded with cotton so she knew exactly which ribs were broken. The stitches showed the trail of the bullet. It was amazing he wasn't dead. He's got his own angels looking out for him, Mandy thought. Thank you, God.

"Do you think I could take him outside if he can get up?"

"I'm sure that would be good for him," Alana said. "Let me get you a leash."

"We won't need it. He won't leave me." She turned back to the big dog.

"Wanna go outside?" Mandy sat back to give him room. He got up on his front legs and pulled himself forward until his head and shoulders were out of the kennel. Then he could get his good leg under him to stand. He stood for a minute, tried to put his injured leg down. That hurt too much so he followed Mandy on three legs out the door to the small yard outside.

He sniffed and marked over other dogs' markings. It was only a few minutes but Mandy could tell that took everything he had. He came back over to Mandy but she did notice that his leg was on the ground, though he wasn't putting his full weight on it. They went back inside and Max went right to the kennel and laid down. Mandy hugged him and told him she'd be back to get him in the morning. He was asleep before she had the door shut.

Mandy drove carefully home. It wasn't that far and it just felt good just to have a little time to herself. She was surprised at how much she enjoyed Michael's company. She thought by now, she'd be screaming for space but she was looking forward to getting home and seeing him.

Lord girl, she thought. You've got it bad. She giggled for the first time in days. She felt so good. Max was coming home tomorrow, Brad was on the mend and she was going home to an incredible man. Maybe it was okay to think about a future.

She checked the rear-view mirror. There was a red Dodge pickup behind her. She has seen it at the vet's office. A shiver ran down her spine. She was about two miles from home. The roads weren't bad and the truck wasn't coming up on her. Just following. She pulled her gun from the console, never taking her eyes off the road or the truck. It may not be someone after her but Mandy wasn't taking any chances. The guys would be in the driveway when she pulled in. That was her best bet.

As she turned in the drive, the pickup slowed and followed her in. Instantly, there were five guards around the truck. Mandy had stopped about 50 feet in and got out.

When Mandy got to the Dodge, she saw it was the Hispanic lady from the vet, her dog in the back seat. She had both hands on the steering wheel and was speaking to Michael. He turned as Mandy walked up.

"I think we just found out why all this shit's happening."

Mandy was standing beside Michael. She looked at the woman. She was a very beautiful woman, somewhere from mid 40s to early 50s with black hair that had an auburn hint to it. Her eyes were a deep rich brown. She spoke to Mandy in accented English.

"Mandy, I am Angelica Contrereas. I think I am the reason behind all that is happening now. I am hoping we can find a way to stop all of this for good."

Mandy watched her as she spoke. She didn't appear to be nervous or upset. Her eyes were calm. The dog in the back was sitting up, on alert but not threatening, just watching. Angelica noticed Mandy's glance.

"Chica won't do anything unless I tell her. She is a half- sister to your dog. Same mama, different papa. I'm the one who turned him loose a month ago when he first came to you. I knew he would protect you."

Mandy looked at Michael, then back to Angelica.

"Follow me up to the house but know there will be a minimum of five rifles on you at all times and three guns on you in the house." She turned and walked back to her truck. Michael got in on the passenger side.

"Are you sure you want to do this?"

"No, but I want answers and I think she may have some. If nothing else, we'll find out where Max came from."

At the house, Mandy waited on the deck for Angelica to park. Chica whined when she got out of the truck. She spoke softly to her in Spanish and Chica quieted down but watched her as she went up the steps. She watched as Angelica walked up the back steps and into the house behind Mandy. Then she leaned against the seat, facing the house and keeping her watch on the back door.

With everyone at the dining table, Mandy poured fresh coffee and sat down. She studied Angelica. She wasn't a large woman by any means. She didn't look like she could weigh more than 120 lbs and only stood about 5'2". Mandy noticed her forearms were strong, the skin smooth and tight. There was only a light sagging along her jaw line and nothing that deteriorated her beauty.

"So what have you done to put a bulls-eye on my back?"

"My ex-husband is the head of the Contrereas Cartel. We were married for 22 years before I left him. That was seven years ago. I've been running ever since. I know what you have been through as I have been through the same. Had I known what he would do, I would have contacted you a long time ago but I couldn't find you. No one could."

"That was intentional. I didn't want to be found."

"I know." Angelica looked down at her hands. When she looked back up, there were tears in her eyes but she refused to let them fall.

"My ex-husband is not a good man. I had met several of his business associates and that included your husband."

"Ex-husband."

"Yes," Angelica agreed. "Your ex-husband. At the time I met him, you were still married. It was a happy marriage. You could see it on him. He was a happy man. A contented man. He never spoke of his family. Instinctively, he knew better. But you could see it." She took a deep, shaky breath before continuing.

"Jorge forced Jim into moving drugs for him by threatening you and the children. I was in the house when he told Jim he would kill you all, cut you in pieces and scatter you across the desert but not before he did unimaginable things to you. Jorge did not know I was in the house or that I heard what he said. I will never forget the look on Jim's face. When I saw that, I knew that I had to leave. It took me a very long time to gather money and make plans that would not be found out. My children were small. I would not jeopardize them so I waited and planned. Finally, the day came. My children were grown and out of the house. They had been for a few years – both away at college in the United States. That kept them as safe as could be possible. I walked out the door one day, dressed to go shopping with my girlfriend. In my purse was money and a gun. I would have killed him to get out of that house. I left with the clothes on my back." Angelica took a sip of coffee.

"I had gotten fake ID from a contact in Juarez. I colored my hair dark red, added padding to make myself look about 50 lbs heavier, wore grubby clothes and ratty tennis shoes and walked through customs with a cane. I knew there would be cameras everywhere so I waited until I had walked to a small restaurant on the U.S. side. There was a car I'd had delivered there. I went into the restroom, changed my clothes into some jeans and a man's work shirt, got into the car and left. I figured Jorge wouldn't look for me in anything, umm…. how you say, low keyed?" Mandy nodded. "I had been a very spoiled wife. There was a price to pay for that. I have the scars to prove it. Not like yours."

"Scars are scars," Mandy said. "Pain is pain."

Angelica nodded, hands wrapped around her coffee mug. Mandy could tell how hard this was for this woman to come here and tell her story to a complete stranger. She didn't push her. She would let her tell her story in her own time.

"I had applied for a work visa as a translator in Flagstaff, AZ. All the paperwork and the visa were under my fake ID. I am like you. I learned how to hide. I was coming out of a restaurant there one day about five years ago and ran into Jim. I had been talking to a lady and didn't see where I was going until I literally ran into him. It shocked the both of us. I begged him not to tell Jorge he had seen me. He promised he wouldn't. To this day, I don't believe he has."

"No," Mandy said. "If Jim made a promise, he kept it. He'd lie through his teeth about anything but if he promised something, he stood behind it."

"He asked if he could see me. I told him no. He was married and it was too dangerous. He told me he wasn't married anymore. We made plans to have coffee later that night. I told him to be careful not to be followed.

"That was the beginning of our relationship. He didn't try to have you killed. That was Jorge. I have never known all the details but from what Jim has told me and what I knew of what was going on at the time, that is what we know. I am divorced from Jorge. It is extreme what I did to get the divorce but it is done. When Jim went into protective custody, he got word to me. As of yet, I don't think Jorge knows I am here. I just bought the truck so I don't even think it's in the system yet. Plus, it is under my fake name. But the reason Jorge has held you over Jim's head all these years is because of me. I am not sure if he knows definitely of our relationship but I do know he suspects Jim knows where I am. He went after you for the simple fact that if his wife was gone, so would Jim's. I know that sounds so…….. pathetic, I think is the word, but that is the truth."

Mandy had sat, sipping coffee and listening. She believed this small lady. She gave off the energy of someone who had been abused and Mandy could recognize that only too well.

"Why are you telling me this? Why do I matter?"

"I have wanted to find you for years. I knew you were a strong woman, as am I. Otherwise, neither of us would have survived. I want all this to stop. I know you do, also. We both have endured enough pain, as have all of our children, though they are grown. Jim is no angel. I know this. But neither is he evil as Jorge is."

Mandy leaned back in her chair, playing with her coffee mug. She looked at Michael and gave him a slight nod that he returned. They were on the same page. They believed her.

"How did you find me?"

Angelica smiled, took a sip of coffee. "By, how you say? Chance? I was talking to my son on the phone. We have those ones you can throw away. He is in San Francisco. He made a remark that Jorge had said there was some connection to your son and Jackson Hole, WY. I knew in my heart you were here. I did not tell Jim I was coming here. I wanted to be sure before I said anything to him. I drove up here with two dogs and just started driving around. I saw you one day working your horse. I knew it was you. You don't look anything like the pictures I had seen of you but there was something about you. I knew in my heart. I watched you for a while and then went back to the motel to think. I knew I couldn't approach you then. I didn't think you would believe anything I said I was scared that if I could find you, so could Jorge. Two days later, I turned Meho loose and told him to take care of you."

"Wait a minute. You sent me Max?" Mandy stared at her in total disbelief.

"Yes, that is what I did. Maybe I better explain about Meho."

"That would be a good idea."

"About six months ago, I came across some people who train guard dogs for the border patrol. They had come to my job and wanted to put on a demonstration. I got to be friends with one of the handlers. They do not know that I am illegal. The handler asked if I would like to come out and see some of the training at the property. I said yes and I went. It was very interesting to me. We went out to the kennels and Chica found me immediately. She was very sure she wanted to go with me. We talked about my buying her. As we were leaving, we walked by this kennel and she sat down in front of it and whined. I didn't understand what she wanted. Meho was laying down in the back of the kennel. He made no effort to get up. The handler told me that he was going to be put down the next day as he wasn't going to make it as a guard dog. I decided that wasn't going to happen. I went into his kennel and made friends with him. I told him I would find him a good home if he wanted to come with me. He got up and followed me out. He and Chica are half brother and sister. They have the same mama. I had no idea of who was going to get him but I could not let them destroy him. That made no sense to me."

"I will forever be grateful to you for saving him," Mandy said, leaning forward. "Last night, he took a bullet for. That is why I was at the vet's this morning."

Angelica gasped and brought a hand to her mouth. She stared at Mandy. "Is he going to be okay?"

"Yea. He's got some broken ribs and lots of stitches but he'll be alright."

Angelica sat slumped back in her chair.

"Jorge is a bastard."

"I won't argue with you on that. Angelica, I have no doubt what you have told me is the truth. I have my own time frame for things to fall into place. I also agree with you that we can do better together to bring an end to this. But I need you to know something and this comes from me, from my heart. I hold nothing against you for your relationship with Jim. I'm still trying to wrap my head around the fact that he didn't try to kill me. Our marriage was over long before I left. If the two of you can find some happiness with what all of us have been through, I say more power to you."

Angelica looked up from her coffee mug and reached for Mandy's hand as tears fell from her dark eyes.

"Gracias. You do not know what that means to me. I think now I can tell Jim what I've done by coming here to talk to you."

"That would be choice!" Mandy laughed. "We might make him stay in the hospital longer!"

They chatted for a few more minutes about nothing. Both Michael and Marty were sitting at the table, gun re-holstered. Michael watched Mandy as she went from being skeptic to believing this woman who was her ex-husband's girlfriend. She never ceased to amaze him.

"I need to get to the hospital. I need to see Jim for myself. I know that it will soon be known that I am here. I think I will stay at the hospital. I know Jim is guarded so perhaps I will be safe there, also."

"I need to go there, too."

"Should we act like we know each other?" Angelica asked.

"For now, until the sheriff knows who you are and clears you, no. I think the more you're not seen with me, the safer you'll be. I'll call him and let him know you're on your way up to the hospital. He'll be discreet. He doesn't want anyone else hurt. Are you going to change clothes or can I describe what you have on?"

Angelica laughed. It was a musical sound.

"I just got cleaned up after quatro…. I mean, four days. These feels so nice. I think I will keep them on, at least for today."

Mandy laughed. "I understand completely. Do you have a phone with you that I can call you to let you know about the sheriff?"

"Of course. It is the throw away that my son got for me." She rattled off the number. Mandy put it in her cell phone.

"Here. Let me give you mine."

"No, Mandy. If, by chance, Jorge finds me, he'll go through my purse. The phone will show your number and he could find you. Only call me if it's important."

Chapter 18

On the way to the hospital, Mandy called Hank and filled him on Angelica. She asked him to be discreet as Jorge may not know she was here and didn't want a target on her back. He would be extra careful. She asked how his deputies were doing. They both were in serious condition but expected to make a full recovery. She sighed in relief.

At the hospital, in Brad's room, Mandy and Michael told of the meeting with Angelica and of Max being shot.

"What do you think, mom?" Marie asked. She had been very quiet through the telling, listening intently as the story unfolded.

"You can feel the fear radiate off her. She's very determined and seems to be pretty much a straight shooter. No drama. Maybe I recognize some of myself in her. I don't know."

"Do you believe her?" This came from Alex. She looked at both Michael and Mandy with this question.

"It feels like the truth," Mandy said. "What would she have to gain by lying? I sure in the hell don't want Jim back. If she loves him as much as she puts on, she'd want all this to end. She doesn't get to have him completely until it is. To answer your question, I'll trust her guardedly until I have a reason not to." She turned to Michael. "What do you think?"

"Right now, about the same. I had Marty run the temp registration on the truck and he'll see what he can find out about her. Until then, I figure just roll with what we've got. There really isn't much more we can do until we know more about her."

"I think all of you need to meet her. You need to know what she looks like, how she is around Jim. That will show a lot. But just be careful 'til we know more."

Brad had been quiet all during the conversation. His leg was wrapped in gauze and vet wrap. She knew the hospital would call it something else when used for people but it was the same material she used on the horses when they were injured. It was vet wrap to her and Brad had the masculine color of dark purple.

"Good thing she verified they got together after you left. Might have been another issue I would have to speak to dear ole dad about." Mandy looked at Brad. "Yes, mom. I plan on having a talk with him. And since it may not be real nice, no one else is invited." The anger was coming off him in waves.

"Are you sure you're up to it?"

"Doesn't matter. Needs to be done." Brad smirked. "He's not in any better shape than I am so we can't beat the shit outa each other."

Marie looked at her brother and rolled her eyes.

"You are such a moron,"

"Best one you know, baby sister," came the retort, still with the smirk. That broke the tension that had begun to fill the room.

Alex leaned over and kissed Brad on the cheek.

"Might want to wait 'til you're no so loaded on pain meds, buddy."

He looked at her.

"Yea. It can wait 'til maybe tomorrow. It's waited this long. I'm trying not to take anything but Tylenol starting today."

"Don't like fuzzy brain?"

"No, I don't. Feels like I have no control over myself. If the pain is tolerable with Tylenol, I'm going with that."

"When are they going to release you?" Mandy asked.

"I think tomorrow. The doctor wanted to be sure someone would be with me 24/7. Alex and Marie said they'd work in shifts."

Mandy laughed. "Yea, right." She stood. "I'd come to pick you up but I think you'll be safer at Michael's than with me. The farther you are from me, the better. You've already been shot and I don't want anything more to happen to any of you." She looked at all of them. "I love you guys too much."

Marie came over and hugged Mandy hard.

"We'll be fine. Personally, I want all of us to be together so we can shoot all the bastards at once and be done with this shit." She released Mandy and leaned back.

"Oops---did the attorney just say that?"

Alex came to stand next to Marie.

"She sure did and the other attorney is her back up."

Mandy laughed and hugged both of them.

"Keep up your target practice, girls."

"Are you going to bring Max home tomorrow?" Brad asked.

"I hope to. The house seems so empty without him." She walked over and hugged him.

"I love you. I'll get over to Michael's as soon as I can."

Brad hugged her back hard. "No worries, mom. Just wish I could be there with you. I'm with Marie on this. We all need to be together."

Mandy looked down out her son and touched his face.

"You be safe. All of you. That's all that matters."

"No, mom. You matter."

Walking back to the truck with Michael had Mandy thinking.

"We need to find Contrereas."

"You're serious about going after him."

Mandy looked at him as he opened the door for her.

"Any better ideas?"

"Oh, yea," he grinned as he leaned in to kiss her. "Several."

Mandy laughed.

"I know you do."

Michael called Marty as they were driving out of the parking lot. As he turned towards the outskirts of town, he noticed a black Ford F150 turn two cars after him. A shiver went down his spine. They were being followed. He couldn't see the driver as the windows were tinted too dark. He could only get a partial plate number.

"Hey, Marty. Could you see if you can get a line on where Contrereas is? Yea. It's time we took the party to his house. Hell. It's Mandy's idea, remember? And while you're at it, check on a black Ford F150. I've only got part of the plate-WY257. Yea, I know there's a million of 'em. Just see what you can find. See ya in a bit."

Mandy pulled down the visor and check the mirror. Sure enough. The black pickup was two cars back. Michael changed lanes. So did the pickup.

"Tighten your seat belt." Michael slowed to make a left turn, punched the gas and took an immediate right. He immediately pulled over to the curb under a massive maple tree and threw the truck in Park so the brake light wouldn't show. No sooner was his hand off the shifter than the Ford flew past the intersection behind them. Traffic had blocked the truck from making the righthand turn. Immediately, Michael slammed the truck into gear and hit the gas. He took turns, back tracked and finally headed out of town an hour later. All the while, Mandy hadn't said a word. He'd glanced at her several times, each time her hand stayed on the gun in her lap and her mouth set in a straight line of determination. Never a change.

They finally made it to the house. Mandy hit the garage door opener and Michael pulled in. Hopefully, they wouldn't think they were back since her truck wasn't in the drive.

It was dark out. The security light by the barn didn't light up the deck. It was lighter with it on but only produced dim light at the house. Suddenly, Michael pushed Mandy into the shadows of the overhang of the house. He was looking out towards the horse pens. She looked over his shoulder and saw a flash of light. The both froze, waiting for another flash. Mandy thought it was the reflection off a rifle barrel. That was the only thing that made sense to her at the moment but she knew it could be any number of things. Just then, Michael's phone vibrated.

"Yea. Okay." He put the phone back in his pocket and relaxed.

"It's one of Marty's guys. No worries."

Mandy sighed. Good to know the good guys were out there.

The house smelled of lasagna and garlic bread. Marie and Hank were talking at the island. She looked up when Mandy and Michael came in.

"Hey, mom. I came home to get showered and change clothes. Alex is still at the hospital. I have to take them dinner. Brad says if he has to eat another meal of hospital food, he'll throw it out the window."

Mandy laughed. "Guess your brother is feeling better. Are they still releasing him tomorrow?"

"Yea, tomorrow morning, after the doctor sees him."

Mandy nodded. She leaned against the island and poured coffee for her and Michael. He nodded his thanks.

"We had company on the way home."

"So I heard," Hank replied. "Black Ford F150 with WY plates. We ran the traffic cams and got a picture of the guy driving. See if you recognize him." He handed Mandy his phone.

Mandy gasped. "That's the guy who stabbed me."

At first glance, she would have sworn that it was Rafe but then she remembered Jim said his brother worked for the cartel. Chills ran down her back as she stood looking at the picture on the phone.

"Let me see that." Marie took the phone out of Mandy's hand. "Damn. He looks just like Rafe."

"Jim said they were brothers."

"Okay," Michael said. "Now we know who the son of a bitch is. We find him and let him lead us to Contrereas." Michael's face was set in hard lines.

"You okay?" Mandy asked, stepping closer to him.

"Yea," Michael sighed. "Didn't realize I was letting these bastards get to me."

"It's okay. I know the feeling." Mandy squeezed his hand and was relieved when he squeezed back.

The sound of a car coming in the drive stopped everyone's conversation as Michael's phone vibrated. He answered and put it back in his pocket.

"Allison and Alan."

Marty had come in. He was standing between Michael and Hank.

"Damn. They always show up. Seems like they know we're planning a war."

"I didn't hear that," Hank grinned at him.

"I know. You're the deafest sheriff I ever met."

Hank stepped up beside Marie and took her hand. She looked up at him, grateful for the warmth that touched her skin. She was terrified for Mandy, for all of them, and beyond angry at the whole situation. There were so many players. She checked to be sure her gun was still holstered in the small of her back, under her hoodie. She knew it was. Could feel the holster but feeling the gun was reassuring. She had meant it when she had told her mother that they were good to go. Mandy just didn't know how far that meant.

Allison and Alan were let in. They stood around the island.

"What do you want." Mandy didn't make it a question. The only reason they were there is because they wanted something. She was angry beyond words that they had come back. She had so hoped she was done with them. Fat chance.

"To tell you that you were right. The leak did come from our office. We had an agent who was bought to give information to Juan Garcia. He's been arrested in Washington." Allison acted as if that was the greatest gift she could have given Mandy.

"So? I told you that. You wouldn't have even have looked at your own office if I hadn't told you. You're telling me nothing I didn't already know."

"I thought you would give us some information since we proved that we have your interests as a priority."

Mandy stood up so fast, the stool she had been sitting on flew behind her.

"I cannot believe that for a federal attorney, you are so fucking stupid! How many fucking times do you have to be told that I don't know anything!" Mandy was shaking now. She was close to losing it completely, of going black. "I have nothing to give you!" she yelled. Michael had moved beside her before the stool hit the floor, Marie on her other side. She saw Alan start to reach for his gun under his jacket.

"Don't you dare pull a gun here. You have three on you here and another four outside. Don't." Marie's voice was low deadly calm. Alan brought his hand back out from under his jacket.

"I'm a federal agent. You'll be jailed for the rest of your lives."

"Well, being an attorney, I'm sure I could find a few loopholes in that. Ask your wife. I'm sure there's several. Put your hands on the counter."

Alan never took his eyes off Marie but put placed both hands, palms down, on the counter.

Mandy was breathing hard. She felt her heart pounding in her chest, felt Michael's strength as he stood beside her and Marie's calm energy. She took a deep breath and lowered her voice.

"I am not speaking to you again. You will leave this property now and if you EVER set one goddamn foot on my property again, I will shoot you. I don't give a fucking damn if you are feds or the fucking president. Do I make myself clear?"

Allison looked smugly at Mandy.

"As this property doesn't belong to you, you cannot make that statement. You either talk to us now or we arrest you."

"Who do you think this property belongs to?"

"Diane Leeds. And that sure as hell isn't you."

"I speak for Diane. I live here for Diane. Get over yourself, Allison. You don't get me. You don't get to break this case and be the great AAG. The government didn't do their job to begin with. So, as I said before, get the hell off my property. Now. If I have to ask again, I won't be so nice."

Allison looked at Michael for help. Again, he gave her none.

"Let me walk you out," Hank offered. He wanted to be sure they left and to make a few calls of his own. He'd call his friend at the FBI. Maybe he could find out more as to why Allison and Alan were pushing at Mandy so hard.

Alan slowly stood. He reached for Allison's arm and they made their way to the door. Michael watched from the doorway as they drove out. He heard Marty on the phone, telling Josh to be sure that car left and to keep an eye out for it throughout the night.

Marie looked at her mom. She knew better than anyone that Mandy could and would have gone black. She had only seen it once. Not in all the years that Jim had beat on her. It had been when he was drunk and had gone after her and Brad. They had been 12 and 10 at the time. She never wanted to see that again.

"You okay, mom?"

Mandy looked at Marie and gave her a shaky smile.

"Yea, or I will be in a few minutes. Came real close to not being, though."

Marie nodded and hugged her. "I got your back, mama." Mandy hugged her back, hard as tears streamed down her face.

"I know, baby."

Michael came back into the kitchen just as Marty came back in.

"We may have a lead on Contrereas. There was a flight plan filed to Billings. That's not that far away. He wouldn't attract attention there as he would here."

"Do we have anyone at the airport?" Michael asked.

"Yea. Josh's brother is there. IF it's him, he should be landing within about two hours."

"Do we have plane numbers?"

"I'm not sure of what all he's got. I do know he has the most current picture we have of Contrereas."

"Okay. Get someone at our airport just in case Billings is a diversion. He must know Jim and Brad are in the hospital and anyone else, for that matter. Plus, he has guys in jail. He could be figuring that he needs to do this himself or needs to bring in his own legal team. Whatever reason he's coming, IF he is, we need to be ready." Michael paused. "Get someone at the Idaho Falls and Pocatello airports. He could fly into either one of those and be a hellva lot closer."

"Done." Marty moved back outside to make calls.

"I want to deal with this bastard." Mandy had come to stand by Michael. He looked down at her. Her eyes were calm now, not flashing in anger. She wasn't asking permission. She was stating fact. She deserved to deal with him. Michael nodded. He'd back her. Hell. In for an ounce, in for a pound.

Mandy turned to Marie. "I don't want Hank to know about this and I don't want you to feel torn. You don't have to stay."

"Hank and I already had this discussion, mom. This jerk has tried to kill both you and my brother and shot your dog. This is about us. We're family. Hank will either get it or he won't."

"He'll get it," Michael stated.

"We need maps, something we can write on. Maps of WY and MT. We need to cover every road from all three airports. He'll have to hire people from the area. There's no way he can come in here quiet. Not with all the bullshit connected to him. Do you think you can get Angelica to talk to you? She and Jim know how he thinks, what his moves would be."

"I'll go over to the hospital and see what I can find out." Mandy needed to do this. Two hours wasn't a lot of time and that would be the soonest he would be here. They needed to prepared.

Chapter 19

Mandy walked into the hospital. The nurse on duty knew her by now and smiled when she came up to the desk.

"Hi, Mandy! We moved Brad to another room. I do believe he's going to be discharged soon."

"Really? I didn't think that was until tomorrow morning."

"I don't know any of the particulars. I just got the orders. I'll be taking them up in a bit for him to sign."

"Good thing I got here now," Mandy smiled. The nurse gave the room number and Mandy and Marie headed to the elevators. They rode to the 11th floor, got out, waited for the car to go back down and pressed the "DOWN" button. The next car came and Mandy pressed the 4th floor.

On the 4th floor, they walked to 412. Brad was still close to the nurse's station but on the other side. The guard nodded as they walked in the door. Brad was standing on his crutches by the window, in the shadows. Alex was sitting in the chair. You could feel how bad he wanted out of the hospital.

"Hey, big guy," Mandy said as she came in the room, going over to where Brad was. She hugged him. "You need a shave."

"Yea, I know," he grinned. "Alex says it's like kissing a grizzly."

Mandy laughed. It was so good to see him up and around.

Alex had gotten up from the chair as soon as they came in and hugged them both.

"I'm so glad to see you guys and know you're okay. How's dad? How's Max? Tell me! We've been going nuts just getting bits and pieces."

Mandy smiled as she sat in the extra chair. Marie took the one Alex had vacated as she sat with Brad on the side of the bed. They both listened intently as Mandy filled them in on what had happened in the last 24 hours. She stressed the fact that Michael was fine, was busy covering all possible aspects of Jorge's arrival. The worry lines on Alex's face eased. Brad's face was dark and angry.

"Who the hell do they think they are?" His anger regarding Allison and Alan was magnified by his frustration. If his leg was better, he would have paced. "They can't come in and take anything from you. If they were such great investigators, they'd know the house is in grandma's name. They are pathetic. No wonder the cartels can come and go as they please." He looked at Alex. "Sorry. I know it's your mom."

"No apology needed. She's acting like a moron and I barely know her. I can't believe they tried that crap. Either they've forgotten this family has two other attorneys besides her or that must've slipped their little brains." She reached for Brad's hand. "She only gave birth to me. That's all I can thank her for." Brad nodded.

"When are you going to the ranch?" Mandy asked.

"As soon as I get the papers signed. Hank is going to escort us back and make sure the house is cleared, since I can't. Marty's guys have kept watch on all of the ranch property. I'd be more of a hindrance than a help at your house and you have enough going on without me adding to it."

"No problem, honey. I get it. BUT you have never been nor will you, or any of you for that matter, ever be a hindrance. I'm glad you'll be at the ranch, though. I won't worry so much. I would rather your sister be there, too, but she's decided to be my shadow." Mandy looked at Marie who only grinned at her. "Which brings me to another question, missy. Where the hell did you get so bold with a gun? And a holster in the back of your jeans?"

Marie smiled. "Told ya. We're good to go." She looked at Brad and winked.

"Oh, shit. You actually let mom know we had the guns?" Brad rolled his eyes. "You know what we're in for now."

"There really wasn't many options at the time, bubba."

Alex suddenly laughed.

"What?"

"You guys remind me of me and my brothers and dad."

"Wonderful," Brad muttered.

"Do you know what room Jim's in?" Mandy asked.

"Why, mom?"

"Well, obviously I want to talk to him."

"With his girlfriend there?"

"Like I care. What room is he in? I need to talk to both of them with Contrereas coming in."

"He's in 302 but they may have moved him."

"Then I'll find them. Oh. Did you meet Angelica?"

"Yea. She seems to be on the level. Jury's still out."

Mandy looked at Alex.

"What do you think?"

"I think she's a straight shooter. I never got any negative vibes off her."

"That what both Michael and I got, too. I'll trust her until I have a reason not to."

"Watch your back, mom."

"No problem. I got your sister."

"Well, you're good then. She can kick some serious ass."

Mandy put her arm around Marie and hugged her.

"That's my girl." They all laughed. Then Brad turned serious and turned to Marie.

"You're gonna have to be both of us on this one. Sorry. Never intended for you to handle it by yourself."

Marie looked at him as only a sister could could- part smirk, part smile.

"You goof. I got this. We drilled. Both of us. And we knew one of us could be out of commission. I will do ya proud, big brother."

"I know you will. Just watch your back."

"No worries. You watch yours."

"What I can't, Alex will." He looked at Alex and smiled.

"I'm going to go talk to Jim and Angelica. If we can't come by tomorrow for whatever reason, I'll call you. I have to get Max in the morning. He should be able to come home, too."

"Great! We can recoup together. I'm sure he'll be going about as crazy as I already am."

Mandy hugged both Brad and Alex one more time.

"Be careful you two."

"We will. You be careful, too, Mandy. Dad will be checking on us so what you don't hear directly from us, you'll hear from him." Alex hugged her hard one more time. She filled a spot Alex didn't know was empty. All three of them did.

At room 302, Mandy nodded to the guard that was posted and knocked on the door.

"Jim, it's Mandy and Marie."

Jim opened the door. A shadow crossed his face for a split second, then was gone. He smiled or rather tried to. His face was battered, bruised on both sides of his jaw and both eyes, though his eyes weren't as swollen as they had been. Mandy imagined he's had cold packs on them so he could see. He stepped aside so they could come in.

Walking into the hospital room was strange. Mandy couldn't tell exactly what it was. Maybe because Angelica was there. They had been sitting side by side in some chairs. Angelica rose as they came in and smiled.

"I am so glad to see you," she said, reaching for Mandy's hand. She turned to Marie.

"You are as beautiful as your mother. I am so glad to finally meet you."

Marie smiled back. She wasn't sure of what to make of this little woman. She didn't feel anything negative from her, only happiness. There was a slight shadow to her. Not negative. Cautious. Couldn't blame her for that.

"I have some news." Mandy began, "and I wanted you to hear it from me so maybe, together, we could figure something out." She let them know what they knew so far and what they could possibly help with. Jim looked at Angelica when Mandy was finished. He reached for her hand.

"We knew this was coming."

Just then, there was a knock on the door and Hank walked in. He nodded to everyone and came over to Marie.

"Hey, babe. You guys okay?"

"Hey, yourself. You talked to Michael, huh?"

"Yea. He let me know what's up. Between Marty's guys, the locals and my guys here, we have all three airports covered that he would most likely fly in to."

"I just let Jim and Angelica know what all we know so far. Thought maybe they could give us some insight as to how Jorge would operate once he's here." Mandy was very calm as she spoke. She could feel that this really was the end of it, however it ended. And she was glad. Eight years of this was more than enough.

"He's very good at strategy. He's also good at doing the unexpected." Jim paused, looking at Angelica. "He'll do anything in his power to do whatever it is that he feels he needs to do. He's very ruthless. It's good that all the airports are covered. He could send in a decoy to the ones he's not flying in to just to throw you off. If the Feds are still involved, they should do whatever they can to stop him before he gets here. He'll have his top men with him and they are as dangerous as he is."

"He won't care how long it takes to get here," Angelica added. "He looks to the result. If he had to ……. how you say?…. detour for five days to get here but would know he would be able to kill us when he got here, then that is what he would do. The men with him are, as Jim said, dangerous like him. They will be his top men. I do not know who they are anymore. I do not know how many he has left, between the jail and who have died or been hurt. I would stay alert. We will be here as there is no way of knowing who he hired here."

Hank nodded. Angelica had confirmed what he was already thinking. Jorge was a sneaky bastard. No doubt about it. He knew they would have to be sneakier and deadlier. He looked at Marie. He knew she had the gun in her waist band in the back of her jeans. He knew the hospital personnel knew they were armed. Their indepth conversations of this whole mess had told him all he needed to know. This was her family. She'd do whatever she had to. Now, with the information regarding the Contrereas Cartel on their way here, he knew the only way this would end would be in a lot of blood. He also knew Mandy wasn't going to play nice anymore. Her son and dog had been shot. From what Michael had told him about the meeting with Allison and Alan, he had the feeling Mandy was going to be a one person tornado if anyone else got hurt.

He couldn't blame her. He was trying to juggle the law and justice. It was a difficult feat.

"Okay. We're getting things set up with the information we have. We also have the information as to how we were found at the safe house. A tracking device had been put on my deputy's cruiser. Now, all vehicles are checked before they're moved. So, that being said, no plan is set in stone. We may have to change direction at a moment's notice. I know how hard all of this is on all of you and I think you know that my men and myself will do whatever we can to end this without anyone else being hurt." He looked at each of them, ending with Marie. She nodded and reached to squeeze his hand.

"We're going to move you today, Jim. You are going to be transported on a stretcher with a nurse at your side." He paused and nodded to Angelica. "That's done all the time. We'll take you to another medical facility in Pocatello and then you and Angelica will go to a safe house in Idaho Falls. Brad and Alex are going back to the ranch. Alex knows the back roads and will be coming in at her Uncle David's. They'll spend the night there. I don't think Brad will be able to make it all in one day but he could surprise me. He has a couple of times already. Michael and Marty called in a couple of snipers they know, who will be bringing in a few more men each. We'll have Brad and Alex covered all the way to Michael's." He paused and looked at Mandy. "I know what you've been through. I get it. But, Mandy, you may end up being bait for this bastard."

Mandy looked at him. He was a good man and a good sheriff. And he cared for Marie so that made him family. She knew this was getting harder on him each day. They were becoming family to him.

"I know, Hank. I've always been the bait. It'll be okay. Whatever way this ends up, it's the way it was supposed to. But I pray to God, I get to kill the bastard." Mandy spoke with quiet determination. Her dark eyes had turned black. Hank knew she meant every word she was saying.

"Can't blame you," was the only response he gave.

Mandy couldn't leave the hospital fast enough. She felt there was a bull's eye on her back and it targeted everyone around her. If she could get Marie to stay with Brad and Alex, she would. But Marie wasn't having any of that. She'd made sure Brad was on the mend and now she was going to be sure Mandy made it through this.

The drive back to the house took longer as Mandy drove a round-about way, making sure they weren't followed. Michael met them at the door.

"You made it back safe. Anyone follow you?"

"No, I don't think so. I took a longer way just to be sure and I checked the truck to be sure there wasn't any tracking devise like what was on the cruiser. Any news?"

"Not yet. We have the airports covered and Hwys 26, 30 and 89. Unless Jorge is coming in on a four-wheeler, he'll have to use one of those to get here."

Mandy started making dinner. A massive pot of stew, salad and garlic bread. That ought to fill up the guys. The nights were starting to get cold and she wanted to be sure they had enough to sustain them through the night. A hot meal and lots of coffee would hopefully get them through.

The guys started coming in at about five o'clock. There were five men plus Michael around the table. Mandy and Marie made sure everyone had full plates and mugs. They were quiet, too busy eating to talk when Michael's phone rang. She could tell by the look on his face that Jorge had been spotted. Everyone stopped eating, eyes on Michael. He hit speed dial on his phone.

"Marty. Just got word. Come up to the house. I'm calling Hank." He hung up and hit another speed dial.

Mandy looked at Marie. They both knew whatever was coming would be here within 24 hours, maybe sooner. Brad and Alex had made it to the ranch. Brad didn't want to endanger Alex's aunt and uncle any more than what they had already been. They'd gotten there about three. Brad had taken a nap and now was up, sitting by the front window with a rifle in his lap. Alex walked the house from time to time and there were guards outside. They were as safe as could be, under the circumstances. Jim and Angelica had arrived in Pocatello and were on their way to Idaho Falls. Mandy was the bait, along with everyone else in the house.

Marty came in. About 15 minutes later, Hank showed up, out of uniform. He wasn't the sheriff tonight.

Marty put everyone on high alert outside. That meant checking in every 15 minutes. Anything that looked outa line would be called in sooner.

Michael started when everyone was seated.

"Jorge was spotted at the Billings airport. The straightest shot would be I90 to Bozeman and head south from there. There was also a flight from Mexico landing in Idaho Falls and Pocatello, both at about the same time. They weren't direct flight but both originated from Mexico and South America. We know he's setting up a diversion. This was all at about four o'clock this afternoon. He could be here anytime. It's not that far from Idaho to here. All our snipers are here but the ranch and everyone else is also covered. We've set up a two -mile radius around all the properties involved. All vehicles leaving all three airports have teams on them. There are also teams along each highway to pick up the tails just to be sure no one is spotted, or if they are, they have back up. Regardless if Jorge is coming from Billings or another airport, we know all his people will end here, at Mandy's. We also have teams along every county and dirt road coming into this property. If anyone has anything more to add or any more ideas, let's hear it."

Hank had been writing as Michael spoke. He looked up now.

"Marty, I'll have my guys contact you so you know who's out there and where. They'll need your channel so we can all be on the same line. They all have ear buds so there won't be any conversation. They communicate in Morse Code with key three." He looked at Michael. "I have teams along the same roads as you. We all need to be connected so everybody knows who's out there."

Mandy listened. She knew little of military tactics but what was set up was common sense to her. Maybe she should have been a general. Damn. There she went again.... Off on some off the wall thought process. Well, it was time to pull it in and focus. She checked her gun. A full clip and one in the chamber, three more clips in her pocket. She grabbed two more clips for the other pocket. She checked all her hiding places-all guns loaded with extra clips. The house was quiet. Michael and Marty were out walking the perimeter around the house and the through the woods. Hank and Marie were checking the barn. She was alone in the house and wished that Max had been able to come home. But he was safe at the vet's. That was a comfort.

Knowing she had done all she could, she went into the living room and sat on the couch. The room was semi-dark, the only light on was over the dining table. She was as safe as she could be. Her stomach was tied in knots as the wait began.

Hank had checked the barn. All the stalls, the tack room and the loft were clear. He came and sat on a hay bale next to Marie. She reached for his hand.

"I know you're not here tonight as the sheriff. I know you're here as one of us."

Hank looked at her. He sure hadn't expected to fall for this gorgeous attorney, or any attorney for that matter. But she wasn't about manipulation of the law. She was about justice and that appealed to him. Marie was brilliant when it came to the law but her common sense would not allow for any of the manipulation he had seen. She had such heart and would stand strong. She wasn't a woman to be taken care of. She could take care of herself. With her, it would be a true partnership. He also admired that.

"You're right. I've gotten pretty attached to all of you in a very short period of time. You said it all when you said this was your family. Nothing more needed to be said, Marie. I get it. I'm with you. I didn't expect you. Didn't expect to ever meet someone like you. But here you are."

Marie looked at him. She knew he was speaking of his dead wife. She knew that traumatic death had scarred him.

"I know about your loss, Hank, and I know how hard it's been. Maybe when all this over, it will be a bit easier."

He leaned in and lightly kissed her.

"It already is."

Chapter 20

A step hit the deck. Mandy tensed until she saw the silhouette a split second before Michael came in the door.

"It's okay. It's just me." He came in and sat next to Mandy.

"Everything okay?"

"We got calls from all the teams. All the cars are heading here. We don't know what car Jorge is in as everybody is bundled up like it was Alaska." He laughed. "Should know better than to head north in the late fall. Anyway, everyone is on alert. All we can do now is wait."

"I'm not doing very well with that lately, in case you hadn't noticed."

"No worries, babe. We're all pretty tense."

Mandy looked at him in the shadowy light. She took hold of his hand, rubbing the top of it. There was so much she wanted to say that was stuck in her throat. Not knowing if they'd be alive in the morning gave life a surreal and desperate quality.

Michael turned her face towards him.

"I can see the thoughts going through your head. We're going to be okay. This is going to be done soon and we won't have to deal with this jackass again. He'll either be dead or in jail."

"Not wounded and in the hospital?"

"No. Dead or jail. Only options open." He said it with such conviction that Mandy believed him, mostly. She was too much of a realist to think there was no room for something else. "Anyway, we have things to do and this bastard is making us put our lives on hold. So, he has to go."

Mandy smiled. It sounded so easy.

Just then, Marie and Hank came in and sat on the other sofa.

"You okay, mom?"

"Yea. Just wish it was over with."

"It will be soon."

They all seemed to settle in for the wait, dozing on and off. It was a few hours later when Michael's phone buzzed. He listened, then hung up.

"Show time. They're on their way. Marty says they all met in town. Two SUVs are coming this way and they have about six to nine men each. One headed south. We'll know soon enough where that one is going."

Everyone moved to the shadows and let each other know where they were. Mandy sent Marie to watch from her bedroom window. Hank was at the living room, Michael in the mud room and Mandy was at the dining room. She shut off the light and stood to the side. She could see out but no one could see her. The house was so quiet. She could hear the soft clicks of the Morse Code as Marty gave Michael updates.

She saw a shadow moving on the side of the barn, another by the horse pens. She felt the air tense from the living room. She knew Hank had someone out front, in the woods.

"Barn," Michael said softly.

"Pens," Mandy replied.

"Front woods. Friendly?" Hank whispered.

"Woods, yes. Back here, no."

A quiet footstep on the deck caught Mandy's ear. She took aim and braced herself for the shot. She never thought about pulling the trigger once she saw the face of the man who stabbed her. She fired through the glass. Three shots to the chest. He dropped. She cautiously looked outside. She knew they couldn't see her with the house so dark but also knew someone could get a lucky shot.

"Mandy? You okay?" Michael called quietly.

"Yea. I'm good."

Mandy saw another figure start to come towards the house from the barn. Two shots from her room told her Marie had seen him. There was no return fire. She heard more shots from the front of the house, not from the inside. She heard Michael's gun fire twice and a thud on the deck. Three down for sure.

Suddenly there was breaking glass from her bedroom. Mandy started down the hallway. Marie. Someone had gotten Marie. Her heart dropped to her belly. Michael grabbed her arm. She started to jerk away but looked up at him. He placed his finger to his lips. She nodded and they went down the hall, Hank behind Michael.

"Hey, puta," came a heavily accented voice. "Tell me where that low life bastard of a husband of yours is with my bitch wife and I will let this woman go. Don't tell me and I will kill her."

Mandy stepped into her bedroom and hit the light. Jorge had Marie pulled up against his body as a shield, his arm across her shoulders. Marie was grabbing his arm and looked more mad than scared. She stared directly at Mandy.

"I don't know where he is. I divorced him years ago." Mandy sized him up in a split second. He was a solid built man, maybe 5'11". He could've been nice looking except hatred screamed out of every pore in his body. He held a gun to Marie's head. Mandy had no doubt he would pull the trigger.

"You know, puta, I know you have been to the hospital to see him."

"No. I went to the hospital to see my son that one of your men shot."

"I can have him shot again if you do not tell me what I want to know."

"Do you think I would risk anyone's life to protect him?" Mandy wanted to keep him talking. There was something in Marie's eyes and Jorge hadn't noticed that Mandy's right arm was at her side, gun in her hand behind her leg. Marie had a plan to do something and it scared Mandy to death. But she knew this couldn't go on much longer.

Marie looked at Mandy, then shifted her eyes behind Mandy. She gave a slight nod and then went completely limp, slipping out of Jorge's grasp to the floor. Jorge wasn't expecting dead weight and staggered back. Mandy raised her gun and fired, twice. Two shots to the head. Jorge was dead before he ever hit the floor.

Michael rushed in, gun drawn as Hank checked Jorge and kicked his gun away from the body. He turned to Marie, who was just standing up. He grabbed her and hugged her tight.

"Damn. You did that perfect but you scared the hell outa me." He didn't want to let her go. "You alright?"

"Yea". She hugged him back and looked to her mom. Michael was just taking her gun and setting it aside. He hugged her.

"You did it, babe. You're the one who stopped him." He looked at her. "I wondered if you could pull the trigger on a person and you said you could after Brad was shot. I never doubted you. I knew you could do it."

Mandy looked at him and grinned. She went to Marie and hugged her hard. Then the tears came.

"I was so scared he was going to shoot you."

"I was too pissed to be scared. That ass literally flew through the window. All I could think of was how many windows we're gonna have to replace."

There were footsteps on the deck and before anyone could take another breath, Marty came. Josh was behind him

"That him?" Marty asked.

Michael nodded.

Marty went over to the body of Jorge.

"Damn. Two shots, side by side right through his forehead." He looked up, questioningly.

"Mandy," Michael stated.

Marty stared at her. He'd thought she was capable. Now he knew she was. She'd be good for his friend.

Hank went into sheriff mode and cleared everyone out of the room. He called his forensic team and put in for the cleaning crew to be there the following afternoon.

Everybody went back to the kitchen. Mandy put on fresh coffee. There were 11 dead altogether. The rest were in custody. The SUV that had headed south had been detained. It was going to be hard to convict them of anything as they weren't on the property at the time of the shootings and all papers were in order. For the time being, they were being guests at the county jail, being held on suspicion.

Brad and Alex showed up as the coroner was leaving. The sun was coming up and the mountains were incredibly beautiful. The pink, orange and purple seemed especially vivid. Mandy made sure everyone was settled and went out on the deck. She wanted just a few moments with the sunrise.

Michael came out and stood beside her.

"You okay?"

"I think so. You know, I never thought about it when I pulled the trigger on both of those men. It didn't even cross my mind not to. I really wanted to empty the clip into both of them. Isn't that horrible?"

"No. After what they put you through for so many years, I'm sure you probably thought of lots of creative ways to kill them over the years."

"You have no idea." She paused. "You know, this means I get to go back to normal."

"And what does that mean for you?"

"Oh," she said, turning to face him. "Cows, horses, hay, Costco."

"Costco?"

"Yea. I think I better keep the house better stocked. I think I'll be having more people at my house."

"Feel like stocking two?" Michael put his arms around her.

"Think your house will be needing some?"

"Yea. I think my house needs a lot more than what I thought it did."

"Like what?"

"You."

"Really? I thought we were going to go slow on this."

"After what we've been through together, I don't think we should be waiting any longer on anything."

"Does this mean we're going steady?"

Michael laughed.

"If that's what you want."

Mandy put her arms around him.

"I can honestly say I want you."

"Good. I want you, too."

"Well, okay then. Consider it done."

"We're officially going steady."

Epilogue

Six months later

Spring time in the mountains could make your head soar with all the natural beauty. Wild flowers in full bloom, snow-capped mountains, deer with fawns playing in the meadows. Spring meant new life. No one appreciated that more this spring than Mandy.

She had walked out on the front deck of Michael's house. Well, it was her house now, too. She had moved in February, the weekend before their ceremony at the Justice of the Peace at the county courthouse. All that had happened since just seemed like the natural progression of life.

Max had come home the day after Mandy had killed Jorge. His coming home was very therapeutic for Mandy. She felt safe with the big dog around. He was almost back to normal, could trot to Mandy's old place all the way now. He did take a nap when he got there but he could make it the full way. Mandy had no doubt he would make a full recovery. Less wasn't acceptable to him.

Brad and Alex had moved into Mandy's. Brad still flew down to Flagstaff to check on his business. His manager kept everything running perfect but Brad felt it was important for his employees to know he cared about them as much as the business.

Alex had moved her practice to Jackson. She and Marie were going into partnership. Marie had moved into Hank's. She was one busy lady. She was learning about ranching, studying for the WY bar exam and getting settled in her new office. But no matter what anyone's schedule, it was always Sunday dinner at Mandy and Michael's with the whole family.

Jim and Angelica were in protective custody, along with Rafe and Juan. Sally still had their families hidden but there didn't seem to be any retaliation planned. Even Angelica's kids were glad Jorge was permanently gone. Juan Garcia had just quit the drug business. He would have been the likely person to take over. Rumor had it that his wife refused to let him end up like her brother. She had been the one to invest their money and they hadn't lived a lavish lifestyle. The whole family had up and vanished.

Marty was back at his ranch in MT with Josh as his foreman. He wanted to meet Sally when she came out to see Mandy in June. He wanted to meet this friend who had stuck by Mandy all these years.

Mandy had finally been able to contact Katie. It had been a three hour phone call with a lot of tears and laughter. So much catching up to do. Katie was planning on coming out in August as it was so hot then in LA and WY would be such a nicer place to be. Mandy couldn't wait.

Her days were filled with everything she loved. Michael her kids, horses, Max and a family she never knew had been waiting for her. Alex and the boys had accepted her with open arms and called her "mom", sometimes joking, sometimes in all seriousness. She was so incredibly blessed.

Michael was everything she had hoped for and then some. She didn't know she had been waiting for him until that dinner date. Goes to show you never know what life has in store, she thought as the sun rose over the Tetons. Life is good.

www.ingramcontent.com/pod-product-compliance
Lightning Source LLC
LaVergne TN
LVHW091545060526
838200LV00036B/716